**"JEALOUS? MY BEAUTIFUL MARA? OF
YOUR OWN YOUNG SISTER-IN-LAW?"
JUSTIN LAUGHED.**

"Don't call me 'your Mara.' I'm not. I—" She
broke off, staring at him from eyes suddenly
wide and so brilliantly blue he was dazzled.

"Aren't you? Then whose? Do you mind telling me—"

Once again she had won. An irrational upsurge of resentment filled him. He pulled her to
him roughly. "Explain, if you please, Mrs. Tregallis."

Her tilted elfin lips and wayward rebellious
glance taunted him.

"You'd like to know, wouldn't you, Justin,
darling?" she mocked. Already the stimulus of
her own defiance and her ability to discomfort
him was rousing the old impish instincts in her.
She lifted a hand to his cheek—a delicate touch
now, flowerlike in its softness. Then, with a gurgle of light laughter, she broke from him and
sped up the stairs. . . .

**Dell Books
by Marianne Harvey**

STORMSWEPT

Marianne Harvey
writing as Mary Williams

A DELL BOOK

Published by
Dell Publishing Co., Inc.
1 Dag Hammarskjold Plaza
New York, New York 10017

This work was first published in Great Britain by William
Kimber & Co. Limited under the title *The Tregallis
Inheritance*.

Dell ® TM 681510, Dell Publishing Co., Inc.

ISBN: 0-440-19030-4

Printed in the United States of America
First U.S.A. printing—January 1984

*TO BILL
WITH LOVE*

Introduction

The house was almost obscured by sand when I found it; great dunes reared their humped shapes above. Rushes waved in the chill sea winds where once the back portion of the ruin must have been. It was said that through the centuries a whole village had been taken and buried by the elements. Occasionally spikes of timber and other relics of former habitation poked through the bumpy ground sloping upward to the moor. When great gales blew from the Atlantic, or there was a freak storm, further drifts of sand were churned from the ocean bed to encroach hungrily upon the ever-changing coastline. On the far side of the estuary where the hamlet of Polgwidden did its best to strengthen defenses, the church had been taken a hundred years before, and a new one built farther inland. But no one bothered about Boscarrion any more. Boscarrion was doomed; a ghost place of stories unproved because no one remembered.

It had all happened so long ago.

Yet somehow an atmosphere remained.

The light was dying when I saw the ruin of Boscarrion that first time. Only a jutting corner of granite structure and broken timber was visible. A sluggish stream of red-colored water coursed slowly around its corner to the wider river bed and the sea. The Red River, so called by natives because of the tin. But in the fading gleam of autumn sun the effect was more of tired blood still coursing from an old wound.

As the last streak of day died quite suddenly behind the brooding line of distant moors, I shivered. Every sound in that lonely place became intensified —the whine of rushes and the insidious trickle of water; the rhythmic breaking of waves from the incoming tide, and the fitful moaning of the rising wind.

I turned and left. From the darkening sky a seagull cried. The climb up the hill was slippery and precarious. When I glanced back, it seemed to me that the tossed waves were already threatening and thick with sand.

All that night I was haunted by the memory of "place" and what I had seen. Next day, I decided, I would return.

But in the morning, following hours of wild storm, the vista had changed beyond recognition. Great lumps of coast had been torn and gulped by a freak tide—and as if to impress its identity upon the forlorn scene, the storm had left empty, ruined windows tangled with seaweed and scattered shells gaping from under a holed roof. The remains of a broken chimney stack were tumbled under the weight of years. The mutilated relic of a doorway was agape and dripping—a dark cave of forgotten things.

I stared, and felt my spine stiffen.

The atmosphere was haunted, compelling.

Hardly aware of my own movement I stepped inside the passage. There was little to see or sense but the dark green of crumbled walls, of shadows massing, and the dank cold, which was intense. The flagstone beneath my feet was slippery and clogged with sand and subterranean growth. Cobwebs flapped my cheeks, yet I went on. Though dead and decayed for so many years the smothered interior had a curious life of its own. At odd places, and around corners where the passage curved, I fancied movement. Sometimes I had to climb or push through mounds of rock. As my eyes grew more accustomed to the darkness I saw broken pots and household implements entangled in the debris. Something fell and just missed my face. I glanced down. In the thick mud a shield projected—scarred but showing a coat of arms. And at that moment an icy shiver of wind whistled through the corridor, stirring the silence to a whispering chorus of echoes.

I waited then, staring into the distance. Forms began to move and subside ahead of me. It was like looking on a mirage or a scene through water or distorted glass. Nothing was tangible; but as I stood with the palms of both hands pressed against the granite wall, a shaft of light penetrated the shadows, curdling into the sickly pallor of a man's face. It was long and wan, with narrowed eyes and a thin mouth twisted into a sneer. A handsome, evil face framed by dripping black hair, suspended, it seemed, in a void of darkness.

I was fascinated, but appalled. Fear made me rigid. Then, breaking the silence, a thin high scream pierced the cloying air. A woman's voice. And for a brief instant I imagined I could see her—a ghost form with staring dark eyes and wild pale hair blown wraithlike behind her. It was only as the man's countenance gradually disintegrated and faded that I realized the cry had been my own.

I forced myself to turn and somehow make my way back to the broken doorway. When I looked around again, there was nothing to be seen but a yawning gap of fetid darkness.

That night I dreamed.

I know now that the dream took me back in time to a place and happenings long gone and forgotten.

How do I know?

There can be no answer except small snippets of history picked up at odd times from various sources, and put together with my own mysterious experience, into a credible kind of pattern.

No proof remains. The ruin now has completely gone.

Only a hump of sand and earth is left to indicate the spot where Boscarrion once stood. Rushes wave above like frail, thin banners of the dead; and across the sky sounds the mournful everlasting crying of the gulls.

1

1800

Christin Tregallis stared at his newborn child with distaste, and at the exhausted young mother in condemnation.

A daughter.

After her three miscarriages and a stillborn son in six years of marriage. He was already forty-seven, and his wife, Elaine, twenty-three. He had expected better things of her. It was essential he had an heir. Life at his age, in those stormy times of complicated European relationships and intermittent war with France, was uncertain—especially since that unpredictable but stubborn little Corsican officer, Napoleon, had bobbed up again declaring himself head of the French government as first consul.

Christin did not doubt England's capacity to survive any European attack, but he was fiercely proud and possessive of his own heritage. If he died leaving no son, his Cornish estate would revert to his nephew Rohan, whom he considered a wily and avaricious character—mercenary in his dealings and capable of bringing only dishonor to the family name. His loyalty to the Crown itself could be suspect, for he had been born of a French mother. She had died—mercifully, Christin told himself—when the boy was but seven years of age, and the father, Ellis, Christin's younger brother, had died a decade later.

Since then Rohan had lived the life of a rake and womanizer, squandering his fortune at the gaming table and with riotous trips to London, yet always managing by fair means or foul to reimburse his pockets when needed. Rumors of dark deeds committed at Boscarrion, his house at the foot of the North Downs facing the sea, had been more than justified. But the natives kept quiet, because Rohan was a powerful man with devious ways of taking revenge on those who threatened him.

So Christin was adamant that a boy child must somehow be brought to Penraven. The Tregallis family seat for centuries, Penraven had to be made secure from Rohan's corrupting influence. There was also a deeper reason for Christin's obsession—a secret known only to Rohan and one other, which would make them forever enemies.

Observing his wife's unconscious face—its sickly pallor against the pillows of the great bed—Christin knew he would beget no son of her. She was delicate, and a sad disappointment in every way except for the considerable dowry she'd brought from her father, Sir Charles Bennedict, when they'd married. Her pink and white beauty had been quick to fade, her sexual responses too obviously no more than cringing obligations. She had tried, no doubt, he told himself morosely, watching her quick, exhausted breathing. But trying was not enough. He must, and *would*, have his heir.

This last birth had been slightly premature, which helped matters. The girl child must be disposed of, discreetly, and in as humane a way as possible. He bore her no ill-will, poor little creature, but she would inevitably turn out as a replica of her mother.

A second Elaine about the house would be unthinkable. So he called old Dorcas, for consultation.

Dorcas, wholly dependent on Tregallis bounty, was an old servant who in her way was a bit of a midwife, with a fund of ancient cures and herbal remedies at her disposal. She also had a certain knack of foretelling the future, which more often than not came true—whether by chance or luck, Christin had never determined. But she was fiercely loyal to him, and he'd no doubt at all that under these particular circumstances she would somehow provide a solution to his problem. She had as well a quick ear and knew most of what was going on about the countryside. Another advantage was that in a year, perhaps less, she would no longer be able to breathe a word about his affairs, even if she were so tempted, because she would be dead. She had a tumor. The apothecary knew it, and Dorcas herself knew it. Therefore the matter could be safely left in the old woman's hands.

After he summoned her return to the bedchamber, there was whispered conversation for a few minutes, and presently, aided only by the fitful light of a single candle, a hunched, dark figure passed unobserved down the wide corridor, with a bundle carefully concealed under her black cloak. There was a high wind that night, so none could have distinguished the thin crying of a newborn babe from the whining of the elements and screaming outside of birds disturbed. The old woman's feet were swathed in wool to prevent any sound; the servants had been abed many hours, and the watchman was heaving in sleep at his post from liquor taken to warm him.

Dorcas, despite her ailment, was well used to hard work, and knew every lane and byway of the district. When she'd passed through a side door she made her

way across the courtyard and through a path leading
to a rock-strewn field. There was an eerie washed-out
moon in the night sky that at intervals threw the
ground into clarity, enabling her to pick her way
carefully to the road above. Once she reached it, she
waited a bit to get her breath.

The sound of wheels and horses' hooves approached, and through the gloomy light she saw a
farm cart driven by its drunken owner. His large
form swayed behind the broad rump of his horse;
pigs and fowls were screeching and clucking at the
back. As he drew near he took another swig from his
bottle and started to sing. He did not appear to notice
her until she stepped from the roadside, jangling a
bag of coins her master had given her.

With an oath followed by a sly change of mood, the
bawdiness passed as though by magic. She untied the
bag, handed him a couple of sovereigns, and after
conspiratorial directions he turned the cart again in
the direction of Truro. At a crossroads on the moor
she ordered him to stop, and, keeping her face well
hidden under her hood, she dismounted with her
bundle. A second later the farm cart was on its way
back, but she made no movement until it was completely lost to sight around a bend in the road, where
it waited.

A mist was rising, and that was good, Dorcas
thought. With a fair on at Truro more night revelers
might appear unexpectedly. This could be dangerous
to her mission, were she recognized. So she hurried
ahead, bent and panting heavily, until she reached a
thick copse of willow, elder, twisted sloe, and oaks, at
the foot of Trencawl hill. She pushed through the
branches guided by the rosy glow of a fire. She knew
of a hovel and van there occupied by old Sarah
Gwarves and her daughter, Lillith.

Both were fortune-tellers and acclaimed witches, though no natives of those parts had as yet testified against them, for fear of dread reprisals. They lived as best they could—weaving baskets, dyeing, making pegs, stealing, and enriching their pockets at fairs. The younger woman, Lillith, had but the previous day been delivered of a male child, a fact that Dorcas through her contacts had learned the same evening.

Lillith appeared as the bent figure of the midwife approached, with the bundle still safe under her cloak. She was a wild-looking woman with black windblown locks, fiery green eyes, and a voice that could be coarse and cursing, or full of sly sweetness and charm. Her breasts were ripe and bursting with rich milk under her shawl. No babe in her care would be without food or sustenance, Dorcas thought shrewdly. Women of her sort bred well; a son of hers would be lusty and strong; and the puny creature from Penraven might thrive in her charge. So the exchange could be well worthwhile for all of them. The squire was not entirely without conscience.

"Let her be cared for," he'd said before the old servant had started off. "I wish her no harm. Just find her a home, but tell me none of it—neither name nor place. Get me a son, that's all."

So Dorcas now went ahead with the deal. There was further whispered conversation, defiant refusal at first, until the bag of shining gold coins was produced. Then all argument subsided. As the older woman ran gnarled fingers avariciously over the money, Lillith went into the hut, and returned with the boy in her arms. He was bawling lustily, and one glance of his face in the gleam of the fire and a lantern was sufficient for Dorcas.

The arrangement was completed, the girl child handed over without further ado, and five minutes later Dorcas was mounting the cart to be driven on the return journey to the manor. The driver, who had sobered a little during the interval, had no idea of what had occurred. Neither had Elaine Tregallis.

When she recovered consciousness at dawn, it was to find her husband staring at her critically, but with warm words on his lips.

"You have done well, my dear," he said. "A fine son lies in your arms. Look how contented he sleeps beside you."

The tired woman glanced down.

For a second as the infant's black almond eyes opened, she was seized by a vague unaccountable apprehension.

"I thought it was a girl," she murmured. "Somehow I thought it was a girl."

Her husband flushed. "Don't have such stupid thoughts, wife. 'Tis a boy and a hardy one at that."

She smiled.

"I must have been dreaming, then."

"Yes."

Relief surged through her. "Oh, Christin, I'm not such a poor wife after all, then."

He patted her hand lightly. "Feed him well," he said. "If you can't—we'll have a healthy wet nurse. There are plenty of them around. My son must have only the best. Attend to his needs and I'll ask little more of you."

He kept his word, and from that time demanded only rare wifely sexual obligations. It was ironic that one such occasion should lead to the birth of another daughter—a cross-looking baby—dark and olive-skinned, who cried a great deal and from the start seemed to take a dislike to her father. He was mildly annoyed, but in no way hurt. His thoughts were already so preoccupied by the boy, one plain girl child could be discounted as a minor irritation in the household.

So it was that the name of Justin Tregallis was added to the family tree, and new blood brought to its heritage.

When the girl was two years old, it was apparent, even to Christin, that in stubbornness and character she was a typical Tregallis—a fact that was to prove irksome in the years to come, and bring considerable dissension to the household.

2

On a spring day in 1818 Olivia Tregallis watched her brother, Justin, ride up the drive from the stables of Penraven, their home, and take the way eastward over the moors toward Camborne. He was a clean-cut dark figure against the clear sky, seated proudly astride his young stallion, Blackfire, and Olivia was envious. Not only because of her deep attachment to Justin, but because she knew where he was going. He was heading for the fair at Camborne, and she loved fairs, with their giants and dwarfs, tumblers and puppet-shows, gingerbread stalls, and marvelous display of wild beasts and waxwork shows.

She was also a good horsewoman despite her mere thirteen years, and would not have been a burden on her brother. But Justin, who had appeared so fond of her when she was a little girl, seemed to grow daily

more withdrawn and remote from her. She told herself that when he left university at the end of the
following year and was back in Cornwall for good,
they would surely become closer again. But a year
and a half was a long time to wait, and by then she
herself would be almost grown up, with a year of
boarding school behind her. Watching Justin, she
remembered with longing past times when he'd
teased her, hugged her, and taught her to ride. He
had been her hero since she'd first learned to walk
and run. He was so tall and strong and handsome,
with his crisp black curling hair, firm features, and
black sparkling eyes that could be laughing one moment then flashing with anger the next.

Not that Justin had often lost his temper. There
had been certain occasions in his younger days when
he' had disobeyed his father defiantly and been
thrashed severely for it. But such times had been
rare, and Justin had never cried or asked for mercy.
He was brave, and the imp of mischief in him was
secretly admired by Christin—Olivia knew that. The
two of them, her aging portly father and his stubborn
young heir, were very close. That was natural, Olivia
often thought rather wistfully, because when her father died, Justin would be master of Penraven, sole
owner of its wild acres and pastures, its tenant farms,
the two mines Wheal Dolly and Wildellen, and the
stately Cornish home itself. Already the eighteen-
year-old young "master" was a popular figure with
natives, the miners themselves, landworkers, farm-
ers, and lesser gentry. He was regarded as "one of
them," in bars and inns, though commanding at the
same time an air of respect as befitting his status.

"Mix well, and show consideration to all who deserve it," Christin had said more than once, "but
don't go too far. Remember you're a Tregallis, and

not of the common herd. You're here to run things
and take responsibility. Once you show you can't
hold the reins they'll despise you for it. Another thing
—keep yourself free of cousin Rohan. He'll come to
a bad end, and that's his due; the sooner the better.
If I ever hear you've had dealings with him, I'll have
the hide off your back so you'll remember it to your
dying day—so help me God."

And Justin had known he'd meant it. What exactly
the feud was between Christin and his nephew, Justin did not know except that Rohan kept a French
mistress known as Melusina, who was said to have
contact with the devil, and that he had squandered
much of his father's fortune in riotous living. His
mother, also French, had been a Catholic—which
had increased family hatred. It had been rumored
that Rohan was even financially involved in slaving
and had been part owner of a French slaver driven
ashore by a freak storm near the rocky promontory
bordering the dunes of Boscarrion. Rohan had contrived to extricate himself through devious means,
and had taken a poor Negro boy into his service
under a show of charity.

Natives thereabouts who could possibly have endorsed accusations against him held their tongues.
Rohan was a powerful man in his way, one who re-
warded his friends but had proved quick to send an
enemy to the gallows. So the dark deeds went on.
Boscarrion was shunned by all who valued the goodwill of Christin, the squire—and Olivia, like her
brother Justin, had been disciplined to keep away
from the house near the dunes.

"Sometime the sea will get it," Christin had pro-
phesied darkly, "and that will be a good day for all of
us."

Olivia, who had an inquiring mind and stubborn

will, frequently wondered about the large dark building huddled in its shadows on the far side of the estuary. Many times she had been tempted to ride there on her young mare, Moonbeam, but fear of the consequences had so far held her back. Her father was a man of his word, and she knew if he found out, she would be tied to a chair facedown and soundly whipped by her stern governess, Miss Cobbet, who had a cane in her desk that she used severely if the occasion arose.

All the same, Olivia thought rebelliously that day, watching Justin ride across the moor, it might be worth the punishment. She had little interests or fun at Penraven, especially now Justin seemed so withdrawn from her. Her father hardly ever noticed her; his affection was all for Justin. And her mother was no company, keeping mostly to her own apartments, either resting on her bed, arranging her hair while singing in a silly high voice, or dressing herself absurdly in fancy clothes far too young for her. Elaine was still a pretty woman in a faded way, but obviously slightly mad, and Olivia felt little relationship to her.

It would be exciting for once to get away from them all, just to have a peep at the forbidden house where cousin Rohan lived. Perhaps he would be dark, devilish, and exciting, like Lord Byron. And perhaps Melusina, his mistress, would be as wild and passionate as Lady Caroline Lamb. Olivia knew about Byron, though his work was forbidden at Penraven. She had read "The Prisoner of Chillon" and "Childe Harold" in a book of newspaper cuttings and snippets of current history brought in by a newly employed linenmaid, who had been instantly dismissed for the offense. The dismissal, however, had been too late—the seed of curiosity had firmly taken root in Olivia's mind. Adventure and a longing to see other people and other things possessed her. She would have accepted her restricted life at Penraven peacefully enough—even when Justin was at Oxford —provided she could be certain of her brother's attention when he returned. But he had shown her all too clearly that she could not.

The fair, for instance.

It would have been such fun visiting all the odd sideshows and seeing the strange people there. Sally, a kitchenmaid at Penraven, who'd been to it the previous night, had told her of a tiny woman there only two feet high who wore a silk gown and a crown and was called the "Windsor Fairy." There were bears that danced, and a funny man with a nose a foot long. Then the gingerbread, and sweetmeats, the waxworks and tumblers, the wizards and dwarfs! Oh, Justin had been mean not to take her.

But if she were willing to accept the consequences, she could still go. And once she got to the Camborne fairground, she'd look for Justin. When she found him, she could surely persuade him to make things right with their father on their return to Penraven. He would have to lie a bit, of course. And Christin was very stern about lying. But Justin was so clever. He could generally find an excuse for any escapade if he had to. And anyway—her jaw set and her eyes brightened to fiery gold at the thought—if that horrible old shrew Miss Cobbet tried to whip her, she'd bite her hand before she'd a chance to tie her up. And that would mean a beating from her father. The thought sobered her; but only for a moment.

Shrugging doubt quickly away, Olivia ran speedily and almost soundlessly upstairs to her room, carefully avoiding Miss Cobbet, who was correcting exercise books in the schoolroom. At the bottom of her chest was a pair of old breeches used by Justin as a boy. She'd found them pushed away in a hayloft and secreted them for just such an occasion as this. She'd ridden in them once before, although no one except Joe Tregurze, the stableboy, had known. It had been an exciting experience speeding along astride behind Moonbeam's flying mane instead of sitting correctly sidesaddle with long skirts flapping round her ankles. The moorland winds had smelled so much sweeter; even the colors of sky, sea, and distant purple hills had appeared clearer and more vivid. Her heart had sung, and her rich dark hair had streamed like a banner through the wild air.

She smiled to herself mischievously as she recalled the incident and her luck in not being found out. Perhaps it would be the same this time. But of course it would, she told herself again—with Justin's help.

When she was changed into her velvet jacket with the breeches tucked into boots, she took a red ribbon from a drawer and tied her thick locks back. They were long and waving, reaching to her waist. In the light from the window the dark masses seemed to hold all the molten copper glory of autumn, merged with the bluish-black gleam of deep mountain pools. Her lips were full and red, tilted in an impish smile. Her golden-brown eyes danced. She was tall for her age, and already gracefully rounded. In a fleeting flash of knowledge, she knew one day she would be beautiful, and then she would marry someone brave and handsome, and as much like Justin as possible.

Her smile faded as she thought of Justin. He would be nearing the fair now. He might even be there. So she tore her eyes from the image, and after making sure no one was about, she ran along the wide landing to a narrow staircase used only by the servants, and went down. She paused at the bottom, listening.

Clatters of pots and the chink of cutlery intermingled with muted conversation echoed from the kitchen, followed by a sharp command from Peters, the butler.

Olivia rushed ahead down a short passage to a side door, and in a few seconds was cutting down a drive past the kitchen gardens and stokehole, to the stables.

Adam, the senior groom, was not about. She'd relied on that—knowing his habit of slipping along to the kitchen at that time for bread and cheese and a drink. But Joe was there. He gasped when he saw her.

"Oh, Miss Livvy," he said, "what you'm be about? Wicked you look—real wicked in them lad's clothes —" but his voice was admiring.

Olivia's color deepened. The dimples came to her vivid cheeks. "Don't say anything," she begged. "Just saddle Moonbeam—quick now, quick, quick. Please, Joe."

"But—"

"I'll love you forever—cross my heart I will," she promised recklessly, "in a friendly way of course—as a special friend, Joe."

Joe, who could never withstand her pleas, reluctantly gave in, and a few minutes later Olivia, astride her mare, was cantering through a gate leading into Wildacre field, and onward up a slope that took her quickly out of view of the house around a bend. From there she cut to the right and up the hill toward Camborne. She had several miles to cover, but the ride was a challenge.

When she reached the high ridge, she paused briefly, drawing the tangy sweet smell of heather and fresh young turf into her lungs. The flash of a gull's wings were bright in the sunlight; larks rose into the sky above her, dipping quickly again to the ground. Moonbeam snorted, nostrils joyously flaring. Olivia flicked the reins and kicked her mount on again, giving the horse its head. Unconscious of danger they sped ahead, galloping wildly past humped boulders and tangled gorse, skirting precariously the lurking dank pits of hidden derelict mine shafts and sudden obstacles of bent windblown trees stretching withered arms from the bracken.

At times she had to change course abruptly to avoid black pools of yawning bog. Once, when she glanced toward the coast, she had a glimpse of Boscarrion's huddled towers silhouetted close against the sea. The land above it was a patchwork of blown sand and reddish earth. The scene was desolate, reminding her of the dark, enchanted wastelands of some frightening nightmare or fairy tale.

She urged Moonbeam to her right, taking a narrow track downward toward a lane leading eventually to the main moorland road. But she had not counted on the animal's wild response to the elements. Without any warning, forelegs rearing to the challenge of freedom, and with a whinny of joy, Moonbeam took a header over a great boulder tangled in furze and briars, and Olivia, trying to rein, was thrown—landing with one ankle bent under her as the mare galloped at increasing speed along the moor.

For a minute she lay still, aware only of shock and a sudden pain. Then, realizing she was not dangerously hurt, she sat up, staring blankly around her. She tried to stand, but the movement of her foot was agonizing; faintness overcame her. She fell back, screwing her eyes up, trying to ward off the wave of giddiness. But it was no use.

There was a blinding flash of light, a sickness that drowned her in perspiration, followed by a sensation of the sky coming down to meet her, and nothing registered anymore. She lay with her head turned to one side, black hair tangled in heather and ferns, a leg bent at the knee to her stomach. A bird pecked curiously by her face; a fox barked.

She had no idea how long she lay there. But when she recovered consciousness it was to see a dark face staring down at her—lean-featured and pale, framed by black hair, and a scar running down one cheek. The man was handsomely dressed in a fawn velvet jacket and twill breeches, wearing a cravat at his neck held by a diamond pin. Laughter lurked round his lips in a grim smile. But his black eyes were narrowed. It was as though he wore a mask defying recognition of either good or evil. And even in her sorry plight, Olivia sensed who he was.

Cousin Rohan.

She blinked, and, easing her up, he said, "You've had a bad fall. Lucky I found you. Where were you going?"

"To the fair," Olivia said, wincing. "I fell. My horse ran away."

"Ran?" The man laughed. "Galloped, you mean. A good thing, too—or I mightn't have found you. Don't worry, the filly's safe."

"Moonbeam? Oh." She tried to move, but automatically a little scream left her lips. He glanced at her foot, then bent closer.

"Well," he said finally. "It may not be broken, but you certainly won't be able to ride anywhere. What's your name? Olivia-Jane is it? Dear Uncle Christin's daughter?"

"Yes. But, how did you—?"

"My dear"—the calm voice was cynical—"I have means of knowing these things. So, little coz, we've got to think of a way to get you home, haven't we?

And without too much trouble either to you or to myself. How shall we do it? Eh?"

Olivia shook her head miserably. There would be trouble whichever way it was. She might be spared a beating when her injury was known, but there would be a terrible fuss, and she'd probably be kept in bed on bread and water until the ankle was healed. And Miss Cobbet would probably use her cane when she was better, and she'd be watched so carefully there'd be no freedom at all for her anymore at Penraven.

"Could I come with you?" she asked. "To your home?"

He stared at her briefly before answering lightly, "Why not? Yes. A most stimulating idea. And quite amusing under the circumstances."

So presently, with a scarf tied round the injured ankle and pain comfortably dimmed with a strong dose of brandy from a flask, Olivia was lifted on to the back of his tall horse. With her arms round Rohan's waist, hands clutching him from behind, they started off for Boscarrion.

The room was long and rather narrow, with an ornate marble mantelpiece at one side framed by erect, large, praying figures inlaid with various colors, and carved in Italian style. The leaping flames of the log fire in the grate gave the forms a macabre sense of life that was emphasized by the dying sun streaming fitfully through tall Gothic-type windows. There was an oak refectory table against the opposite wall. It was already laid for a meal, with glass and cutlery gleaming through the transient light and shade. Candles flared wanly from silver chandeliers. The chairs were monastic-looking, with tall, domed backs intricately carved with leaves and flowers. Rich tapestries were hung in every available space, and rugs of Persian design were laid at different angles on the floor, which was mosaic and of black and red inlaid marble.

As her eyes became accustomed to the exotic interior, Olivia noticed a sword hanging close to the entrance door, beside a shield and an immense stag's head. There were also numerous mirrors about, which cast odd reflected shapes from unexpected angles.

A dog that was lying in front of the fire lifted its head, growling, as Rohan led the child in.

"Down, Brutus," she heard a feminine voice saying quickly—so quietly and softly one would have thought no animal would obey. But the mastiff settled instantly in its place again, and a tall figure moved from her seat in a shadowed recess and came forward gracefully with a rustle of silk and waves of exotic perfume. She had black hair, very highly dressed with flowers and ribbons, and scarlet lips that emphasized the creamy pallor of her face and white powdered shoulders. She was not young. The neckline of her gown was so low and wide the ripe breasts were hardly covered and were supported above a narrow black velvet belt. Below the shoulders, puffed sleeves edged with frilled lace were fitted above tightly shaped elbow-length embroidery. Her skirt was straight, flaring only slightly from full hips to the ankles. It had a fancy embroidered hem of gold and black that emphasized the pointed shining slippers. In spite of her height and all that fashion could do, it was obvious Melusina. Countess of Lefrougé, had a ripe and mature figure that could one day run to stoutness.

At the moment the woman had a sophisticated allure that reduced Olivia to sudden shyness. The

strange impression of being in some other world
overcame the girl—a world reflected through water
The constant ebb and flow of the sea outside provided a mournful accompaniment to the blurred
mirror images, the jingle of crystal, and spitting logs.
She was excited, yet a little afraid.

As though in a dream she heard Rohan introducing
them and saying formally, "My dear, this is Olivia
Tregallis, a young cousin of mine. Olivia, you'd better
rest while I make arrangements for your return to
Penraven. If my presence would not be so exceedingly unwelcome to your family I'd take you myself.
But I won't add to your suffering. How is the foot
now?"

"It hurts," Olivia answered bluntly.

"I'm sorry. But it's very unwise for young ladies of
your tender age to go galloping over the moors on
their own. Melusina"—turning to Lady Lefrougé
—"give the child a glass of wine. It will soothe her."

He turned abruptly and went out. Melusina
fetched two goblets and a decanter from the cup-
board, poured wine into the glasses and handed one
to Olivia. Taking the other to her chair by the great
fireplace, she seated herself, leaning back languor-
ously with the crystal goblet between her long white
fingers. There was a drawn-out silence during which
the woman regarded the child reflectively. Then she
said with a hint of amusement in her soft, husky
voice, "You're very young to be my—to be Rohan's
cousin."

"I'm thirteen," Olivia said, lifting her head proudly
and a little rebelliously. She knew Melusina did not
like her, and she was resentful of the countess's
condescension.

"A very great age indeed, to be sure," Melusina
remarked.

Olivia flushed, and gripping the two arms of the chair heaved herself to her feet.

"I think I could ride back all right if someone helped me mount Moonbeam," she said stiffly, trying not to wince.

"Moonbeam?"

"My filly." As soon as she'd spoken, Olivia vividly recalled being thrown, and the horse's wild plunge away from her through the bracken.

"Oh, but—I forgot. Where is she? Rohan said—"

At that moment Rohan returned.

"And what did Rohan say?" he asked, with a tight inquiring little smile about his thin lips.

"My filly. You said she was safe."

"So she is. A groom has her outside and is ready to take you back. He's a trusted servant and will lead you both carefully."

"Lead us?"

"My dear child, don't imagine for one moment he'll trust you with the reins, and don't argue, if you please. I'm no friend of your father's or your bold, lusty brother's, and I have no wish to provoke a bloody duel. That you're here at all is challenge enough. So the sooner you're off, the better. Penraven's a considerable distance. Well?"

"I don't want to stay," she said defiantly. "I didn't ask to come—"

"But you did. If I remember correctly, you said, 'Can I come with you—to your home?'—those were your very words."

"Oh, yes, of course." She was confused. "Well, then —thank you. I'm sorry I've been a nuisance."

He patted her shoulder.

"No, you're not; except for the sprained foot I'm sure you've enjoyed the adventure, as any adventurous young chit of your age would. But I don't advise it a second time. I'm afraid that might mean serious trouble."

"With my father, you mean?"

"Exactly."

Olivia wrinkled her brow, then asked bluntly after a short pause, "Why don't you like each other?"

Rohan's face darkened. A dangerous glint lit his eyes below the frowning brows. The thin lips suddenly twisted into an ugly line.

"That's my affair. Mind your manners and keep your thoughts to yourself. Do you understand? My word is law at Boscarrion, and no questions asked—especially by a brat of a child. Now off with you."

He pulled a bell. A servant appeared almost immediately at the door. Rohan gave instructions, and Olivia was helped from the room. Leaning on the man's sturdy arm, she glanced back once. Rohan was watching her, his figure silhouetted fitfully against the rosy glow and leaping shadows of the firelight. For a second the lean countenance was thrown into fleeting clarity—the set jaw, cruel mouth, and hawklike nose. The effect, though only momentary, held such hunger, such concentrated bitterness of desire, that she was suddenly frightened, and longed for home. She pulled her gaze from his, and clutched the servant's arm. The shadows seemed to deepen and reach after her as she made her way painfully down the wide hall.

A little later she was seated on Moonbeam's back, being led by Rohan's man. It was an uncommunicative return journey. The last daylight had already faded when she was deposited at Penraven stables. The man cut off quickly, taking the narrow footpath through a field toward the moors. Only the young groom saw him, and accepted without question Olivia's explanation that she'd had a bad fall and had had to rest for a long time.

"The nice man found me," she lied as her cheeks flamed, "and brought me back."

Well, in a way it was true, she told herself in an attempt at self-justification, except that the man who'd found her had not really been the nice kind.

Cousin Rohan.

Supposing Justin had seen them together?

Luckily for her Justin had been otherwise occupied in dallying with a very beautiful stranger at the fair.

The lady was an exquisite creature with vivid orange curls peeping from under a tall cylindrical black hat topped by extravagant waving plumes and tassels. Her shimmering lilac-shaded gown fell narrow and straight to her delicate ankles, in accordance with the most up-to-date fashion. A silk cape was held by a clasp at the neck and pushed back over her shoulders. Jewels glittered around her cream neck and from the lobes of her ears. In one mittened hand she carried a richly embroidered reticule shining with tiny pearls. Her features were perfect—a slightly tilted nose above lusciously red yet finely sculptured lips. Her eyes, azure blue and long above the high cheekbones, shone alluringly between thick dark lashes.

She was already causing a sensation when Justin spotted her—a young lady of wealth and breeding, obviously—coming out of a gypsy fortune-teller's tent some yards away. What she had been told must have pleased her, for she was smiling, and the smile enchanted Justin. He pushed toward her through the little crowd gathered there. Some were still staring, some frankly gaping with admiration.

"Ah," he heard her say, "she is truly wonderful. All she told me so right—so veree accurate—" There were whispers, and a cessation of chatter as the graceful figure swept by. One by one others moved into the fortune-teller's tent. Several followed the magnificent visitor, eyeing her with increasing curiosity. Justin wondered about the accent. What was it? French? But surely not. The French were decidedly unpopular in Cornwall at that moment. Then who the devil was she?

He quickened his pace but did not manage to reach her side before a shrill feminine cry rang out.

"My reticule! Thief—thief! Someone has stolen my reticule."

By the time Justin was close on the scene, the lovely creature was being supported by a young farmer, with a number of locals offering stimulants and the greatest concern for her. No one noticed a small Negro boy who pushed his way between the skirts and legs of the crowd and quickly disappeared.

Justin dismissed the farmer with a few words and took charge of the young woman himself. "If you will allow me," he said, "I'll see you to your coach. Or would you prefer me to make a search for the thieving villains first?"

She stared up at him. Her innocent clear gaze set his senses alight.

"My coach will not yet be here," she told him, "and I do not wish to make trouble over the reticule. I was careless, and perhaps some veree poor person who needs it—oh so much!"—she lifted her small hands like quivering butterflies in distress—"has taken it. No, no. Please leave matters as they are, sir. I will just wander around a little. Yes? Until my man comes to the lane below. . . ."

"Nonsense," Justin told her sharply. "You must have refreshment. There's an inn toward the moor. Quite close to the lane. I'll accompany you and see you're rested before you leave." He paused, then asked, "Won't you tell me your name? And where you're going . . . ?"

His hand was already gently propelling her ahead by her elbow. She did not attempt to resist him.

"My name? You won't know it. Some call me Clarissa, others 'your ladyship' . . ." Her voice died on a subtle note.

"Clarissa then," he said boldly. "And I hope very much you won't always be so mysterious."

She didn't answer. The faint air of coquetry combined with her obvious secrecy both irritated and fascinated him. He'd discover all about her in the end, he vowed to himself as he untethered his horse from a tree. He placed both hands around her slender waist and lifted her to the saddle. She glanced down. Her voice was a little amused when she said, "I know how to ride once I am upon a horse."

"Nevertheless," he insisted, "from now on—until you're safely in your coach—I'm in charge."

After that she submitted obediently, and a few moments later, followed only by a child and a few half-drunken stragglers from the fair, he was leading the horse and girl toward The Star of Prussia. As they crossed the narrow lane cutting down to the moor, the group dispersed, and by the time they reached the inn, the dip in the wild landscape was deserted except for themselves and the animal.

The light was quickly fading from the gray sky, showing the inn at first as a mere huddled shape pinpointed by glimmering eyes of lighted windows. There was no wind anymore, and no sound from within—only the distant jingle of the fair from over the slope above.

Inside, a seaman was slumped drunkenly over a small table. A stout yellow-haired woman who looked like a prostitute leaned against the bar counter in the

arms of a rough black-bearded customer wearing a
patch over one eye. The interior had an un-
wholesome air about it, thick with the malty smell of
beer and sweat. Mugs and empty bottles stood about
in the flickering lights of candles and one swinging oil
lamp.

Justin thumped on the counter. A heavily jowled
man with small piggy eyes lumbered in from the
back. When he saw Justin, his scowl turned to an
ingratiating grin. His teeth were large, blackened,
and uneven, his apron stained.

"Yes, sir—m'lord—" he muttered through husky
wheezing. "What can I be doin for 'ee, surr, an' for
th' fair lady?" His expression turned to a vulgar leer
at Clarissa.

"A private room," Justin said, "quickly, and proper
attention. Look sharp about it, man, and see you've
cleaned yourself up, or I'll have you thrown off the
premises in no time." The slits of eyes narrowed and
became ugly, then the man heaved his heavy form
away, limping as he went.

A minute later Justin and the girl were ensconced
in a small room that, though tawdry and dark, had a
less redolent atmosphere. A wan fire burned in a
grate. A stained, shabby plush tablecloth covered the
round table. On one wall hung a yellowed map and
an engraving of some past wreck. Justin drew a chair
up to the feeble flames.

"Rest yourself," he told his companion, "while I
see about some refreshments. I'll get that oaf to bring
logs too."

He had no chance of noting the mocking little
smile about her mouth, or the reflective glance in her
green eyes when he left the room. Had he done so,
he might have delayed leaving her.

When he returned only minutes later, the room

was empty. She had unaccountably disappeared, leaving only a faint drift of perfume behind.

He stared incredulously before striding back to the bar. The piggy-eyed man was drawing ale at the back.

"Where is she?" Justin demanded. "Where the devil's the lady gone?"

The man stared at him.

"Gone, surr? Gone?"

Justin swept a glass aside, leaned over the counter, and grasped the fellow by his dirty cravat.

"You know what I'm talking about. The lady I was with. You tell me or I'll have your hide, by God I will."

The fellow wrenched himself free and thrust his ugly chin out threateningly.

"Be careful, I'm warnin 'ee. Jasper Tollan edn' the man to threaten. Friends I have, as'll tek care of 'ee ef they do have to." He gave a significant glance toward the black-bearded customer who was already rising from a bench. "So doan 'ee mek trouble. Ef the lady edn' theer—she bin an' took 'erself off, an' that edn' my doin'—see?"

Justin turned away in disgust. He left the bar and went back to the small room, hoping to find the girl had returned. But she hadn't. Only a tired elderly woman with a cringing expression was there, putting cheese and bread on the table.

She replied to Justin's questions with a frightened negative shake of the head, and, "No, surr. There wasn't no lady here when I comed in, nor at the back neither. I haven't seen none, mister, not any."

Irritated and dejected, with a curious sense of loss in him, Justin left a quarter of an hour later; it was only when he went to untether his horse that he discovered his wallet was missing. His first instinct was to blame the unsavory-looking landlord. Then he realized with a shock that his only close contact had been with his fair companion.

Irritation slowly deepened to increasing anger and the frustrated determination somehow to find her again, and make her confess the truth. After that he would demand payment through complete submission to his will, according to the mood he was in when they were at last face-to-face.

3

On an autumn morning Olivia stood in the hall of Penraven, waiting for the family chaise to draw up below the terrace. That day she was traveling to Plymouth and the dreaded boarding school that she knew she was going to hate. A large valise stood by her, and her brother Justin was trying in vain to cheer her up.

"You'll have fun there," he told her, giving her stubborn chin a little flick with a finger. "There'll be other girls of your own age to talk to, and when you come back, you'll be quite a fashionable young lady."

"Fashionable? Other girls?" She looked up at him with such unhappy emotion flooding her brilliant eyes, he was momentarily taken aback. "I don't want fun," she said, "or other girls. I want to be here, at Penraven. With you."

"But I won't be here, Olivia. Now be a good girl and don't make a scene."

She stamped her foot. "Don't talk to me like a child—"

"You are one," he told her. "Thirteen—"

"Nearly fourteen. Girls can be married at fourteen."

Something about her direct stare filled him with unease. He pulled his eyes away from hers, realizing with a sudden flash of knowledge that she was quite right, and that during the last few months there had been a great change in this wayward daughter of Christin Tregallis. She had grown taller. Her childish figure had ripened considerably, already showing subtle but unmistakable signs of approaching womanhood. Her skin, which in early youth had been so dark, now glowed in her cheeks as deepening rose. Her features, finely carved like her mother's, held nevertheless all the haughty pride and strength of the Tregallis family.

She was not beautiful—yet. But one day she easily could be, and Justin felt a discomforting challenge in her that mildly unnerved him. He had never really understood her as a brother should understand a sister. Her affection for him had always been too intense. Occasionally, during the past few months, he had felt there was a stranger in the house, that no true kinship existed between them. At other times her bursts of enthusiasm and sudden wild moods had touched a secret spring in his heart that he had sternly dispelled. The truth was that he knew any unbending on his part would be to court danger. Olivia could never be more to him than his young sister to be guarded and advised, even disciplined when required. Certainly he did not intend his future to be obsessed by her demanding temperament.

So his voice was stern when he said, "You've a great deal to learn before you're ready for marriage, Olivia. Men don't like spitfires or spoilt brats with no manners. If you try hard at school, maybe one day some unsuspecting young man will fall for you—God help him."

"And that's a horrid thing to say," Olivia told him sharply. "Sometimes I hate you."

Her childish temper reassured him, quickly dispelling embarrassment. He laughed. "Hate on," he said. "And maybe you'll feel better. I've got broad shoulders. I can stand it."

Her face drooped. She turned away, suddenly looking dejected and very very young.

He slipped an arm round her shoulders. "Cheer up, Livvy dear, you'll be back for Christmas, and so shall I," he said in gentler tones. "We'll go riding then. So be a good girl now, and for my sake and your own don't make a scene. You know how Father hates them."

She did not reply, because at that moment the sound of carriage wheels and horses' hooves echoed from the drive. Almost simultaneously Elaine's thin figure shrouded in a gray silk wrap appeared at the top of the wide staircase. Silvery-pale fair hair escaped in ringlets from a flimsy lace cap. She looked vague and woebegone, with protruding blue eyes and pouting lips overemphasized by scarlet lip-salve. Any beauty she had once possessed was now quickly fading. An aura and odor of spirits blended with too much perfume hovered about her. Her posture was unsteady, her expression vacant.

Clinging to the banisters, she made her way totteringly down the stairs. She lifted her arms toward her daughter. They were trembling, and the movement brought pale fire to the diamonds glittering on her hands. Her slender fingers were so heavily beringed, little flesh could be seen.

"Oh, my dear child," she moaned, "my d-darling d-daughter—what will I do without you? How will I en-endure it? Such long wasted hours . . ." Olivia steeled herself to bear the brandy-thick embrace, the quivering touch of trembling lips and cold flagging skin against her cheek. Then she pulled herself away, firmly saying with a touch of contempt, "You'll be all right, Mother. We don't often see each other. You've got Queenie anyhow—"

"Ah, yes, Queenie—where's Queenie?" Elaine demanded fretfully, dabbing the tears from her eyes.

Christin's portly figure emerged from the library door on the right, carrying a yelping too-stout Pekinese dog. He threw it at her unceremoniously. "Here's your confounded Queenie, madam, and see the messy creature doesn't get into my library again, or I'll wring its neck."

The little dog wobbled unsteadily to her mistress. Justin picked it up and thrust it into Elaine's arms. She bent her head, cradling it against her with a flood of incoherent endearments. A moment later, completely forgetting Olivia, she had turned and was trying ineffectually to mount the stairs. Christin touched a bell, and a maid came scurrying from the kitchens.

"Help your mistress to her room," he said curtly, "and see that damned dog of hers is kept safe from my sight."

By this time the chaise was at the front door and Olivia was rebelliously facing the first stage of her journey to Plymouth and the hated school.

Justin watched the chaise rattle away, ruminating on his sister's departure. He was chagrined to find his

heart so suddenly low in his boots. He'd miss the little
jade. The only sensible course, therefore, was to turn
his mind in other directions.

Clarissa.

Since the day of the fair, though he'd searched
intermittently and frequently thought of her, all
efforts at locating her had failed. He'd traveled the
district extensively from time to time, making inqui-
ries and describing her delicate rich beauty, fashionable dress and manners, foreign accent and flaming
red hair.

None seemed to have heard of her. Or if they had,
they didn't say. Yet with uncanny shrewd insight, he
sensed she was somewhere not too far away. So an
hour after Olivia's departure he set out astride
Blackfire for yet another exploration of that wild
area.

The air was cool and windless, pungent with the
heady scents of brine, blackberries, and tumbled rotting leaves. Overhead the light was leaden under the
lifting morning mist. The trees and bushes dripped,
almost naked now, silhouetted as humped grasping
shapes by the crouched boulders, or clawing starkly
to the lowering sky.

Blackfire's nostrils flared with energy and wild animal delight as Justin gave him his head. When stallion and rider reached the ridge above Penraven, the
glitter of sea below emerged fitfully as blurred glass,
fading into the uncertain line of cliffs and dunes.
Justin reined for a moment or two, scanning the landscape.

Nothing was clearly discernible, only the moorland
heights stretching toward Camborne, and on his left
the uneven slope downward leading to the humped
bridge over Red River. The roofs and turrets of Penraven were now mostly hidden by the fold of moor

beneath them, half shrouded in the milky veil of thin fog. This was not really the proper light for searching, Justin decided. All the same, he was ready for a good gallop, and his mind and imagination were alight for adventure.

So he started off again, taking the track over the bridge to the slightly lower ground above the shadowed territory of Boscarrion. Westward the moors continued much as before, except for darker patches of marsh blackened in places by pools of dangerous bog and abandoned mine shafts. He did not care for that particular area and generally avoided it when possible. But already a queer hunch was niggling at him that something could be waiting for him if he followed his instinct rather than reason.

He kicked Blackfire to a gallop again, taking a wild narrow track so tangled with gorse, bramble, and hidden boulders that the horse reared several times, and Justin had to pause in order to get his bearings. In the misted light this was not easy. He realized after some minutes that he'd covered more mileage than he'd thought, and that he was already approaching a stretch of dense, tangled forest land known locally as "Pookswood."

As he neared the fringe of the shadowed area the stallion jibbed and would have galloped back in the opposite direction if Justin hadn't allowed a detour, circling to the left of the huddled trees. Above them coils of mist crept to the distant ridge, imbuing the standing stones with uncanny secret life—a life emanating from the earth itself, dark and elemental. The black trunks of the trees below held a wasting quality —a force that despite Justin's lusty good health and strength filled him with revulsion.

No wonder the place had been named Pookswood, he thought, and no wonder there were weird super-

stitious tales of a witch living in the heart of it with
her evil daughter—conceived, it was whispered, by
the Devil himself. Mere nonsense, of course. The
couple were just tinkers dwelling in a cottage at the
far end. Though outwardly a humble gray-stoned
building little better than a hovel, rumor had it there
were orgies sometimes at night, when lights flashed
and the small windows blazed from within, with
many candles and the glint of jewels. Shapes had
been seen changing from great black cats into
human forms as they slipped through the moonlight
to the open door. Misfortune had beset the district
following such proceedings; a pig, perhaps, had died;
occasionally a cow had been taken by a pool or bog.
Once a neighboring farmer had hanged himself in
his own loft. A twelve-year-old girl—a simpleton—
had spoken in strange tongues one day, and later
became dumb. She kept a green frog as a pet, and
was frequently tethered by day like an animal to a
stake outside her home. In spite of this she'd borne
a child that later disappeared. No one knew the father, but it was whispered that the witches' spells
were responsible.

Justin accepted none of it. Nothing could be
proved against the women. If that were possible,
they would have been stoned, beaten to death, or
taken by the law. As it was, local folk avoided them
and crossed themselves when they passed their
home. One day, Justin decided, he'd insist on inspect-
ing the premises himself. As heir to Penraven he had
the power. And if anything was going on there that
shouldn't be, he'd get them hounded from the district.

He'd met neither of them face-to-face since he'd
grown up, though he'd come across the older woman

once or twice when he was a boy. She'd been a handsome, buxom, slatternly creature then, with hard narrow eyes that had stared at him with unpleasant hostility. Her clothes, though garish, had been none too clean; her hair—dense black—loose and untidy over her red shawl. Something about her had chilled him. And that chill was about him now as he kicked Blackfire to a fierce speed. To ease his nerves, he laughed aloud and uttered a few scathing words of derision. For some distance horse and rider continued recklessly.

The air grew colder and grayer. The stallion suddenly reared and then stood stubbornly unmoving, head raised, hooves planted firm on the ground. Justin tried pleading and command. It was no use; and then, suddenly, he saw why.

There was a light moving intermittently ahead on the fringe of the trees, a strange, quivering blurred glow that seemed to rise from the very earth itself, resolving gradually to the semblance of a white watchful countenance beneath a mass of shining pale hair.

Justin dismounted and automatically said, "It's all right. I mean no harm to you. Come here, whoever you are."

There was no response for a moment or two, then very slowly a figure emerged from the mist, and moved cautiously forward. A girl. She was carrying a bundle of sticks and was wearing a black shawl over long dark skirts clinging soddenly around her slender thighs and ankles.

One of the "witches," he thought doubtfully, the daughter? Or—? He was puzzled. As she drew close he was surprised—almost shocked—by her beauty. She had not the features of a tinker wench. To the

contrary, her skin, though scratched across one
cheek by brambles, was white and unlined. Her slant
eyes even through the uncertain light reflected the
azure quality of moorland pools. The lips were
full, yet proudly sculptured above the delicate chin.
A string of glass beads at the base of her throat
only emphasized the graceful lines of her slim neck.
Quite suddenly the image of the other beauty—the
one he was searching for, his brief acquaintance
of the fair—was dispelled by the one confronting
him.

"Why haven't I seen you before?" he asked, hardly
knowing what he said.

She smiled, and the smile, in a strange way, had a
haunting quality of familiarity. When she didn't answer, curiosity in him turned to quick, irrational
anger. Still grasping Blackfire's bridle with one hand,
he reached his other arm forward roughly and seized
her by a shoulder.

"Are you dumb?" he said. "Can't you speak?" The
feel of her cool, soft flesh inflamed him. His pressure
increased.

She flinched, and pulled herself away.

"You leave me alone," she said. "You leave me—
do you hear?" The words came out quietly in a soft
hiss.

He frowned, letting her go suddenly.

"What's the matter? I shan't hurt you. . . ."

Her expression changed. From defiance her lips
relaxed almost to a smile again. The frown lifted
above the clear eyes. She hesitated before saying,
"Why've you come here? What d'you want with us?
We've done no harm."

"I never said you had. Your name—that's all I want
—tell me your name, girl. I've a right to know."

"Rights? You've no rights with us."

"I think so," he told her, with lips hardening. "As heir to Penraven, I have power to question and make my own judgment on those wandering round our lands."

"This isn't yours. It's common land. King John gave it—to the people—folk like us, forever."

He stared at her, surprised.

"So you know your history."

She lifted her head. "Why shouldn't I?"

He smiled sardonically. "Indeed. Why not? I've no doubt you know much ordinary people do not. You're her daughter, aren't you? The tinker's wench?"

Her lips closed. Then she said, "If I am, what then?"

He was suddenly tired of fencing and argument, so he answered coldly, "One day you may need my help. You have a bad reputation. A little politeness from you now may stand you in good stead in the future. I'm a good friend but a bad enemy, girl, and I like to know who I'm dealing with. Your name— what is it?"

"Mara."

"Ah. Very apt." Justin's dark eyes glowed. "Since you know so much, you perhaps know there was once a gypsy girl also called Mara who fell in love with a gorgio gentleman and sold her family and her own soul to the Devil, in exchange for power over him. That is the legend, Mara, and to entrap him she was given a magical violin. Have you a violin, Mara? Do you play strange tunes at night to lure me from Penraven? Is it your music I hear sometimes when the chill wind whistles through the trees and the owl cries?" He was laughing. "Are you set on charming me, wild one, with your witch's melodies and moon-bright hair?"

He plunged forward again and grabbed her by the waist. Her hair fell back in a silken stream over her shoulders. The shawl dropped to the ground, and the dark bodice slipped where his hand clutched it, revealing one white breast. Desire overcame wisdom. With a rush of passion his lips were on her tilted mouth, traveling heedlessly to the rose-red nipple. She struggled, and as he suddenly released her she brought a hand sharply against his face.

He drew back abashed. But his voice was hard when he said, "Go on, little devil—run. One day I'll be back, though, and you'll come to me gladly, with humble sweet words on your lips. Penraven men do not forget."

The next moment she had turned and gone, slipping like a pale shadow into the encompassing darkness of the trees. The stallion, momentarily freed, was about to gallop away, nostrils flaring, head erect, ears pricked to the stirring of a rising wind. In three strides Justin had him by the mane. Clutching the bridle, he heaved himself into the saddle, and seconds later was cutting back toward Penraven. At the bend of the marshy track bordering the wood, he had a brief glimpse of another mount and rider, statically watching him from the moor above.

The figure was gray—gray as the cold stones standing starkly against the wild landscape. No features were clear. But Justin felt a sense of such concentrated malevolence, he reined a few yards ahead to take a second look. The horse and rider were moving then with a deliberate steady motion downward, toward the spot where Mara had been.

Cousin Rohan.

The truth registered through Justin's mind with

sudden impact, and with it was born a decision that eventually was to change the course of his life and the whole of Penraven's.

Somehow he had to save Mara from his licentious cousin, even if it meant resorting to the wildest, most outrageous means.

A measure of composure had returned to him when he reached his own stables.

But with Rohan it was quite different.

In the darkest clearing of the wood he had Mara's half-naked figure in his arms. His cruel hands bit hard into her buttocks, his mouth and body ravished hers mercilessly. His need was a weapon draining desire and life from her. And when it was over, he said, "That's to teach you who's master. Play with him if you like. Yes—I order you to. You'll listen and learn, and later you will recount to me every small detail, any scrap of knowledge you've heard. Look at me, before I take the whip to your back."

Her strange eyes opened. Her white arms reached to his shoulders. If she hated him, she also desired and knew herself to be forever in his power. Her lips parted placatingly. "Yes, Rohan," she said.

"Good."

He freed her, but before she attempted to move he said, with a bitter smile on his lascivious face, "Remember this, you are mine. Play the whore and madam where you choose—with my permission. But when I call, you come."

And again she assented.

He gave her a push, and threw her skirt at her. "Run away now to your hovel. Tonight I'll see you— at Boscarrion."

"Will my lady be there?" she asked, clutching the shabby garment to her breasts. Her trembling amused him.

"No. My lady is gone."

Her eyes widened. "Oh—where? For how long—sir?"

"That's none of your business. Off with you now; your questions bore me."

A second later she'd left him. The smile deepened on his face, then slowly died, leaving only darkness there, and a hatred bred from many years of frustration and greedy, unfathomable suspicion.

No one knew the jealous thoughts that from his youth had haunted him—the hints and veiled odd words dropped by servants here and there, that had started the enigma of a secret jigsaw in his quick mind. There had been no one to talk to, or plant the seed of reason and acceptance in his heart. So all his life he'd felt himself deprived, and so had been determined to take and savor everything that was offered.

Penraven one day should be his, as was rightful and his due. He had no facts to go upon. But the conviction itself was proof enough. And when the day came, he would have no mercy on anyone—least of all Justin, or the wild beauty of the wood who was merely a pawn for his ambitious and insatiable hurt.

The servants had been dismissed to their quarters. The large drawing room was warm from the fire and redolent of the heady smell of wine when Mara, wearing a large dark cape, entered the hall of Boscarrion.

Rohan, in a loose embroidered wrap, was waiting for her. His brain and body were already aflame from spirits he had taken to dispel the events of the day.

"Come in, wench," he said, with a mock bow at the door of the room.

She entered.

On the carved gilt back of a Louis Quinze chair lay a flimsy gown *à la Récamier* style.

"Put it on," he said. "And throw those rags away."

She obeyed mutely. Her pale form as she undressed was a shiver of silver and rose in the candlelight. She stepped from each garment gracefully, and was about to slip the elegant shift over her head when his savage arms encircled her from behind. He lifted her up, savoring her beauty avariciously for some moments while desire mounted in him. One hand felt through the thick sheen of her hair, fondling her skull as though he would crack it. Then he jerked it back, breathing heavily, watching the fear in her eyes gradually change to longing. He carried her to a chaise longue and threw her down.

"After this," he said, "you'll have no desire for any other man. And if you try to leave me, I'll kill you."

An hour later she was seated on her donkey riding back toward Pookswood along a secret narrow track shadowed by windblown nut trees.

Lillith was still moving about the cottage, a stooping, oldish woman now, with untidy gray hair, yet richly clad, her thick fingers heavily beringed by jewels.

"Bin there, have you?" she inquired. "The rich, cruel one of Boscarrion?"

Mara nodded mutely. She was tired.

A brown hand shot out and grasped her wrist. "Where is it, then? What've you got? And no cheating now or I'll have the skin off your back."

The girl handed her a small wallet of gold. The woman counted it. Then she looked up. "What else?"

Mara showed her a star-shaped brooch studded with a circle of rubies.

"I'm keeping this."

"You what?"

"I'm keeping it," the young voice said firmly. "It's mine. A pledge to him. He said so—and to match the stain. See . . ."

She slipped down her dress, showing a curious purple birthmark the shape of a circle that could have been a coiled reptile on her thigh.

The woman did not speak for a moment, then she said, "He noticed, did he? You showed him that?"

"He saw," the girl said fiercely. "Everything about me he saw and liked." She paused before adding, "And I liked him."

"That was well," Lillith told her, "because it's the Devil's mark, the mark of a witch. So just you see no one else hears of it, or we'll be hanged at the crossroads."

She did not know—no one did, except Christin Tregallis—that his own lady wife bore the same telltale mark on her thigh, and that for many generations it had been a peculiar characteristic of her early noble ancestors, who had seen that it was interwoven in the family coat of arms.

4

During the following weeks Justin contrived to see Mara several times, but not so frequently as he wished. Her beauty haunted his imagination. The

mystery of her personality both irritated and enchanted him. She said little about herself, and when
he pressed her for information, she would be evasive
and slip away with the sly speed of some frightened
wild thing into secret hideaways of the woodland. He
resented the hours when she was away from him, and
continuously planned how to install her at Penraven.

Marriage, he knew, would present almost insurmountable problems. Christin had already made his
wishes clear on this point. When his son left Oxford,
he would be expected to wed Annabella Fearnley,
the daughter of Sir Martin Fearnley, mineowner,
shipping magnate, and one of the richest men in the
whole of Cornwall. He had, as well, aristocratic con-
nections that would give ballast to the dignity and
pocket of the Tregallis family. Annabella was no
beauty; she was large and buxom but possessed a
sense of humor that Justin had enjoyed as a youth.
They had become good friends. He had been a frequent visitor to the stately Fearnley home near Falmouth during vacations and at periods when life at
Penraven became mildly boring.

Annabella, he knew, would be only too ready to
throw herself into his arms. She had done so once
already, following a fall from her horse when they
had been riding. She had not been hurt, but the
excuse of a sprained ankle had been sufficient for him
to make a thorough examination of her leg. As the
boot had been removed she'd given a little squeal
and fallen on her back. The white plumpness of her
firm flesh had sent a thrilling tremor through him.
Such a wealth of it—and with her rosy large mouth
glinting up at him, her pale blue eyes so expectant
and wildly excited, he'd done only what a chivalrous
young man could do, under the circumstances, he
told himself later—taken what she offered with oblig-

ing gratification. As she stood up afterward, smoothing the silky satin pink drawers before adjusting the thick dark skirt, she'd said, "You're quite a fella, Justin," and laughed uproariously.

He'd laughed too. The event had really been quite enjoyable. But as a wife! Doubts had gradually gnawed him during the days that followed, intensified by niggling concern about the consequences. He needn't have worried. Annabella had soon reassured him.

"As if I'd do that on you," she'd said with a wink. "I'm a big girl now, Justin. Babies are strictly for marriage. And you might not want to marry me, might you?" She'd given him a second wink, a hefty dig in the ribs, and a sidelong glance that induced him to say rashly, but with reserve, "I'm sure any man would be proud to marry you, Annabella."

"Sure?"

"Sure."

After that, friendship between the two families had become decidedly warmer. Sir Martin and Christin laughed together a good deal when they met, and there were secret convivial meetings in Penraven's library when the two men, cheerfully imbued with vintage brandy and cigars, made mutual plans for founding a wealthy and fruitful family dynasty.

It was unfortunate for Christin that on the evening before Justin left for Oxford the young man became engaged in a drunken brawl at a country fair near Penjust.

The event was held on Sarna's village green, which was a large one, enabling space for a number of booths, cheap-jack stalls with the usual conjurer, and a fortune-teller's tent. There was, as well, a platform erected for a group of players, and a crowd had gathered to watch the wrestling. When Justin arrived, a

black-clad minister—one of John Wesley's followers
—was already preaching doom and hell-fire to the
revelers, fist raised in condemnation, Bible in his
hand. Nearby a dwarf with a false nose was perform-
ing somersaults, to the amusement of a handful of
miners already raucous from too much mead and ale.

There was shouting and singing interjected with
the noise of argument from the door of the dram
house, The Goat and Star. Justin pushed his way toward the players' platform, but was interrupted by a
frenzy of shouts and a female scream.

He turned quickly to see a woman in a scarlet
gown being roughly handled and hoisted in the air by
two rascally-looking sailors. They muttered oaths and
obscene threats as her two slim legs kicked frenziedly from a froth of white petticoats and torn drawers. As Justin watched, horrified, she was flung from
one to the other, to the hilarious appreciation of the
crowd. He sprang forward with his cane raised. "Let
her go, you ruffians," he shouted, reaching with his
other hand for his pistol, "or I'll have you in the
stocks—or worse!"

Something in his manner and voice penetrated the
bawdy scene. There was a brief pause before the
muttering and shouting started up again, but on a
lower key.

"A thief—that's what she is—" one cried, "a
wicked trollop cheatin' poor folk—"

"Shai should be tek an' dragged by cart through th'
streets," a woman shouted.

"A whip to her tail-end, that's what the likes of her
do need—"

"Or burnin'," yelled another, "that's et—burn 'er
—burn 'er—"

"Hold your tongues," Justin shouted, "or by God
I'll see every one of you lands in jail!"

He raised his pistol threateningly. "Let me have the wench, and if she needs a beating, I'll see she has it. You can trust me. I'm a Tregallis. Justin Tregallis of Penraven."

The name caused a sudden lowering of voices. There was a confused hush followed by subdued muttering. The woman was released and the two men made their way back to the dram house after giving the tumbled figure a contemptuous push with a boot where the scarlet skirts and frills lay in a disordered heap on the ground.

Eyes watched with furtive anticipation as Justin stepped forward and picked her up. Many had looked forward to seeing her publicly whipped and raped. But none had expected to witness what did happen. As the girl lifted her head for a glimpse of her protector, the mane of thick black hair tumbled off—revealing a sudden flashing glint of streaming gold. At the same moment a bag of silver fell from a pocket, spilling over the trodden grass. Eager hands were outthrust greedily—the mass of fair hair hardly registered, as eyes popped at the clinking coins rolling about the ground. But Justin recognized her. Mara, the tinker wench.

In the confusion he managed to get the girl to the lane where his horse was tethered. He lifted her to the stallion's back, took his own coat off, and covered her head and shoulders with it.

"So it was you," he said accusingly before they started off. "*You* who misguided and beguiled me at Camborne with your high and mighty airs and false accent." He laughed contemptuously. "My lady Clarissa!—a thief—that's all. A lying tinker girl who airs her charms to cheat harmless villagers and gentry. How long have you been doing it? Eh? How long— you wicked chit?"

He paused, looking down into her strange eyes willing her to answer. Then suddenly, she spoke, like a young wildcat driven to defend herself.

"As long as I was old enough. My mother and I have to live. Not all folks are born to wealth like you." Under the red silk the panting motion of her uptilted ripening breasts was obvious. He felt desire stirring him. But his voice was controlled and hard when he told her, "In future you'll behave or I'll inform the law about you, and you'll be deported, or worse. So we shall have to decide what to do about you. Understand?"

The wildness of her face turned to gentle beguiling sweetness. "Oh, yes, sir, I understand."

Justin forced his eyes away from her.

"Take me to your home, then. I have something to say to your mother. And remember—there'll be no more wigs or dressing up. No more airs or pickpocketing. In future you'll behave, young woman. And before I leave for Oxford tomorrow, I'll see you safely in the care of our housekeeper at Penraven. She has a quick eye and a hard hand. Like my father also."

So it was, that after arguments and much bargaining with Lillith, Mara was taken to Penraven that same night, to start her hard training as maid to Elaine Tregallis.

Elaine took an instant liking to the girl, but Christin from the first was discomfited. He saw no reason for having a wench imposed on his household simply because his wild son, who was returning almost immediately to the university, had probably indulged in "a roll in the hay" with her, as they put it. Besides, she bore an uncommon resemblance to his lady wife, which started a string of conjectures in his mind— ideas that could prove damned difficult, if true. Another problem was her reputation. Mrs. Bohenna had confided to him after her brief interview with the girl that she was Lillith Gwarves's daughter from Pookswood way, and everyone knew that the couple were a wicked pair—disliked by the whole district and even feared by some.

He'd told Justin to take the wench back where she belonged, but Justin had answered with a flash of his dark eyes and belligerent set of his jaw that if she went, the Oxford session was over.

"I'm not leaving her without protection," he'd said fiercely, "and you can keep your cane to yourself, Father. I'm a man now, and not prepared to take any more of your bullying."

"Are you threatening me, you young scoundrel?" Christin had thundered, although secretly proud of the noble, fierce stance of the youth, the proud curve of his lips and challenging air.

"I'm telling you," Justin had answered. "And you may as well hear the rest of it. When I return at Christmas, I expect to find the girl well fed and happy and fully trained to her duties, or the marriage to Annabella is off—" He'd broken off, suddenly aware of the implication of his words.

Christin, seething with anger mixed with a gratifying sense of triumph, was mopping his brow vigorously. He walked to the window and stood there for some moments, staring out. While he got his thoughts in order, the rage in him died. Then he said, turning, "If I give my promise, you give yours, eh? About Annabella? You'll wed her as soon as your studies are done?"

A sudden dull red suffused Justin's face. He realized he'd been caught. A swift vision of a life bound to the bouncy Annabella Fearnley with her loud laugh, rollicking humor, sporty ways, and eternal horse-talk flooded his mind. She could be fun but also domineering. A large girl who would grow larger with the years. Still—a man could have a worse fate. She would bear strong sons, and if he married her, she'd see from the beginning he was master. She might fling her airs about now; but in bed—a quirk of humor softened his lips.

"Well?" he heard his father say impatiently.

"All right," Justin agreed with a show of heartiness. "I'll marry Annabella—if she'll have me."

Christin grinned. "She'll have you, boy. From what her father says, she's already thirsting, and ripe, and more than ready."

The analogy, for a moment, dimmed Justin's enthusiasm. He turned away abruptly. Christin called him back.

"Your hand, sir!"

Justin grudgingly felt his fingers and strong palm gripped by the older man.

The deal was settled. The immediate future of Justin Tregallis was secure. Neither man would break his word. Justin's only consolation was that in the meantime Mara would be safe at Penraven, and when he returned to Cornwall she would be there, waiting.

Mara was quick to learn the ways of Penraven, and with the shrewd insight taught her by Lillith, she instantly assessed Elaine's inherent vanity, and pandered to it with all the subtle skill of a born actress. Gone was the grand lady who had lured unsuspecting clients to Lillith's tents, and slyly pocketed others' gold. There were no curls or ringlets of black or red to arrest the eye. The masses of her own pale hair were discreetly hidden under a white cap. The fey wraithlike creature of the woods—who had so taunted and enchanted Justin with her fawnlike

grace and spitting tongue—had retreated magically
under a veneer of polite, well-mannered servitude.

No one would have suspected the wild heart beneath the calm facade. No one knew, either, of
moonless nights when she managed to creep unseen
from Penraven's granite walls and speed to Boscarrion for passionate hours in Rohan's arms. She had
her own wild pony of the moors that was quick to
sense her presence and obey her high call. Sometimes—only occasionally—the young mare would
not respond and so Mara crept back to her own bed
in the attic of the great house. Then she would lie
wakeful for a time with rebellious desire seething in
her, knowing that with Rohan it was the same. Much
as he taunted and ill-used her, his need of her was as
great as hers for him.

There were times when they hated each other,
when she scratched and defied him until he subdued
and ravished her cruelly. Then in the aftermath of
passion her delicate body would relax under his.
He'd tilt her chin, staring into her long azure eyes
with his own narrowed, and a sardonic smile on his
mouth, whispering, "Wildcat, wanton. Mine, aren't
you? See you remember."

And she'd answer, bemused. "Yours, oh, yes. Yours
—Rohan."

There'd be a pause until he pushed her away,
jumping up with some hard remark on his lips such
as, "Sir to you. And don't forget it. In all things you'll
do as I say. All things. Understand?"

Once she'd asked, feeling suddenly young and desperate, "Do you love me, Rohan?"

And he'd laughed. "Love? Don't be a fool. Who'd
love a gypsy's by-blow?"

She'd sprung from the bed, pushed past him fleet
as a panther, and at the door had turned and cried

as her blue eyes changed to feline jade, "If you call me that ever again, Rohan Tregallis, I'll kill you."

He'd laughed scornfully. "You try it, wench—and it will be the last time you try anything on Rohan Tregallis or any other lusting male."

In a flash she was gone, her throat suddenly thick with tears, knowing that in spite of his cruelty and harsh words Rohan would always win. They were bound together as inextricably as the cold granite to the wild moorland turf—as the gaunt cliffs were to the relentless ocean forever pounding their shore. Yet somewhere deep within her a voice told her she had been born to better things. Justin?

Her thoughts were frequently with him during the period he was away at Oxford. The memory of the passionate moments when he'd held her in his arms —the warmth of his kiss and dark flame of his eyes though filled with desire—held a protective quality she'd found in no other man. Many had admired and lusted after her—especially during her escapades at wild and lively gatherings when she'd played the high-and-mighty lady, flaunting her charms under a guise of wealth and rich attire.

To a certain extent she'd enjoyed the adventure of ensnaring and robbing the unsuspecting, although escape afterward had sometimes proved tricky. But there had always been Nelson, Rohan's little Negro boy, to assist and provide a diversion when necessary —Nelson, the link and messenger between the gypsies and Rohan. When Rohan had discovered Mara's thieving game, he had been quick to take advantage, accepting payments of her body for the fine garments provided. The sport amused and intrigued him. His knowledge of it put both tinker women firmly in his power. And as he'd pointed out frequently with heavy sarcasm, his attention and protection—so long as Mara behaved—provided safety from the law. If she took it into her pretty head to deceive him, that same head would soon have a rope round its neck.

Mara shivered whenever the terrible picture came to mind. At such moments wild plans possessed her to run away and hide herself on a boat sailing from Penzance or Falmouth for France or Ireland. But the idea quickly faded. She knew she could never be free of Rohan; neither did she wish to be. Had he been kinder—oh, then perhaps they could have found real love together. A little gentleness sometimes would have made such a difference. But she had found none of that in any man, except perhaps Justin. Justin—so broad and strong and handsome, yet with a sensitive streak in him that had induced him to bring her to his home, Penraven.

She was very often surprised at her own weakness and acquiescence in staying there. Having her charms hidden by heavy working clothes and caps was not at all to her choice. But apart from her promise to Rohan to stay and keep her eyes and ears open for any shred of gossip concerning family history and affairs, she was becoming daily more attached to her delicate, alcoholic, and neurotic mistress. A bond was steadily developing between them that was hard to understand.

In the middle of a drinking session, with the brandy bottle halfway to her lips, Elaine would suddenly pause, blink, and gape at the girl, as though seeing her for the first time.

Once she said in a burst of sobriety, "Your face reminds me of someone. Now who can it be, I wonder? Who?" She fumbled in her pochette and brought out a tiny gold-rimmed mirror studded with turquoises and having a slender gold handle.

Smoothing her hair with her thin beringed fingers, she peered into it and continued, "We have the same eyes. Yes, yes. How very funny. Odd, is it not, that you, a serving wench, should bear the slightest resemblance to a—a lady of quality such as myself?"

"Very strange, madam," Mara agreed composedly.

Elaine's pale cheeks flushed suddenly. She thrust the mirror aside and said crossly, "You are lying, girl. Don't lie to me. There is no resemblance. None—none, do you hear?" She took a quick drink of the brandy, sighed heavily, and fell back against the pillows, eyes closed. Then she came to life again abruptly. "Answer me, you impertinent wench."

Controlling a quick rush of temper, Mara replied, "Of course there's no resemblance. I was only agreeing with you, madam."

"Hm! Then don't. Liars are as bad—worse—than braggarts. Not to be trusted. And I do so need that— a friend, Mara. A friend I can trust in." The brandy was already beginning to work, sending tears of emotion down the haggard cheeks. She lifted a thin wrist. "Take my hand girl, and p-promise to be my f-friend."

Mara took it. It felt like a skeleton in her own firm palm. She shivered, but managed to say steadily, "I will always be your friend when you want me to be."

·And strangely it was true.

In a curious unfathomable way she felt drawn and obligated to the pathetic relic who must once have been beautiful, before life with Christin Tregallis had so cruelly disillusioned and embittered her. Yet it was Christin who had allowed Mara to stay at Penraven, whereas he so easily could have had her whipped and sent back to face Lillith's rage. There would have been a further beating then, for Lillith enjoyed the tidy weekly sum Justin had arranged for her. Rohan, too, would have been more than a little displeased.

So all things considered it was Christin who deserved Mara's gratitude. But she had none for him. Beneath the rubicund stern facade she sensed a ruthless quality, an assessing cold glint in the eyes far more deadly to her than Rohan's threats. Experience had taught Mara to be a shrewd judge of character, especially of men. She was seldom wrong, and decided therefore that the less she imposed herself on Christin's notice, the better. So with the competence of her acting ability she played the servile part, dressed discreetly and kept her personable attributes well hidden. She was cautious in her ways, though secretly watchful and always on the alert—listening. For the first weeks at the great house the other servants were suspicious in her company, lowering their voices when she approached and keeping any gossip to themselves.

But one thing she did learn—that Christin Tregallis doted on his son and resented his only daughter quite fiercely. To be proud of Justin was quite natural, Mara decided, remembering with a rush of warmth the young man's handsome looks, his strength and air of command. She already felt a stirring of affection and longing for him herself, although not for the world would she have dared to let Rohan know. But the girl! Why should a father dislike a daughter? Unless she was so ugly and stupid her presence was actually offensive.

Mara had subtly questioned Jenny, a kitchenmaid, about Olivia and discovered that, far from being even plain, Miss Olivia was growing into a real handsome young lady.

"Tall, she is, proud and a bit haughty, you could say," the girl had remarked, "and real fond of her

brother. A bit of a firebrand though. Wild—that's it.
If you ask me, there'll be fireworks here when she
leaves school, specially if Mr. Justin weds that stuck-
up bitch Annabella."

"Marry?" Mara had echoed. "I didn't know he was
going to be married."

"Why should you?" Jenny had said tartly. "You
doan' know nuthen 'bout Penraven yet."

"No." Mara's voice had been conciliatory. "I'm not
so lucky as you. But then you've got a safe position in
the house."

Jenny had flushed pleasurably. "You could say that,
I do s'pose; one day mebbe I'll get raised to housemaid. That'll be the day. Providin' she don't start
bossing folks around."

"Who?"

"That Annabella Fearnley, that's who. Big she is—
bossy—all ha-ha! big bosom and behind, and a way of
stickin' her fat chin up as makes you sick. I tell you
this though—ef she do think she's goin' to madam et
over Mr. Justin, she'll soon find et's the other way
round, an' I only hopes I'm there to see et."

The enlightening conversation had ended at this
point, interrupted by the unexpected entrance of
Mrs. Broome, the elderly cook. Jenny had made a
vigorous show of polishing a tray, and Mara had withdrawn discreetly with a tea tray for Elaine.

After that incident Mara had wondered frequently
about the two young women in Justin's life, especially Olivia.

Shortly before Christmas she had to wonder no
more.

Olivia and Annabella both arrived at Penraven.

Olivia was the first to appear, having traveled by
post chaise from Plymouth. She had been met at
Redruth by the family coach and driven cross-coun-

try along a maze of narrow lanes that had eventually
deposited her with her valise and luggage at the
doors of her home. The journey had been a bumpy
one and had taken longer than was usual, because of
the chill fog seeping from the moorland hills. Her
hands and feet were cold, in spite of the brown serge
cloak and her unbecoming thick dress, but elation at
being at Penraven brought a rising flood of warmth
to her stiff body, brightening her eyes and cheeks
and driving her to embrace everyone on the scene
with wild enthusiasm.

Everyone that is except Miss Cobbet, who was hovering about in the background looking frigidly disapproving of such abandoned behavior. Instinctively
Olivia's underlip protruded in distaste. Her chin took
a stubborn thrust forward. Silly old thing! Why had
her father insisted on retaining the creature when
lessons were no longer required? Just for a year, he'd
said, until Olivia proved she was capable of deporting
herself in a proper manner.

Olivia had inwardly seethed. Going to school was
bad enough, but to have Cobbet on her trail all the
time during the holidays was just too bad. One thing
Olivia had already decided—Cobbet would certainly
not be allowed to use her cane anymore. If she tried,
Olivia would pull it from her hand and snap it in two.
"Poor old Cobby"—Justin's name for her—was after
all only a miserable thin stick of a creature, no taller
now than Olivia herself, who had added inches to her
height during the months at school, and had thrusting pert breasts already stretching the bodice of the
restricting dress.

So she swept past her former jailor with merely a
slight inclination of her head, after throwing her
arms wildly around Mrs Broome the cook, embrac-
ing Dora the housemaid, even standing on tiptoe to

plant a kiss on Willy the under footman's cheek, and giving a hearty hug to Jenny. All gaped with astonishment and a lurking fear. Oh my dear Saul, Mrs. Broome thought. Whatever would the master say to this?

The master, fortunately, did not see, although Miss Cobbet attempted to have a disgruntled word in his ear. He was coming out of the library, and pushed her away irritably. Approaching Olivia, he noted with surprise how she had matured in such a brief time. Quite good-looking, too. Hm! A true Tregallis, which was something in her favor, he supposed.

He went forward and gave his daughter a cool dutiful kiss. "You look well," he said. "School's done something for you, I hope. Making a hole in my pocket—all that education."

Olivia smiled a little coldly. "I'm sure I'm learning the things you want, Father—how to primp and curtsey and how to catch a rich husband—"

"Don't be insolent, miss."

Again the taunting, slightly wicked smile. "I'm so sorry, Father. I thought that's what you wanted."

Christin, very red-faced, turned away, snorted, and walked back to the library. At the door he turned.

"See you're in a better and more dutiful frame of mind when you come down to dinner," he said shortly. "I'm having no ill manners from a slip of a girl in my house."

The door slammed. Miss Cobbet stepped forward with a flurry of black skirts and caught the girl's arm. "Behave yourself," she said—almost hissed—through narrowed lips, "or you'll be severely beaten, do you hear? I'm in charge of you still, and if you defy me I'll see you pay for it."

Olivia wrenched her arm free. "You'll do nothing,"

she said with cold emphasis, her brilliant dark eyes challenging the insipid gray ones haughtily, "because you are nothing anymore. *Nothing*. And if you try to make trouble for me, I shall tell my brother and he'll see you're dismissed."

A hand went to Miss Cobbet's lips in frustrated fury. For once the unhealthy pallor of her face turned to dull brick red. Under a poor attempt at dignity she turned and marched toward the school-room. There were muffled giggles and hushed comments from the servants, who were quickly ordered by Mrs. Broome to attend to their own duties. Olivia waited a moment for Willy to go ahead of her, carrying her valise, then she followed at a discreet distance, mounting the stairs quickly, smiling to herself and wildly pleased by the outcome of her confrontation with Miss Cobbet.

When she reached the landing leading to her own room, she saw a pale figure emerge from the shadows and a moment later was drawn into her mother's arms.

"Oh, my dear—my dear Livvy," Elaine gushed in a quivering voice, "how truly w-w-wonderful to have you back. My darling child—they are trying to kill me, did you know? Oh—it has been so terrible—if it had not been for Mara—but you don't know Mara, do you? Such a kind friend—such a—such a . . ." The voice faded incoherently.

Elaine's skeletal arms fell away; she blinked, closed her eyes, and clung momentarily to a gilt banister. With distaste Olivia noticed a strong scent of spirits blended with that of heavy perfume. An arm slipped instinctively round her mother's waist.

"You're ill, aren't you?" Olivia said. "I'm sorry." She tried to infuse sympathy into her voice, but could not help cringing distastefully against the quivering form. Sickness always mildly appalled her, and it was all she could do to help her mother back to the stuffy bedroom.

At first Olivia was aware only of the muted pinkish light and heavy air—of the thick rose-colored velvet curtains drawn across the windows, completely shutting out any remaining glow of twilight. There was a wan fire burning in the vast marble-topped grate. Candles flickered from a chest and bedside table, throwing eerie shadows around the cream walls, emphasizing the towering dark shape of the huge wardrobe and immense canopied bed. Mingled with the smell of spirits and scent was the peculiar odor of eau de cologne too liberally applied.

As Olivia guided Elaine to her bed she noticed an array of medicines and lotions arranged on the walnut table.

A bowl of late roses stood on the carved chest.

Steeling herself against the atmosphere, Olivia helped her mother to mount the bed and ease herself between the sheets. "Don't you want fresh air?" Olivia asked. "If I opened the window a little—"

She was interrupted by movement from a shadowed corner at the far side of the room. A slim shape emerged, wearing a mob cap and apron.

"Madam feels the cold," a soft voice said, "and does not wish there to be a draft."

Olivia stared, surprised.

"Who are you?"

"This is Mara," Elaine said, and her tones, though frail, were firm, even a little obstinate. "I told you about—about M-M-Mara, didn't I? Come here, my dear—my daughter does not understand. No one understands except you . . ." she sighed, "and yet there was once a time when I was the toast of—of—where was it? I forget. But did you know about the—the

Prince of Wales?" Her lips curved in a secret faraway smile. "Oh, he admired me very much before that silly woman—who was she now? I forget—I forget so much these days." Tears filled her blue eyes as she fell back against the pillows.

"Don't try to remember," Mara's soft silky voice urged. "You must rest and sleep a little. What about your medicine, madam?" The pale face nodded weakly. Mara poured a teaspoonful of liquid from a small bottle and placed it to Elaine's lips. A second later the eyes closed, there was a heavy sigh, and Elaine was already in a half doze.

The two girls stared at each other.

"What is that stuff?" Olivia demanded.

Mara's delicate brows arched above her lovely eyes. "Just medicine," she said, "ordered by the apothecary."

"Are you in charge, then?" Olivia asked with faint challenge in her voice.

Dark fringes of lashes, so unusual for the very pale skin, and locks of gold hair escaped from beneath the cap, shadowed the luminous eyes as Mara replied coldly, "No. I am merely a servant; only too pleased to fulfill any service required of me for madam."

"Who engaged you?" Olivia demanded, more blatantly than was polite.

A slight contemptuous smile tilted the perfectly modeled lips. "I hardly think that is anyone's affair but my own."

Olivia flushed. "I'm the daughter of the house. I have a right to know."

There was the glint of pearly teeth before Mara gave a sarcastic little bow.

"Very well, then, it was your brother, Mr. Justin Tregallis."

"Justin?" Surprise momentarily shocked the

haughtiness from Olivia's voice. "Why? How could he? He's at Oxford."

"He was not at Oxford when he arranged with his father for me to work here."

"I—" Olivia struggled with her emotions. There was something about the young woman that dismayed and confused her. For one thing she did not speak like a servant, and for another, looked at more closely she was very pretty, in spite of her ugly clothes.

"Oh, I see," Olivia said, childishly bewildered. "Still—" She drew herself up. "When you speak to me you should say 'Miss Olivia.'"

Again the secret sly smile.

"Certainly Miss—Olivia."

"And don't look like that."

"What?"

"As though—as though I was a child."

"But you are, aren't you?" the girl said, turning away. "Otherwise you wouldn't dare talk to me in that way."

"What do you mean?"

"I have friends here."

"Justin?"

Mara did not answer the question in words, but her look was sufficient. Following an awkward pause she added, "We shouldn't argue when madam's dozing. She needs rest."

Olivia stared down at her mother's sleeping form. What had happened over the years to so completely change Elaine Tregallis? When had the drinking started? The lassitude and alternating moods of extreme possessiveness or sudden turning away from her children to the shadows of disillusionment? Olivia recalled, when she was about six years old, asking Justin about her mother.

"Why is Mama so funny?" she'd said. "Why doesn't she love me like she once did? Why is she different?"

And the boy had said, shrugging, "Is she different? I hadn't noticed. To me she's the same. She never liked me anyhow. It doesn't worry me. Oh, stop brooding, Livvy. You're always on about nothing."

"Why doesn't Mama like you?" Olivia had persisted stubbornly. "I think you're the nicest person in the whole world, Justin. And the wonderfulest."

He had flushed.

"Now you're being a softy. Leave me alone and go and play somewhere."

Tears, unpredictably, had filled Olivia's dark eyes and brimmed over down her round cheeks. Justin had seen, and put his arm round her, then taken his own kerchief and wiped them away. The contact had filled him with compassion, and an alien queer feeling—never entirely to leave him—that he felt no true kinship with her, only a deep affection. There was nothing similar in looks about them, no trait or characteristic of personality. In fact, it was very hard to accept she was his sister at all, but was something more—something more potent than blood, and far more dangerous.

He'd told no one of this, and dismissed the haunting thought later as passing foolishness. Once or twice he'd vaguely pondered on the suggestion that Olivia could have been the unfortunate result of Elaine's dallying with some secret lover. Such a state of affairs was not uncommon, and would explain his father's apparent hostility to the child. It could be the answer also to the steady decline in his mother's health and her addiction to the bottle, which had driven Christin from the marital bed, or vice versa. Whichever way it was didn't matter. The fact remained. His parents no longer slept together.

It had occurred to him as he grew older that Cousin Rohan might be at the root of the trouble. Then Justin had dismissed this suggestion. There had been no friendly contact with the two families since Ellis's early death. Boscarrion, "the dark house on the dunes" as it was known, was a place of ill repute, and Elaine would have had nothing to do with Rohan.

Naturally there had been fleeting confrontations from time to time when Rohan and Justin had passed each other riding the moors. Neither had stopped or acknowledged the other, though Justin had been aware of his cousin's striking looks, which though unpleasant had an aggressive pride and bearing mildly discomfiting to the younger man. Rascal he might be, Justin had decided, but during the brief interval it had seemed to him that something of the very nature of the elements—relentless, wild, and granite-hard—had swept by.

Mild regret had stirred him that there could be no contact or adventurous spirit shared. However, with Justin's departure for Oxford, new interests had proved the folly of giving Cousin Rohan a second thought. "I am my father's son," he had told himself determinedly. "The heir to a respected name and house, and I'll damned well do my best to honor it."

During his first year at the university he'd tried.

But the truth was that studying history and English bored him. He felt an honors degree would be beyond his powers, and that he would have been of far more use to Christin dealing with the affairs of Wildellern, the family copper mine, and the problem of reopening a further one reputed to be still rich with ore on the site of the old Crannick Mine. This mine had been discontinued working in 1814, owing, it was said, to the finance needed for sinking new and proper shafts and providing fresh adits for a quality of ore that in the end might not prove worthwhile.

Crannick was situated on the edge of the cliff, northward beyond Penraven. Justin's imagination had long been fired by its possibilities, and during the tedious studies at Oxford the matter had haunted him. As he entered the family home on the day following Olivia's talk with Mara, he was debating with himself how best to put a certain proposition to his father—a kind of tempting blackmail: marriage to Annabella not at some future date, but immediately —providing he would be allowed to leave the university and devote his considerable energies to Crannick.

Olivia, as usual, was excitedly lingering about to meet him, and he was surprised at his warm response to her soft lips on his cheek—the abandon of her arms reaching to his shoulders, and the excited stirring of affection between them as her young breasts pressed close against his velvet jacket. When the first greetings were over, he took her hands and let his eyes flicker admiringly over her ripening form.

"Why, Livvy," he said, "you have changed. Quite a young lady."

"Yes, Justin," she agreed, fluttering her lashes and looking falsely demure. "I am. Am I not?"

He laughed outright at her adult manner of speech.

"I don't believe it for one moment," he said. "And stop pretending. Once a minx, always a minx. But I must say you look quite a charming one."

Two spots of fiery color burned in her cheeks. Any compliment from Justin was so pleasing to her she also felt acutely embarrassed. She shrugged, and the laughter died from her face. "It's the dress I suppose," she said. "Do you like it?" She turned this way, and then that, to demonstrate effectively the green silk emphasizing the tiny waist, and the creamy shoulders beneath the full puffed sleeves graduating to the slender wrists. The neckline was low—rather too low, Justin decided, for her age—and edged with a cream embroidery frill. The skirt fell gracefully to her ankles and was also frilled. With her dark curls parted in the center and drawn to the top of her head by a satin ribbon, she looked very unlike the girl who'd driven off months earlier to boarding school.

"Charming, Livvy," Justin said. "Where did you get it?"

"A friend gave it to me—a school friend," his sister said.

"She's very rich. Her father owns two shipping lines and lets her have just what she wants—loads of money and clothes. Her name's Verity. Verity Clare."

"Hm! She sounds the sort of girl I ought to know," Justin remarked. "If it wasn't for Annabella, I'd take a trip with you to Plymouth just for the pleasure of making her acquaintance."

Olivia frowned.

"Annabella? Do you mean Annabella Fearnley? What's she got to do with it?"

Justin paused for a moment before answering calmly, "I'm going to marry her."

"You—what?"

"Marry her, sister dear," Justin continued, looking away in pretense of adjusting his cravat. Olivia's expression exasperated him—so suddenly shocked and drained of happiness. It was as though life had been sapped out of her at one blow. Then he heard her saying in a very quiet voice, "It isn't true, is it, Justin? You're playing with me. You don't mean it?"

He turned around quickly, staring at her with a frown drawn close between his dark eyes.

"Of course I mean it. Why shouldn't I? It's always been expected of me—"

"What does that matter?"

"Believe me, Livvy, such things matter a great deal. Besides—I like Annabella. She's fun."

"Fun? Fun?" Olivia almost choked on the word. "If you marry her, you'll be a fool, Justin. Just a stupid, silly fool. I won't let you, I won't—" All resemblance to the refined young lady from finishing school had vanished. Olivia stamped her foot and was about to carry the argument further when Christin appeared from his favorite sanctum, the library.

"Now, now," he said, "what's going on here? Ah, Justin, my boy, I'm glad to see you. Where's that man to carry your baggage up? And what are you making a scene about, young woman?" He eyed his daughter coldly. "Go upstairs immediately—and take that fancy thing off. You should be ashamed of yourself. Any trollop would know better than to greet your brother in such a—such vulgar array. Miss Cobbet—"

It was unfortunate that the governess should appear at that very worst of moments. She had been spying and listening of course, Olivia decided darkly.

The irate woman, with a spiteful glance of triumph, came forward and took Olivia's arm. Olivia pulled herself away immediately. "Let me go, you old cat. Don't dare to touch me." Miss Cobbet stared aghast at Christin, who was about to raise his cane. Justin sprang to Olivia's defense.

"Leave her alone," he said to the woman, and to Christin, "Livvy didn't mean anything. She was just surprised at my news."

"News? What news? Not been sent down, have you?"

Justin took his father's arm placatingly. "No, no,

nothing of the sort. I was just mentioning about Annabella."

Suspicion flooded Christin's eyes for a moment, then faded to expectancy. "Ah! Hm! I see."

He waited.

"I was telling Livvy I'd like Annabella and myself to get married as soon as possible," Justin explained in equable tones. "I've got a plan, Father...." He put his hand on Christin's arm, and together the two men walked back to the library. A servant had appeared meanwhile to take Justin's luggage upstairs. Behind, from the far end of the hall leading to the kitchens, Justin had a glimpse of a pale, ethereal face watching him from the shadows. Mara. He had almost forgotten her during the uncomfortable interim with Olivia. That brief reminder of her presence disturbed him profoundly. What was to become of her in the future? He'd have to solve the question somehow; she couldn't just be abandoned now that he'd taken her into the house. On the other hand, neither could he picture her forever playing the role of underling and maidservant.

Still, his first immediate problem was to have the matter of his marriage settled, and Oxford finally disposed of. Until then even he had not realized how profoundly dull the university had become.

Upstairs in her room, Olivia sat on her bed, stormy-eyed and sullen-faced. If Justin married Annabella, she wondered how she would be able to bear it. Somehow she'd imagined they'd always be together, even when she was grown up. Now, she realized suddenly, that would not be so. If what he'd said was true, Annabella would probably come to Penraven and act as mistress of the house. Elaine was no use, and her father was getting old. There was no way of

averting the situation. Justin himself had chosen his
own future.

After a few minutes of depressing conjecture
Olivia quickly removed the green dress, stamped on
it before flinging it on to the bed, and presently,
when she'd changed into her riding habit, she made
her way to the stables to have her mare saddled for
a ride.

The light was already fading, but she didn't care,
and to the dismay of the young groom she was soon
speeding over the moors toward the bridge leading
to Red River, in the direction of Boscarrion.

5

Olivia was perplexed as she stared down at the house.
A wind had risen during her ride, and clouds of sand
swept from the sea to the shadowed building. She did
not usually indulge in morbid fancies, but it seemed
to her that the whole place brooded with unhappiness and thwarted ambition. The queer mixture of
chimneys and gables appeared veiled and insecure.
She wondered what restoration could do for it, but
could not imagine her cousin's home, ever, as a
cheerful dwelling.

She remembered, during those moments poised
on her pony, the bitterness of Rohan's manner on the
one occasion of their meeting—and the macabre in-

terior of the house, so curiously intermixed with valuable relics and sense of approaching decay. It seemed wrong, she thought, that any family should be so divided. It would have been exciting to be able to visit openly and be friends.

Not that Cousin Rohan was the ordinary friendly type of man. There had been something fascinating about him, though. He could be quite handsome if he smiled naturally without the bitter twist to his lips. And he had helped to get her home safely to Penraven on the evening of her fall. Everything had been all right until she mentioned her father. Then he'd changed. Perhaps the Countess of Lefrougé was the root of the trouble. Perhaps Christin was in love with the exotic Frenchwoman, too. Everyone at Penraven knew that Christin did not sleep with his wife anymore. Was that it? A sort of terrible greedy jealousy gnawing between her father and his nephew?

Oh, there were so many possibilities. And how wonderful, she thought with sudden childlike enthusiasm, if she could bring the whole Tregallis family together again.

Just as quickly as it had arisen, her wild idea faded. Obviously, Christin was too stubborn to accept any overture from Rohan, just as Rohan probably would never be so humble as to make it.

Life was so very frustrating. The depressing news of Justin's impending marriage to Annabella seemed to have cast a blight over everything. As Olivia turned and set off again for Penraven, rebellion churned and intensified in her. It would be terrible having to live under the same roof as Justin with bouncy Annabella in charge of things—ordering the servants about, insisting on queening it at the family dining table. The picture was so unpleasantly easy to

imagine—Annabella sitting at one end with Justin,
Christin at the other, and Olivia herself in between,
having to listen to their boring conversation while
Annabella nudged and joked with Justin, rolling her
stupid round eyes at Christin whenever she had the
opportunity.

Of course it was the money, she decided practically, cantering back over the bridge along the moorland track toward Penraven. The proposed mine
needed finance to get it started, and Sir Martin would
probably give a large dowry when Justin and Annabella married—if only to get her off his hands.

Why had marriage to be such a contrived and mercenary business? No wonder that Lord Byron—
Olivia's particular romantic hero—and the poet Shel-
ley kicked against it. The authoress Jane Austen, who
had died only last year, had indeed described
women's lot with accurate irony in *Pride and Preju-
dice*. That silly Mrs. Bennet in the book, scheming
and conniving so gushingly to catch rich husbands for
her daughters! The whole business appeared revolting to Olivia. Of course, Elizabeth Bennet, in the
end, had been lucky in marrying the brooding, dark
Mr. Darcy. But apart from this one pleasant happening, the rest of the girls in the novel appeared terribly flat and uninteresting.

Now Olivia's own handsome and dashing brother
had allowed himself to get involved in a mercenary
marriage deal. She was sure it was that—it couldn't
be anything else. He couldn't possibly be in love with
anyone like Annabella. Well, she, Olivia, wouldn't
allow her father to order *her* life.

The sudden quick decision made Olivia feel better.
She kicked Moonbeam to a faster speed and soon
reached the stables of Penraven.

No one was about there except Justin and the head groom. Justin eyed her suspiciously as she dismounted and handed Moonbeam over to the man.

"Where have you been?" he inquired. "Riding about on your own at this hour?"

"Trying to get that mean creature out of my mind," Olivia replied with a toss of her head, but refused to face her brother's direct stare.

"Who?"

"You know who," she said, flashing a sudden fiery glance at him. "That horrible Cobby. Unless Papa gets rid of her, I'll run away—I really will, Justin." Her mouth was stubborn, a child's mouth. But her eyes, so dark and sorrowful and rebellious, were those of a young woman refusing to submit anymore to the ignominious tyranny of a vengeful governess.

Justin took her arm, giving a conspiratorial look toward Adam, who had a weak spot for his dashing young master. "Come along," he said. "We'll go in together, and if anyone questions you, I'll do the answering. There'll be no trouble. I quite agree with you about that spiteful woman. Penraven would be a happier place without her, and I don't think you'll have to wait long."

They were walking to the drive; Olivia stopped, staring up at her brother with sudden brilliant expectancy on her face. "Do you mean it? It is really true? Is she leaving, Justin? Because of you? Have you said anything?"

Justin grinned. "I've already put more than one spoke in her wheel, as they say. And as Father happens to be in a good mood just now, I don't think her plain face will be with us much longer."

"Oh, Justin!" Olivia's smile was radiant. "Thank you. Thank you. But . . ." She paused a moment as her

expression sobered. "Is that because of Annabella?
Papa's good mood, I mean? Are you going to marry
her, Justin? Really?"

Her voice was so urgent, her breath so quick with
apprehension, Justin released her arm gently.

"Quite true, Livvy," he said. "I've given my word.
I told you, if you remember. So we'll drop the sub-
ject, if you don't mind."

Olivia was silent. Obviously when Justin spoke in
that particular tone, there was no point in arguing
with him. Her mood turned from happiness to cheer-
less acceptance. She did not speak again until they
approached a side door to the house, leading through
a conservatory to the dining room. "I suppose it's
because of Crannick," she said then. "The old mine,
isn't it? Papa needs money, and Annabella will give
it. That's the real reason."

Justin was about to reply heatedly when his attention was diverted by the graceful movement of a
woman's form behind the glass. He pushed the door
open, ushered Olivia in, and followed her, narrowing
his eyes slightly. Mara stood there, holding a pair of
scissors. In the other hand she carried a few white
star-shaped flowers glowing pale among slender curling fronds of fern. The flowers were the night-bloom-
ing type of an exotic plant originally brought from
abroad by one of the earliest Tregallis ancestors. Justin stared.

Against the green verdancy, Mara's face was as
pale and radiant as the blooms. Her cap had fallen
back and lay from its strings against her shoulders.
Candlelight from the adjoining room caught the
glint of her silver-gold hair. Her head was delicately
raised on the slim neck, there was a tentative smile
on the tilted lips. All the colors of the rainbow
seemed to flash in her luminous eyes.

Olivia was aware instantly of Justin's start, his quick reaction to the girl's beauty. No one at Penraven had seen her without her cap, except perhaps Elaine. Olivia herself was startled.

"Mara!" she heard Justin saying quietly, almost on a sigh.

The girl gave a little bob.

"I was told by madam to cut some flowers for her room—sir," she said in explanation.

"Does my father know?" Justin questioned mechanically, his eyes never leaving her face.

"Oh, yes," Mara answered. "I asked first."

"And do you—do you generally take off your cap to do your work?" Justin said, forcing himself to sound cold and formal.

"No, not generally." Mara's manner had changed, she looked upset, even a little defiant. Justin took Olivia's hand again and drew her toward the dining room.

"I suppose you know what you're about," he said shortly. "Come, Livvy." He pushed past the girl, dragging his sister with him. A flower fell from Mara's hand to the floor. Turning to look back Olivia noticed, but Justin did not. When they reached the hall Olivia said, "She's so pretty, isn't she, Justin? What a shame Annabella doesn't look like that."

The remark angered Justin quite unreasonably.

"You don't know what you're talking about," he said, his words grating in his own ears. "Hurry up now and get changed before Cobby finds you with her little stick."

"But, Justin, you said—"

"It doesn't matter what I said. Unless you behave there'll be trouble. So don't argue."

Olivia went upstairs dragging her feet miserably, wondering why Justin had to change so quickly from being nice and helpful to being in one of his bad moods. Was it because of Annabella, or Mara?

Whichever it was didn't matter. But she wished there were something truly dependable at Penraven, something she could rely on to keep her safe from the varying emotional moods filling the house.

Still, Christmas was coming—Christmas and Annabella. Perhaps Annabella's jaunty moods would dispel gloom for a bit. And Justin would have a chance to get to know her better, which might mean he wouldn't marry her after all.

In a queer, unfathomable way Olivia sensed that Elaine's strange new maid could bring far more disaster to Penraven than would Sir Martin Fearnley's daughter. She didn't admit it to herself; the fact was, though, that no one in the world had the right to be as beautiful as Mara was.

In a hazy way these vague thoughts flooded Olivia's mind through the rest of the evening. But by the next day they were completely dispelled, because Annabella Fearnley arrived with her aunt, Miss Elizabeth. Sir Martin had intended to enjoy further planning and conversation with Christin, but at the last minute had been prevented because of the certain mysterious malady of his wife, who had developed migraine and a temperature.

Miss Elizabeth was extremely portly, with a round, primped-up mouth above a number of chins, and very shrewd, small eyes set in a maze of puffed, rouged wrinkles. She had a cultured loud voice but was overdressed, wearing too many rings and an extravagantly befeathered hat on her piled-up hair.

Annabella, resplendent in pale blue velvet trimmed with fur, appeared ridiculous, Olivia thought, watching her dismount from the Fearnley chaise to walk with her aunt up the steps. Both women looked so extremely large. A coachman followed, laboring under the weight of two immense valises and numerous boxes and packages. From the window of the large lounge Olivia giggled. Supposing the aunt stumbled and sent Annabella rolling down, tumbling the manservant and array of hatboxes to the ground? She was sure Miss Fearnley and her niece wouldn't be hurt—they would just roll like blown-up balloons.

The next moment Olivia was ashamed of the uncharitable thought. It would be dreadful if it really happened. Christmas would be spoiled, and everyone would be rushing up and downstairs wailing over poor dear Annabella and her statuesque aunt! There'd be no time for fun or anything else at all. So she crossed her fingers, grudgingly wished the pompous couple well, and left the window to peep through a chink of the lounge door as they entered the hall.

There was a buzz of activity as servants took the luggage. A puffing and panting, followed by high-voiced exclamations from Miss Elizabeth, who proceeded immediately to use smelling salts with a show of exhaustion. Then Christin and Justin appeared. Justin stepped forward, as Annabella, both arms spread, rushed toward him.

Olivia shut the door with a snap. How awful, she thought. How sickening. It was going to be far worse than she'd imagined, and she dreaded the thought of dinner that evening.

However, everything considered, the meal passed off quite well. Most of Christin's remarks were addressed to Miss Fearnley, giving Justin and Annabella little chance to talk together. Occasionally Justin's glance flickered to Annabella's expanse of powdered bosom above tightly stretched green silk, and Olivia wondered what he was thinking. Did he approve or not? It was hard to decide; Justin could be ambiguous and very secretive of his own thoughts when he wanted to be. But there was a curious assessing look in his eyes that told her he was very definitely considering the situation.

"Oh, do let him see how boring, how stupid, she is," Olivia prayed inwardly, though she wasn't aware who or what she was praying to. "Please—please don't let Justin marry her."

In the next few days, though, it appeared that her wishes were going to be ignored. The weather turned crisp and dry, with a flurry of thin snow in it. Justin and Annabella went riding together during the daytime, and in the evenings Annabella proved her accomplishments by singing ballads and accompanying herself at the grand piano in the large drawing room, to the great satisfaction of Miss Elizabeth, and presumably Christin, who applauded vigorously after each item. Justin also praised Annabella's musical ability, and when Olivia dug him fiercely in the ribs, he merely glanced at her coldly and said in a whisper, "Behave yourself, or I'll get Cobby."

After such episodes Olivia sometimes managed to extricate herself by the excuse of a headache or feeling tired. But more often she had to bear the stuffy business until the very end.

Once she slipped out unseen, intending to go for a wander around the gardens or have a breath of fresh air on the moor. But seeing Mara halfway down the main hall, she decided it was safer to go to her own room and lock herself in. After all, the strange girl might say something to Christin. You couldn't tell with servants, and this one had an odd look in her eyes sometimes when they met by chance—a look that seemed to say, "I'm not like the others—I'm different. I could tell you a great deal if I'd a mind to.

I could be a friend to you, but a very bad enemy."

Those long, luminous azure blue eyes always had a compelling effect on Olivia, and that evening before going upstairs she took a few steps to meet the girl.

"What are you doing there?" she asked. "Standing about. Do you want anything?"

Mara shook her head slowly. The cap half fell off. She reached up with one hand and caught it. Her hair fell like a pale shroud around her flower face.

"Nothing you can give, miss," she answered in a low sweet voice.

Olivia stared, stupefied. "What lovely hair you've got."

"Yes." Mara pushed the stream of it under her cap again. "So madam tells me."

"You mean my mother?"

The girl nodded. "She likes pretty things around her."

"You're very vain," Olivia remarked, "calling yourself pretty."

Mara shrugged. "Would you rather I lied?"

"Of course not. But—"

"I've been ordered not to lie," Mara continued, still in those calm soft tones, "by the master."

"My father?"

A wide, sweet, yet faintly sly smile tilted the girl's lips. "Oh, no, miss. Mr. Christin hasn't a thought for me. I meant Mr. Justin."

"But . . ." Olivia hesitated before inquiring with a hint of temper, "what has my brother got to do with it? He doesn't own the house—it's—"

"He will one day," Mara said. "And it was him—Mr. Justin—who brought me here."

Olivia struggled with her indignation.

"Perhaps," she agreed grudgingly. "To be a servant. Unless you do your work properly you won't stay."

"I shall stay," Mara told the younger girl quietly, with an assurance that shook Olivia, "and I do what I'm told to. I look after madam, your mother, and she's already attached to me. So if you'll excuse me, I must go now to prepare her nightcap."

She turned, and without another word retreated to the kitchen quarters, leaving Olivia nonplussed and still wondering.

Annabella and her aunt were due to leave Penraven by the end of December to enable them to be at Falmouth for the New Year. Before the day arrived, however, something unpredictable occurred.

Justin, having resigned himself to marriage with Annabella, found himself quite unable to reconcile his own emotions to so dull a fate, which viewed in solitary moments presented an interminably dreary prospect. He slept badly, in spite of energetic hours riding and tramping the moors with his future wife. Looking back, he found it hard to pinpoint the exact moment when positive acknowledgment of the engagement had been expressed. He had never said to Annabella, "I love you," or "Will you be my wife?" They—or rather he—had simply drifted with the arrangement, through a promise given to his father and Annabella's obvious delight and determination to have the future so satisfactorily settled.

He had forgotten the first time she'd said, "When we're married, darling, we'll do—so and so, or something or other." But it had happened, and he'd complied, and on Christmas Eve he'd dutifully presented her with a diamond ring thoughtfully produced by his mother from her large collection of jewelry in one of her more sober moments.

"I don't envy you," she'd said with a wry twist of

her lips. "But no doubt that horsey girl will provide you with strong sons, and that's the important thing, isn't it? The only thing men really want."

Surprised at her sarcasm, Justin had replied, "Many, I believe, also wish for love."

Elaine had sighed.

"Maybe. But obviously you don't. No matter. No doubt the Tregallis fortunes will be considerably enhanced."

Justin was about to reply shortly when Mara had appeared with one of his mother's concoctions on a tray. He'd flung her a quick glance, nodded curtly, and marched out of the room, slamming the door sharply.

Following this instance he had tried to avoid contact with the girl as much as possible. Yet, although her presence so disturbed him, the thought of sending her away never occurred to him. He had given her his protection, and did not intend to break his word. Also, he was jealous of any other man lusting after her. Deep inside him was a secret desire to keep what he could of her unsullied and for himself only.

Yet, how could he do it, in view of his forthcoming marriage? Later, possibly, when Annabella was conventionally installed at Penraven as his wife, he might be able to arrange someplace for Mara. Provide her with a new cottage of her own, or establish her as mistress some distance away at Penzance or, better still, Truro. When he had taken the plunge and informed his father definitely that he had no intention whatsoever of furthering his studies at the university, work at Crannick would afford frequent excuses for trips up-country.

Lying did not come easily to him. In all things he liked to be open and completely unashamed and master of his own actions. But the circumstances of his commitment to Mara now made this impossible. He sensed she would not forever be content to be a mere servant for his mother. Therefore he had to provide a reasonable alternative for the future.

The problem at times seemed unsolvable. One evening three days before Annabella and her aunt were to leave for Falmouth, Justin set off for a late-night walk across the moors, in an effort to get his mind and nerves at rest. Like Olivia, he was relieved Christmas festivities were at last over. The good food and wine about had made the boring period bearable. There had been hearty amusing moments when he'd succumbed to Annabella's amorous overtures. But the aftermath had been depressing when he realized gloomily what he was letting himself in for.

Women! Botheration to all women, he thought glumly on that certain night as he set off along the track cutting around the hump of moorland hills and precipitous coast of the north cliffs. It was a wild night, with shreds of black clouds blown rapidly across a rising moon. The sea glittered fitfully like dark glass below him. The air was salty and strong. He drew it deeply into his lungs, dispelling all thoughts of dull domesticity, bracing himself against the wind, as the far-flung sting of foam bit face and lips, driving him to wild exhilaration. For a moment he paused, scanning the glittering line of coast. Against the fitful night sky, the stark remains of the Crannick workings jutted from a jagged headland of rock stretching like a giant black finger into the water.

Ambition quickened in him. To have that relic of the past working, with tin and copper enriching Penraven, proving his own ability to himself and Christin —this surely justified his marriage to Annabella. Love? What was love, in comparison with man's con-

quest of earth and elements? And what was love anyway? Did it really exist? In ten or twenty years he'd
be nearing middle age, the period when a man was
fired by comfort in bed rather than useless yearnings
for romance. Besides, he'd never yet met a woman
capable of satisfying his every need—not even Mara,
whose beauty might enchant him, but whose real
worth hadn't a fraction of his own young sister's—
Olivia's. If Olivia had been more mature and not of
his own kin, he could have found release and peace
with her, laughed and suffered with her, fought and
possessed her with abandon and understanding. Yet
all the laws of man and Nature forbade such a relationship. She was not his, nor ever could be. So he
pushed her image resolutely into perspective, turned
suddenly, and cut up the moors toward the high
ridge, where he took a westerly direction along a
high sheep track over Penraven.

He was about to cut down to the right when his
quick ear caught another sound above the wind's
moan—a faint thudding of hooves pounding the
short turf. He stood perfectly still, watching, as a
brilliant flash of moonlight lit the dramatic scene to
sudden clarity. Rocks, windblown humped trees, and
scudding shadows emerged dark against the silvered
ground. And less than a hundred yards away, at a
point above Red River Bridge, he saw the silhouetted
form of a girl on a horse. She was riding bareback, her
black skirt blown back from her knees. Near the river
where it flowed in a stream downward, she halted
the animal—one of the wild mountain ponies, obviously—dismounted, and gave it a slap. The pony
reared, snorting with delight, and a second later had
galloped away into the shadowed evening.

The girl lifted her skirts and stepped carefully but
with considerable speed over a number of stones

providing foothold. Justin knew the place. It was frequently used by shepherds. The stepping-stones provided a short cut from one side of the river to the other, except at flood times, when the water tumbled in a swollen torrent over the moor, leaving the earth boggy for days afterward.

Justin waited.

As he'd expected, the girl, half running, was making her way to the Penraven path down. As she pulled her flying cape free of entangling brambles, her hood, shawl, or whatever it was she was wearing, was torn from her head and the pale gold hair blew out behind her in a flying silver stream.

Mara! He'd thought so.

She pushed the covering back on her head, hiding her face. But with a sharp movement Justin was after her, cutting through furze and undergrowth to intercept her before she reached the house.

For some minutes, due to a sudden massing of cloud and blurring from bushes, he lost sight of her. But as he reached the wider moorland path leading to the drive, he saw her cut around a rock and come speeding toward him.

When she saw him, she stopped short and just stood there staring. He hurried toward her. She turned, holding the hood of her cape tightly under her chin, head bent, and made a frantic dash for the sheltering rocks and undergrowth. But he was too swift for her. By then the moon was out again and before she could slip away, he caught her from behind, swiveled her around, and with his hands gripping her fiercely was speaking between gasps of anger and desire.

"Where have you been, little wildcat? What are you up to? What's this all about—eh? You tell me, do you hear, or I'll damn well have you explaining to my father."

She struggled, then went slack and leaned back over his arm, waiting to regain her breath. He released his grip, took her by her shoulders, and asked, "Tell me, Mara. Where have you been? Why've you been riding about the countryside at dead of night? One of your little thieving tricks? Is that it?"

He waited until she managed to answer against the sighing wind. "No. I couldn't bear that stuffy house —" His hand tightened on a slender forearm. She winced.

"So you go riding a wild horse to nowhere just for the fun of it. Is that it? Is it?" he persisted.

She tore herself free. "Stop bullying me. I'm not your property."

"You're under my protection and you promised to behave," he told her harshly. "Is this your idea of it?"

"What's wrong? I'm harming no one."

"Except yourself perhaps," he said. "Where have you been, Mara?"

"I'm not telling you."

"Oh, yes, you are, or you'll explain to the law."

His threat suddenly quietened her. She shivered. "There's no need for that. I just had to see someone—"

"Who? Your mother? Or an acquaintance of ill repute? Cousin Rohan, perhaps?" The name slipped out almost unconsciously. Until that moment the suggestion hadn't occurred to him.

She gazed at him for a few seconds, chin up, eyes changing from light blue to dark in the moonlight. Then she laughed, with the shrill high quality of a bird crying. He was shocked.

"Yes, yes," she shouted in his face. "Rohan, of course. How did you guess? How very clever of you —" She broke off, turned, and tried to push past him. But he caught her and, placing a hand on either side

of her face, bent his head down and with his breath
hot on her cheeks said, "Is that true? By God, if it is,
I'll kill the bastard."

Her eyes grew wild and terrified. "No, no, of
course not. I was teasing. You should know—" Her
mouth was trembling, her voice, gone suddenly soft
and pleading, was lost on a rush of air. His rage slowly
ebbed. She looked so fey and childlike, so suddenly
forlorn against the elements and his own rising desire.

"I know you're a devilish good actress," he said
grudgingly. "How do I know you're not acting now?"

"You should—you should—"

He did not know what to believe anymore. Neither, just then, did he care. His lips were suddenly
hot and hard on hers, his arms crushing her slender
form wildly to him. Moonlight and darkness claimed
them fitfully. The creaking and moaning of bushes
and heather drowned the rush of incoherent endearments between them. He was about to wrench the
clumsy cloak from her shoulders and take in a rush
of primitive desire what had so tormented and
eluded him for weeks, when a swaying beam of light
that was not that of the moon caught their two
figures in a wavering drunken motion. He turned his
head quickly, and below, from a high window of Penraven, saw the disc of a face suspended, it seemed,
above a candle or lamp, watching. For some moments it remained there, pale, blurred, and motion-
less. Then quite suddenly it was taken back into the
shadows.

"Who was it?" Justin heard Mara asking. "No one
could see. They couldn't, could they?"

"I don't know," Justin answered, releasing her as
desire slowly ebbed into cold common sense. But he
did know. Their figures—his and Mara's—must have

been starkly clear against the pale, moon-washed moor. He'd forgotten how near to the house they were. He could only hope they hadn't been recognized. If so, there'd be the devil to pay.

He gave the girl a little push, while his nerves and muscles recovered. "We'll have to wait a bit, until the moon goes in," he said. "Sit there, on that rock, and don't move until I tell you to. Then run for your life, keeping your head down. I'll follow. And no climbing trees or crawling through windows. I've a key. Wait by the side door till I get there. Understand?"

Mara nodded.

Half an hour later the girl was safely up in her bedroom, and Justin was having a stiff whiskey in the library, thinking that all was well.

But in the morning pandemonium broke loose.

As Justin made his way downstairs for a late breakfast, he saw a crowd of figures in the hall, gesticulating and arguing in a manner that told him something was very wrong. He paused at a bend in the staircase, and as the figures moved to one side, interrupted by two menservants carrying luggage to the door, he was dismayed to see the large figure of Miss Fearnley facing Christin with the manner of an immense galleon about to run down a defenseless craft. Christin, very red-faced, was blustering and making every endeavor to soothe the irate lady, but she would have none of it.

Her words rose shrilly above the commotion.

"A very good thing we found out in time, sir. Your son, as you must surely know, is little better than a dissolute rogue. A-whoring after servant girls when respectable folk are abed. Come, Annabella—" She motioned with her stately arm, and her niece moved forward. Her face appeared puffed, whether from rage or distress Justin could not tell. He thought at first she was going to comply to her aunt's command without argument. But she did not.

"Before I leave," she said, calmly and clearly, "I'd like to know from Justin himself if it's true. What you saw—or think you saw from your window."

"And you shall, indeed you shall," Christin roared. "I'll drag that young reprobate from his bed myself, even if I have to do it with a stick."

"There's no need for that, Father, none at all," Justin said loudly from above. He walked sharply down the stairs toward them.

They all stared.

Christin's face had gone a bluish purple. One hand clutched his side as he commanded explosively, "Speak, sir. Speak. Explain yourself before I send you to Kingdom come!"

"I hardly think I'd reach there," Justin said dryly, and was immediately amazed at his own temerity. "Being such a hardened sinner." He gave a little mock bow to Miss Elizabeth. "A thousand apologies to you, ma'am, for my misdeeds. It was indeed true. A harmless kiss for a pretty wench in the moonlight. No more I can assure you, and"—turning to Annabella—"I'm sure your niece will understand." A certain subtle wickedness lit his eyes. "Since she is so soon to be my wife, it's surely right and proper she should know my weaknesses in time to retract if she wishes."

"If she wishes, certainly she wishes. Whether she does or not is of no consequence," the lady continued irately. "My brother would certainly never countenance such a union in view of what has happened, and if Annabella is stupid and stubborn enough to go ahead in face of family opposition, it will be without a penny for a dowry, that I can assure you."

Justin shrugged. "Then I must accept your decision, madam."

Christin tried to interrupt. It was no use. Annabella spoke first.

"I'm sorry, Justin. You should have waited a bit longer. Until we were married." She gave him a slight smile, half humorous, half ironic. "You've cooked your goose I'm afraid. Papa would create quite a shindy, and you're not all that in love with me, are you?" Unseen to the others she gave him a faint quick wink. Then her hand came out. Justin gripped it. The contact between them was strong, firm, and friendly. He knew with a flash of intuitive relief that they had never been destined to marry, and that only disgruntlement and unhappiness would have resulted.

Five minutes later the Fearnley chaise was rattling away down Penraven drive. At the bend into the lane a white-gloved hand was thrust out in a wave from Annabella. Then the rattle of wheels and horses' hooves died away into the morning mist, and nothing was left but the unpleasantness of the business ahead as Justin faced his father.

The interview was explosive, threatening a violent finale that disintegrated suddenly into something far more frightening. Christin, with one hand to his heart, staggered and would have collapsed if Justin had not helped him to a chair. From purplish red, his face turned a ghastly gray. He was breathing heavily. Sweat trickled in rivulets down his swollen cheeks to his cravat. A rasping, grating sound came from his lungs.

He did not instantly lose consciousness. But when the apothecary saw him later, he was ordered to rest in bed for a month, a treatment accompanied by potions and regular sessions of being bled, to relieve stress and pressure on the brain. Even so, a certain amount of paralysis resulted, and his speech had gone.

Elaine's concern was so excessive, her devotion, between drinking bouts, so all-absorbing, no one except Olivia noticed Justin's increasing attentions to Mara.

When she attempted to interfere or reason with him, he brushed her coldly aside.

"Don't be such a jealous chit," he said. "My life doesn't belong to you. Keep to your place, as a sister should, and leave my affairs alone."

He knew, by the slump of her shoulders when she turned away, that he had hurt her. And the knowledge rebounded on him curiously, causing acute physical pain. But he set his mind and jaw determinedly against her, reminding himself that in another fortnight she would be returning to school. When she came back to Penraven, everything would be settled, leaving no room for argument, because by then, he decided, he would be married.

And so it was.

6

During the weeks following Christin's stroke, an uneasy quiet reigned at Penraven. Olivia, who'd believed at first Justin might allow her to leave school —at least for a term until her father showed improve-

ment or otherwise in his health—found him adamant
that she should return to Plymouth at the appointed
time, refusing to be softened by either pleas or defiance.

So toward the end of January she was packed off in
the family chaise, accompanied by the housekeeper
who had been ordered to see the girl deposited safely
at Fairclose before returning to Cornwall. Olivia sat
stiff-backed with her head held severely upright, jaw
set and cold. She did not once look from the window
or wave, and with a feeling of frustration Justin
turned and went back into the hall. He regretted his
father's illness, but found it hard to feel the normal
sympathy of a son to a parent.

Christin, when told of Justin's plan for sacrificing
the rest of his Oxford period to live at Penraven with
Annabella as his wife, had not at first seemed pleased.
Marriage—yes. He had been more than eager for
union with the two families and if his ungrateful heir
was willing to oblige with such speed, he was not
against the plan. But he had been quick to impose
conditions that allowed Justin no business control in
the matter of Crannick or the other two mines. If he
proved his ability and judgment where the former
was concerned, he would eventually be given a tidy
shareholding in the estate. But this would mean a
considerable waiting period when Justin's hands
were bound, and in everything he did concerning
the estate, permission had first to be given by the
bailiff and overall mines manager, Joe Pollard.

Pollard was good at his job, a shrewd and capable
assessor of tin potential and financial facts. But Justin
did not like him. Fundamentally he felt the man to
be a cold character, unwilling to chance anything for
the sake of its adventure. And what was mining without the fire? The challenge? The risk?

The difficulty was, of course, that Justin had no way of proving his own hunch over Crannick. In technical matters—except for what he'd studied on his own when he was growing up—he was inexperienced, an amateur. And no working miner took to an amateur dabbling in mining affairs. Yet Justin felt a familiarity with granite, stone, and earth that many a qualified engineer had never experienced. With his hand traveling the surface of a Cornish rock, he could almost feel the contact—a living response of elemental awareness to human touch. Something like water-divining, he'd told himself more than once—a kinship with the primitive earth itself. And he was certain—completely certain in his own mind—that Crannick had a wealth of ore to offer anyone possessing sufficient initiative and spirit to tap it.

He had tried to explain to Christin, but Tregallis had not accepted that credence could be given to just a "feeling." Still, one day he'd want Justin securely back at Penraven, so he'd listened, gone with him a certain way, knowing the young man at heart was no scholar or likely to bring intellectual honors to the family, and was on the point of a limited agreement when illness had struck.

Now with his cherished hope of alliance between the Tregallis and Fearnley families crushed at one blow, he lay helpless, unable to argue or properly communicate. Paralyzed down the whole of one side. Yet behind the frozen contorted exterior, his mind was clear on one point. Marriage. Justin must marry and beget an heir. Marry Annabella. Annabella! Annabella! The word rose in constant reiteration, like the waves of the sea, pounding his brain. Once when Justin stood by his bed, he mouthed a soundless *A*, which closed slowly to the semblance of an *M*.

Justin patted his hand. "It's all right," he said, wanting above all to still that contorted grimace. "I'll marry, have no fear." He bent to Christin's ear, echoing more loudly. "I'll marry—marry, Father."

Christin's eyes closed. He managed to nod feebly, then the stentorious breathing started again, and he lapsed into fitful unconsciousness.

Elaine was waiting on the landing when Justin left his bedroom. She looked strained and frightened, and tried ineffectually to hide the small brandy bottle under her shawl.

Justin laughed contemptuously. "Don't pretend, Mama," he said. "Drink yourself to hell for all I care. But for heaven's sake, don't pretend."

A flush stained the pallid face. "You're cruel—cruel. How can any son of mine speak like that?"

Justin pushed past. "How? Yes—I agree with you. Truly remarkable, isn't it?"

He was striding down the landing when Mara appeared from the other direction. She was carrying a small tray with a sprig of Christmas roses on it.

"Is madam upset again?" she inquired coldly. "I hope not—sir."

Justin gave her a long stare, noting against his will the unblinking clarity of her blue eyes under their lashes, the delicate sheen of her white skin, and the single strand of pale hair glinting gold under her cap from a high window.

"You had better ask her," he said noncommittally. "If so, you can inform me later."

A slight smile tilted her lips. "Certainly, sir."

She passed him without another word, and as he retreated to the stairs he heard the women's voices murmuring, followed by Elaine's emotional sobbing as Mara urged her into the bedroom. He did not look around. He felt suddenly irrationally and over-

whelmingly sick of the situation. Master of the house
he should be now, during the period of his father's
sickness from which it was doubtful there would be
full recovery. Yet on every hand he seemed the vic-
tim of women's complaints and subtle tyranny. First
young Olivia telling him what he should do, then his
mother's hysterical accusations. And now Mara, who
was very largely responsible for the whole sorry business and appeared to be subtly ranging the household against him.

Mara! That enchanting slip of a girl to whom he'd
given shelter and his protection in spite of her ill-
deeds and thieving and lying tricks. A playactress of
such talent she'd even managed to enslave Elaine,
who generally had no taste for women. And why?
For what reason, except to ensconce herself more
firmly at Penraven, and make her services so invalu-
able she would be beyond dismissal?

Justin smiled grimly, a tight little smile having no
humor in it, but more than a hint of triumph. In a
flash a plan had come to him, whipping his senses
with the impact of a sudden sting of cold air, to a
foretaste of adventure.

A bride, he thought. Why not?

Annabella was denied to him. But there were others. The world was full of women wanting husbands
of rank, women who would tyrannize and torment
once the knot was tied. There were other types too
—the pliant and weak despots—wailing, fretful crea-
tures like Elaine. God forfend he should take any one
of these. Or the clever beauties who pretended faith-
fulness but who were whores at heart. Never yet had
he met any feminine creature possessing all the vir-
tues rolled into one. Just for an instant a vision of his
passionate young sister intruded on his mind. If only
—but she was beyond him. Forever out of reach; his

own kin; of his blood. That left but one on the visible horizon.

Mara.

However outrageous, the challenge of making her his wife and mistress of Penraven was stimulating. There would be fireworks and criticism on every hand. Cornish society would be affronted by such an alliance. The servants would sniff and whisper, and Christin might easily suffer another stroke when he heard. On the other hand, should Mara early produce an heir, Tregallis might even approve. There was no knowing how a man in his state might react. The future was unpredictable. Any shock—even a small one—might prove fatal. On the other hand, he could go on for years keeping the household on tenterhooks, making a tyranny of his sickness and creating a morgue of Penraven. But not for him, Justin. Life was too short. He was too young to be bound by duty—the fire of youth too hot and strong in his veins to be sacrificed by filial bondage.

So he swept his brain clear of negative reasoning and turned this thoughts again to Mara. He already had a shrewd assessment of her character and recognized she would appreciate acting the grand lady, just as he knew there were mysterious depths in her he had not yet plumbed. Therein would be the challenge. The delight would be in possessing her beauty utterly. He was in no doubt concerning her shortcomings—her aptitude for deceit, for playing the seductress; but if she became his wife, he'd see she behaved. Oh, yes—life with Mara would at least be stimulating.

Once the idea had properly taken root, he allowed it to flourish and took every opportunity of waylaying the girl when no one was about, of flattering her vanity by ardent glances and double-edged speech.

She was responsive in her heart, but puzzled. At moments, when she had not seen Rohan for some days, she felt desire for Justin. She could, she argued with herself, love him, if it were possible to wash all obsessive thoughts of that other dark face from her memory. But there were nights, even in sleep, when the image of Rohan still intruded, and she felt herself drawn by deep insidious impulses to the house on the dunes where he stood in the shadows by the door, waiting to claim her.

She would wake up with the perspiration wet on her brow and face, knowing that never on earth could she be free while he lived still wanting her. His need was a prison entombing her spirit, yet at the same time giving it the power to expand and fly—an elemental force conjured into dark strength by his own. Her breathing would quicken then, as she thought of him. She'd get up and rush to the window, scanning the sky for a glimpse of his form against the cloud—for the sound of his voice calling her—echoing with that of the wild birds crying.

"Rohan, Rohan," she'd breathe, though the words were formless, merely a whisper with the rising and dying moaning of the wind.

She both longed for and hated him at the same time, wishing he'd never crossed her path or her, his, yet accepting that if they hadn't, the most secret deepest needs of her being would never have come to life. And if they hadn't? Well, then, she knew she might have been a better person. Less wicked; more virtuous. But what are such qualities? Of what avail against the primitive forces of that wild district? Of pounding seas and flying cloud? The rush of air, and driven rain—of violent storm dying to fleeting calm, under moors lit to fire from the lifting sun? She was part of all this. She belonged. And in a strange way so did Rohan. Justin was so different—carving his will instead of subjecting himself either to persons or circumstances; and this gave him strength. The strength perhaps to save her from herself?

If only he could.

Occasionally, following one of her secret visits to Rohan, which were becoming steadily more rare, she would decide fiercely to have nothing more to do with him. He was so cruel, so ruthless in his possession of her body, so contemptuous of her wish for words and gentle promises he'd no intention of giving. Then she'd think warmly of Justin and long for security, for the safety of Penraven.

It was in such a mood, when returning from a visit to see Lillith, who was sick, that she met Justin galloping toward her on Blackfire above Red River. She was riding the little donkey that Christin had allowed her to keep at the stables. The wild pony was used only for nightly escapades when she had to be away quickly to Boscarrion.

He drew up as they met and dismounted. She remained seated on the donkey.

"Where have you been, Mara?"

"To see my mother—Lillith. Although that's my own business, surely. Madam gave me permission. I shouldn't have left without."

"Oh, I'm sure," he agreed ironically. "In all things you're so compliant and well behaved. That's what you'd have me believe, I know. But it's not true, is it? There's something in you forever watching and planning and scheming to have your say."

He paused; she didn't answer, just stared at him, biting her lip. Then she jerked the donkey's reins. He grasped them quickly. "Get down, Mara. Give that

poor little beast a rest. We've things to talk about"—
and when she didn't reply immediately—"or shall I
lift you?"

She dismounted abruptly, and stood facing him.
"What do you want—sir?"

"Ah. That's better."

She lifted her chin a trifle higher. The hood slipped
back from her head, and once again he was amazed
at the beauty of her hair—the delicacy of her perfect
features and wild-flower coloring so intensified by
the dark cloak and heavy clothing. At the fair she had
been an alluring, sophisticated young woman of fashion. In the woods, a feline creature spitting defiance.
But here, against the brown moors with the gaunt
rocks and primitive cromlech above, she appeared
suddenly as some shy, lovely nymph frightened of
capture.

Compassion suddenly flooded his desire.

"Don't be afraid, Mara," he said gently. "I shan't
hurt you. You know me. I only wish you well."

"How do I know? No one but madam does that.
You know very well what everyone says of us—Lillith
and me—" She broke off a little desperately.

He took her wrist, and felt his hand involuntarily
slipping up her arm. "That you're a couple of witches
waving spells that take cattle and make women
dumb? That Lillith has orgies with the Devil, plays
leapfrog at midnight over a chamberpot—roasts
toads, and brings the plague to good folk—yes, I've
heard it all. Black cats that fly, and the mark of goats'
feet where no goats are—but that's all talk, isn't it,
Mara? Witch you may be, but not that kind."

She shivered.

"I'm no witch."

"Oh, yes, you are. You've bewitched me, and that's
no easy thing."

She pulled her arm free. "I must be getting on. Madam will be missing me."

He pulled her back, and suddenly his lips were on hers. His hand slid upward to a breast and over it, encasing it firmly through the thick material. The cold January wind whipped around them. Closing her eyes, she felt her arms reach to his neck as he lifted her up. It seemed for a moment that he'd take her there in the dried heather, without words or preamble. Then, to her astonishment, he released her. His voice had an almost cold ring in it as he said, "You're right. You must be going."

"But—"

He eyed her warily. "I'm not having you as village men take strumpets in the heather. Get on your donkey, Mara. Tomorrow we'll talk."

"What about?"

He pushed her toward the placid creature that was nibbling nearby. Once mounted, she stared at him with such resentment his nerves relaxed, enabling him to answer calmly despite the hammering of his heart. "You should know that. Surely I'm not aiming to marry a fool."

At first she thought she must have heard wrong. Marry, he'd said—marry?

"I don't understand. There's no need to mock me, for all I'm only Lillith's daughter and you the master of Penraven."

He put a hand to the reins. "I'm not mocking you. I meant what I said. Wouldn't it please you—being mistress of a fine estate? You've played the part fairly well in the past, if I remember. Well—I'm giving you the chance of filling the genuine role. What about it, Mara?"

For a few seconds she said nothing—merely stared at him, as though unwilling completely to believe him or delude herself. Then she uttered one word.

"Why?"

"What do you mean, why?"

"I want to know. Pity, is it? Because you're sorry for me?"

He laughed wryly.

"I'm not that kind. Young I may be, but man enough to know pity makes no good bedfellow. You understand?"

A sudden wild color flooded her face. This was her chance, surely—the opportunity to rid herself for good of the dark destiny that had so recently threatened to bind her.

"Very well," she said. "All right, if you really want it—I'll marry you, Justin."

A moment later she was on her way back to Penraven, and Justin was kicking Blackfire at a gallop in the direction of old Crannick Mine. When he reached the wild spot of darkish reddened earth and cold granite, first enthusiasm in him had subsided to more commonsense perspective.

He knew he would marry Mara, but there would be no dowry. The estate was not flush at the moment. Both the tin and copper yield of the two other family mines was not sufficient for imbursement of a fresh mining venture. However certain in his mind he was of potential ore, his problem was to interest and induce adventurers to invest. He thought resentfully of Rohan—of the wealth said to be secreted in Boscarrion, and of the evil means used for getting it. Slavery —smuggling—dubious deals with dubious characters from abroad who stopped at nothing—even murder —at the chance of lining their own pockets.

As always, any fleeting image of Rohan evoked such anger in him he had to dispel it in the only way he knew, by some tough physical action. In quieter moments he had pondered over Christin's excessive hatred of his nephew. Ambition and family pride alone could not entirely account for it. Way back, there must be some personal issue that had emphasized the evil rift in the Tregallis family. But Christin had kept an obdurate silence over the matter, forbidding Justin since earliest boyhood to mention the name of his dissolute older cousin.

So a mystery it remained; and as Justin drove his horse hard on that early evening to the high moorland ridge overlooking both the north and south coasts of that rugged granite tongue of Cornwall, he swept all thought of Rohan aside. Exultancy rose in him as he once more reined, his figure dark on its mount against the fading sky. So much of what lay before him was Penraven land and would one day be his. Three mines, including Crannick, if Crannick could be brought to life. And by God, he'd see it done, he told himself almost savagely, even if it meant getting a loan, or taking in as partner a certain Joshua Partridge, a flamboyant but astute character from the Liverpool area who had already purchased large acres of land north of Truro and had visions of establishing himself as "country squire" of the district, with a secret eye to a political future.

Partridge was rich; everyone knew that. A man of business perception rather than of culture or conscience. His excessive fortunes, it was said, had come from cotton. A less charitable opinion suggested his mills had prospered mainly from a two-way traffic of slaving, concerning American cotton plantations and raw cotton brought back to England for spinning and weaving. He had also married well, in terms of worldly wealth—the daughter of a prosperous Plymouth merchant, who, though lacking in breeding, was rich enough otherwise to more than make up for lack of social assets.

It was the social angle now that interested Partridge. Of what use was a fortune without acceptance by the privileged set? Those who could provide the means to enjoy it? So, egged on by Maria, his wife, who wished to settle in the south, he was already shrewdly planning how best to accomplish it. So far, Cornish society had contrived to preclude his invasion of their inner circle. He had little subtlety, and although any financial contribution of his to assist the needy and the community in general had been graciously received, he was still privately regarded as a "furriner," and a brash one into the bargain.

Justin was well aware of his position, and had met him once. Christin, he knew, would never under any conditions agree to an alliance with such a dubious character.

But, damn! Justin thought, as he paused on that particular evening, following his visit to Crannick, he's no longer capable of making judgment or taking action on his own. I'm master now, and I'll prove it.

At that moment, though he was not quite twenty, the decision of a man twice his age was upon him. His stance and strongly carved dark face combined with his magnificent figure astride the stallion gave him a look of maturity quite formidable against the rocky landscape.

As he kicked Blackfire into a gallop, his mind was quite made up. The evening, for him, marked a stepping-stone in his life. In the next two months two things would be accomplished. He would have Partridge as a friend, and Mara as wife.

With money in his pocket, Crannick working, and sons to follow after him, the future at that moment appeared very rosy indeed.

7

Rohan sat idly back in his chair, watching Mara reflectively as she moved gracefully to the table where two decanters and glasses stood—a glitter of amber and cut crystal in the candlelight.

"Pour two," he said, with a lazy yet amorous gleam in his narrowed eyes. "We may as well be comfortable after such a long parting."

"I'd rather have nothing," she said. "I've quite a ride back to Penraven."

"But I'd rather you did," he insisted. "Just to warm your cold senses. I'll not believe you're aiming to play the prude after so long." His voice sharpened. "Do as I say, and tell me what you've been up to."

Her hand trembled imperceptibly as she took the stopper from the brandy decanter and poured one glass full, the other only slightly. She was wearing a soft green-colored woolen dress, fashionably cut, fitting the breasts and falling in graceful lines over the rounded hips. Her pale hair, loosened by the wind, though caught on top by a scarlet ribbon, had a few shining tendrils brushing her cheeks. A ring set with a single large ruby glowed from the third finger of her left hand. She looked beautiful and entrancing, and Rohan's senses stirred. But his voice was cold when he said, "Give me that glass and sit down." When she'd done so, he continued. "Now. Explain."

She faced him, with the flash in her luminous eyes he knew so well. As always, his presence reduced any resistance she'd summoned during her journey to compliance and a desperate unhappy passion that she knew could not be abated until his arms were around her.

"What do you want to know?"

He laughed.

"Playing for time, darling?"

Her heart quickened. "No. It's just—that I have news."

He nodded, staring significantly at her hand.

"So I see. And who is the happy man? Could it be Cousin Justin?"

She paused before admitting. "Yes. He's asked me to marry him."

"Oh. I see. And you have already accepted that conceited young buck."

"It was difficult to refuse," she said truthfully, adding quickly, "but I can think twice about it. It needn't go on . . ." She paused breathlessly, waiting for his reaction, wondering for a bewildered confused moment if he would burst into a torrent of objections, if his jealousy would prove too much for him and he'd betray an inner longing too strong for sharing her with another.

He jumped up and came toward her. But it was not love she saw on his face. He slapped her sharply across one cheek. She flinched. He pulled her to him, and his lips were on hers, burning her mouth and neck and hollow of her throat above the constricting green material. Then he pushed her back onto the chair.

"Why didn't you tell me of this before?"

"Didn't I? I think I did. You told me to play with him and find out what I could—" She broke off breathlessly.

"And is that all it is? Playing?"

She shook her head. "No. He's strong and kind. I like him."

"And you don't like me?"

"Not much," she admitted. "Not *like*. You're a cruel person, Rohan. If I could—I would, but—"

"I don't want your liking. And I don't care a damn about you marrying my cousin. In fact"—he poured another drink and quaffed it quickly down—"it suits me very well. For you to have the trust of a loving husband and me to have you at my command when I feel like it—what could be better, eh? Tell me, Mara. Answer, you little scheming wildcat." He thrust out an arm again and wrenched her to her feet.

Then he said with his face very close to hers, "Just remember you're mine, that's all. Remember, too, that should I choose to, I could see you hanged for the thief and witch you are—you and your lying mother. Or maybe there'd be more satisfaction in punishing you myself. I have a strong hand and a neat switch available. So don't ever play me false, Mara. Bed as often as you choose with that buffoon of a youth. Wed him and play the spy for me. But never forget who I am—your lord and master—"

He broke off and laughed again, to find her trembling. Then he picked her up and laid her on the floor. The world seemed to darken as he disrobed and took her to him, mercilessly. She was shocked and completely subjugated, but even then her humiliation could not quench her desire. He did not love her, he never would; Rohan Tregallis loved only himself and his own appetites. If she could have wiped him from her heart and memory, she would. But while she and Rohan lived and breathed the same air in the same world, she knew he would never be out of her blood or she out of his. Hate as they would, they belonged. The dark knowledge was disturbing, and hard to bear.

When half an hour later she once more set off for Penraven, an exhausted sense of fatalism possessed her. The dark shadows clawing the fitful moon-washed landscape loomed as hungry fingers of approaching disaster.

If she had been seen at that moment, riding the wild pony toward Penraven, she would not particularly have cared. But she arrived safely without being observed, and let herself into the house by the side door, shutting it quietly behind her, and leaving the key safely turned in the lock.

No one heard her tiptoeing to the back stairs or creeping along the landing to her own room. No servant was about. Everyone except Elaine was asleep, and Elaine was too bemused to notice a faint creaking of old wood as Mara passed her door. Even if she had, and had looked out, she would have seen nothing. In the dark cloak, with its large hood hiding the glimmer of pale hair and face, Mara was just a shadowed shape among those other shadows thrown from the gothic windows to make a patterned network against floors and walls.

At the far end of the corridor Justin, in a deep sleep, dreamed. Not of Mara, but of the belching of steam and pumping of engines—of vast mine-stacks rising from a wasteland to bring a wealth of ore and riches to Penraven; and in the distance a young figure watched and cried, lifting her arms unavailingly toward him. Her eyes were dark pools against fire and blackness—her voice a high treble of remonstrance and grief. Olivia.

"Justin—Justin—" The tones died into a wail, and he woke up suddenly, with the sweat heaving on his body, brow and face dripping with a strange, unaccountable apprehension that left him temporarily puzzled and ill at ease.

In the morning, however, he had recovered and put the dream from his mind; for later that day he was to meet Joshua Partridge—an interview that later was to prove exceedingly fruitful for both concerned.

Partridge was a large man with paunch, a North Country accent, small eyes bright as blue glass set deep in a broad rubicund face, and a direct manner that could be deceptive. Behind the well-padded exterior a quick mind darted, assessing—and usually correctly—more than one angle of a situation before he spoke.

He was an astute judge of character, having learned during his fifty-eight years that to know the potentials of both one's friends and one's enemies was one of the first steps to success.

His immediate reaction to Justin could be summed up in three words—"likable but headstrong." His second, that in spite of his youth Justin Tregallis was above all a man of action who had a faith in his own hunches. That also was commendable. But Joshua never went on hunches alone. There had to be something sound to build on, and he had no intention of throwing away good money on a bad mine.

The two men were sitting in the parlor of The Mariner, an inn at Penjust reputed for its good food and liquor. They had a private table near a roaring log fire and were indulging in cigars with vintage brandy following an excellent meal of duck, game pie, and apple tart.

"How do I know this bit of dead land's got anything to offer except stone and weeds?" Joshua asked bluntly. "Why didn't someone open it afore, if what you say's true? Come to that, why was it shut in the first place?"

Justin explained about levels running dry, and the cost of sinking new shafts and opening fresh adits—the expense involved in getting fresh machinery, paying for labor, and the impracticability of even starting such a project without sufficient finance to cover any setbacks or false judgment—

"So you admit there could be errors?" Partridge cut in quickly.

"Of course. You always get a few in any adventurous undertaking like this," Justin agreed. "You don't just strike lucky the first time, not often. But if you have knowledge of tin and copper, it's hardly likely you'll make a second mistake. And I know Crannick's loaded."

"With what? Fool's gold?" Joshua asked ironically.

Justin frowned.

"I shouldn't be troubling to waste time talking to you if I thought that. And if you can't bring yourself to believe in me, then we'd better part company here and now," Justin retorted with some heat.

"Now now, don't take on so," the other man remarked more quietly. "I do believe in you, young man—at least in your sincerity. But the experience isn't there, is it? What credentials have you? What kind of proof do you have a man like me wants before sinking a fortune in something that could be as dead as the dodo? Another thing—" He wagged a finger. "Have you the right?"

"What do you mean by right? Crannick's on Tregallis land. My father's had a stroke and isn't likely to take on anything of a business nature ever again. In fact it's doubtful that he'll live for long."

"And you've powers of attorney?"

"As good as," Justin answered curtly. "Anyway, my

solicitor could see to all that. There'll be no legal difficulties, I can assure you. Another thing—the old man's as keen as I am—or was—about Crannick. And if you want engineering opinion, there's an expert coming down from Birmingham next week. No doubt you'll want a word with him?"

"Quite right, no doubt at all," Joshua agreed. "And that's about the nub of it, isn't it? I'll see this Birmingham fellow, and then we'll talk again. If he's reasonably satisfied—I say if—I may want others to take a look too. Nothing like being on the safe side. In the meantime, you get things straight with your father so there's no snag there."

The interview ended shortly afterward. Joshua Partridge left for Truro, and Justin made his way back to Penraven. The housekeeper met him as he went through the door. There was consternation on her face. "It's the master, sir," she said. "He's been took worse. Can't move a finger anymore, and his breathing's bad. As you weren't here, I sent for Mr. Groves the apothecary—" she broke off, lifting a corner of her black satin apron to an eye.

Justin felt a wave of coldness seize him. He and Christin had not always seen eye to eye. But the old man had been good to him. If he died, there'd be a loss in the house. Things would be easier no doubt, but without realizing it, Justin had been looking forward to proving himself in Christin's estimation—showing him that he'd been right about Crannick and had the character and vision to reimburse Tregallis lands, without Fearnley assistance.

When he entered the room, he doubted he'd have time. The red color had now completely left Christin's face, leaving him gray and drawn-looking lying against the pillows with his eyes closed and his fingers plucking the sheets. Groves stood by him, holding his wrist. He glanced up at Justin, shaking his head. The housekeeper gave a muffled sob behind the two men.

Groves straightened himself. "I'd like a word with you, Mr. Tregallis," he said.

Justin understood. "Stay there, please," he said to the distressed woman. "I'll be back shortly."

"Well? Is there any hope?" he asked the apothecary when they were outside. "Will my father recover?"

The blunt, businesslike question took Groves back. "I think it's extremely doubtful. But while there's life there's always a chance. I shall send for a specialist immediately, with your permission."

"Of course. Spare no expense. Just get the best man possible," Justin said tersely.

"The best man is Pengerthick at Plymouth. Whether he'll be able to get here in time is questionable. However, I'll do what I can. In the meantime, treatment must continue as before, with bleeding and potions. Keep Mr. Tregallis completely quiet, and on no account let anyone but yourself intrude." He coughed. "That is, of course, unless madam— Mistress Tregallis—wishes to sit with him."

"That's not at all likely," Justin said shortly. "My mother's indisposed."

"Indeed?"

"Her usual complaint," the young man added in a curt tone.

"Ah, well, we must pray for a miracle," the apothecary told him ambiguously. "I'll leave now and come back shortly when I've made arrangements for contacting Pengerthick."

But before the specialist arrived, it was already too late. In the last few seconds of his life Christin opened his eyes and stared at Justin with sudden startled comprehension. His mouth opened. There was a gurgling in his throat as he tried to speak. Justin bent down.

"Yes, Father?" he questioned. "Don't worry. Everything's all right. What is it?" No one had ever before heard the young man speak so gently. In the pause that followed it seemed the whole atmosphere was strained with the tension of waiting and listening —waiting for that last communication between two human beings. Justin's heart jerked as three words came from Christin's lips—"you are not—" Then his head fell. There was a drawn-out wheezing gasp, and all was ominously and coldly still.

Elaine was not told of Christin's death till the next morning. She had not yet partaken of "the tonic" that was her support, and was in a comparatively normal frame of mind.

"I suppose I should be sorry," she told Justin in a clear, light voice. "But I'm not." She smiled with icy callous contempt. "He was a cruel man. The house will be better without him. Mara, dear—give me my flask, will you?"

Mara's eyes met Justin's, calm and expressionless as pools on a windless summer's day. There was a faint smile on her lips.

Justin turned on his heels quickly and left the room.

"Damn her," he said to himself. "She's not human. Neither of them are."

But to his shame, desire was mounting in him and his senses already set alight. The sooner he married her, he thought, the better. Then maybe he'd have peace. She'd learn her place, and the torment of sensual need would be over. His mind and body would be free for Crannick and for living in the manner he chose.

A man's way.

* * *

Olivia did not return to Penraven for the funeral.
Justin did not write to her telling the news until the
day before. Although she had never been close to her
father, she had a warm heart, and Justin was anxious
to spare her any unnecessary distress. There was also
another reason. She would be bound to question him
about Mara, and having made up his mind concerning the marriage, he'd no intention of letting her
interfere. Once Mara was his wife, Olivia would have
to accept the fact and show proper respect of the
situation. So the mournful occasion was proceeded
with as quickly and quietly as possible, and Christin
Tregallis was laid to rest with his ancestors in the
family vault at Gwynfa Church.

Elaine did not attend, although she made a point
of appearing in the large library afterward for the
reading of the will. She had kept sufficiently sober to
dress elegantly for the occasion in frilled black silk
with a shred of thin black veiling half hiding her face.
It fell in folds from massed black ribbons arranged on
top of her silver hair, which was luxuriously supple-
mented at the back by a wig of false curls.

Her gait was unsteady; but she sat stiffly erect in a
high-backed carved chair, content for a brief period
to reign as matriarch of the household.

The contents of the document were simple, holding no surprises except that both Elaine and Olivia
were left completely unprovided for, except at the
discretion of Justin, who inherited everything. No
bequests to servants; not even a meager legacy for
either widow or daughter.

There was an ominous silence after the oration,
followed by the rustle of papers as the solicitor fold-
ed them, coughed, stood up, and at Justin's request
took a cigar and a glass of brandy. Then Elaine, with

her hand on the chair arm, got unsteadily to her feet. Shock had rendered her momentarily clear-headed, and there was a certain bitter pride about her as she said through thin lips, "It is just what I expected. Christin never did know how to act with propriety."

Later, when Mara had helped her to her room and onto the bed, she said, "We will now endeavor to be merry, my dear. Have no fear, that hulking, handsome creature who professes to be my son—will see we have whatever we wish. Hard he may be in some ways, but soft underneath; besides, I have a little of my own." Her eyes narrowed for a second. There was a keen flash of suspicion—almost of intuitive knowledge—in them that would have surprised Christin if he'd seen. Then she said slyly, "What do you think of Justin, Mara?"

Mara paused before answering, "He's good-looking, and kind, I'm sure, madam. As you say—he'll take care of you, there's no need to worry."

"Can you see any resemblance?" Elaine persisted. "Do you believe that I love him?"

Mara was nonplussed. "But he's your son, isn't he?"

"Is he?" Elaine's voice took on a dreamy note. "Sometimes I wonder. I was so sure, at the time, that I had a daughter. And I didn't drink then, you know. Not much. Of course, I was very ill. And when I came to myself, I had such a shock. Justin was a large baby. Dark. And he screamed."

"Babies do scream, madam. And they thrive quickly."

"But I couldn't feed him, you know. I had a wet nurse."

"Well . . ." Mara's voice faded. There was something in Elaine's expression—far away, yet intense and thoughtful—that was strange and new to her, and hard to understand. "It was all a very long time ago, wasn't it?" Mara continued. "It can't be good for you, worrying about the past. No point."

"That's true," Elaine sighed. "You're so wise, Mara. You seem to know me so well. Please, dear, help me undress. The day has been exhausting."

Her eyes closed as Mara skillfully unfastened the voluminous frills and petticoats. She had never before seen Elaine's thin body completely naked, and when she did so, before taking the frail nightshift from a drawer, she had a shock.

There, bright and purplish on Elaine's fragile white flesh, was the mark! A mark identical to the one on Mara's own thigh.

"What are staring at?" she heard the older woman say petulantly. "I'm cold. Give my shift. And take no note of my peculiarity. It is a noble one, in case you don't know. The mark of a great family, which none but my kin bear—"

"But, madam—"

"And don't argue, girl. Mara, whatever's the matter with you? My gown, dear, and pass me my flask. I have need of it."

With a sense of bewilderment on her Mara did as she was told. As she handed the brandy to her mistress and saw her comfortably between the sheets, a string of wild conjectures raced through her mind. Later she wondered whether to speak to Rohan of the matter but decided to keep silent, at least for the time being. Until she was Justin's wife, there was no point at all in raising further complications.

Justin also saw the wisdom in keeping the news of his forthcoming marriage a secret, for the time being, from the household. Until all legal matters concerning the estate were satisfactorily settled he wished to avoid unnecessary probing and dissension.

No one except Lillith would approve, unless it was Elaine, and there was no certain way of predicting how she would react. The housekeeper would naturally feel affronted, also the family solicitor, and acquaintances in the "county" social set who already disapproved of Justin's lack of regard for the conventions—especially his unfeeling treatment of Annabella, news of which had been spread and magnified by servants' gossip. Miss Elizabeth also had been quick to add lashing contempt. He was ill-mannered and unprincipled—a character of whom her niece was well rid. Certainly Justin Tregallis had an insolent quality about him—an arrogant disregard for the accepted rules of the "establishment" that set him apart from others of his station.

This alone evoked a feeling of suspicion.

Rohan Tregallis, of course, came into quite a different category. Rogue and libertine he might be, but at least he did not abuse his birthright by intimate and open association with servants and low-class vagabonds. His reclusive life was from his own choice. He was not shunned by the elite—merely an eccentric. One could accept a rascal so long as he was of the gentlemanly order. But Justin! Whenever his name cropped up at social gatherings, secret glances were exchanged, elegant noses sniffed, and young women nudged each other, smiling meaningfully behind their hands while their seniors hastily changed the conversation. Justin Tregallis, despite his name, was an enigma; one on his own, and therefore not entirely to be trusted.

Justin was aware of this, and it ironically amused him. But he wanted no further jibes or provoking innuendoes until the business deal with Partridge was settled. Joshua, after all, would certainly not cooperate without assurance of an introduction into

Cornwall's social set. Once he had that, Justin told himself, it was up to the man himself to establish his own place. He had wealth enough, and wealth, in the end, generally paid off. No doubt, in time, Partridge would earn by fair ways or foul, a seat in parliament and foothold in many of the great houses in the country. An entrée was all that was needed. So it was essential Justin kept his own image as clean as possible, in order to give it. When that was accomplished and Crannick safe, he'd marry Mara, and hell to all the rest.

The business of accomplishing the necessary task to Joshua's satisfaction took longer than Justin had anticipated. Following a discreet show of mourning in respect of Christin's memory, Justin found himself involved with a minimum of entertaining and being entertained. Elaine even made a great effort to appear the elegantly woeful widow on certain occasions, and Partridge did his part in controlling his natural ebullience with a subtlety that made things considerably easier than might have been expected. With his shrewd insight, any allusions to his own prosperity and fortune slipped out—apparently—quite unconsciously. He did not brag. Men began to be interested. Women already were. He played his cards well.

But it was not until the middle of March that the business concerning Crannick was finalized and Justin felt himself free to marry Mara. There was no publicity. No public ceremony enabling the bride to display her beauty. No notice in newspapers, or fashionable reception—just a private service at Gwynfa Church, followed by a discreet return in the family chaise to Penraven.

The housekeeper, who had only heard the news on the previous day, was waiting prim-lipped and disap-

proving in the hall for their arrival. Behind her were
ranged the other servants. One by one they bobbed.
All were surprised, most of them shocked—Mara,
after all, was daughter of that reputed witch Lillith
—but every one of them was taken aback by the
ethereal loveliness of Justin Tregallis's bride. She
wore palest blue that accentuated the azure blue of
her eyes to the deepest forget-me-not shade. As the
couple entered the large drawing room, Justin himself was startled. Elaine was waiting to receive them.
She also was in blue, and as she came toward them
a glimmer of sun from a window caught her face
sideways, lighting the fine features to sudden clarity.
Despite the lines running from temple to jaw and the
slight sagging of her chin above the thin neck, the
likeness between the two women was remarkable. So
remarkable that Justin felt a strange chill creep over
him.

"My children," he heard Elaine saying in a voice
that trembled, "oh, my dear Mara, how truly pleasant it will be having you for a real daughter."

There was no resentment, not the slightest sign of
jealousy or disapproval. Justin was bewildered. He
had expected recriminations and shrill abuse. But
the situation was one suggesting only warm gratification. He supposed, uncomfortably, he should be
pleased. But it was as though some intuitive bond
existed between the two women—some secret understanding that could be used as a force against him
if ever they chose to do so.

He quickly dispelled the suggestion. As master of
the house, he was now in command. He had no idea
of enforcing his power, especially where his mother
was concerned. But he'd see to it that she had another personal maid as soon as possible, and that
Mara and Elaine had no opportunity to become too

close. This would be easier when Olivia returned
from school. He was already considering allowing
her to leave earlier than had been intended. Every
year that passed would give her more assurance and
a sense of her own importance. Justin well knew that
his marriage to Mara would be a shock. The sooner
his sister faced it, the quicker she'd get over it.

Before Easter he wrote to her informing her of the
event, adding that if she felt like returning to Penraven for the comparatively short holiday, he and
Mara would be glad to receive her, but if she preferred to remain at school until the summer, they
would understand.

> The household is not an exactly festive one at the
> moment [he wrote]. Owing to our father's death
> any celebrations have been kept to a minimum.
> You might find the atmosphere here a little
> strained. However, the choice is entirely up to
> you. Next year you may wish to leave Fairclose
> altogether, and I shall not object. Let me know
> as soon as possible of your decision.
> Your affectionate brother.
> Justin

He sealed and sent the letter three days following the
wedding. Mara was watching from a window as he
handed it to a servant for delivery to the mail coach.
She pulled on a gray silk shawl and went into the hall
toward the door. Her eyes held a hint of curiosity
combined with something else. Speculation? Desire?

Justin's brows arched. "You're not going out,
surely?" he said.

"Why not? The house feels close. I'm used to fresh
air, Justin, and—"

"Riding about the moors on a wild pony?" He

laughed meaningfully, pulling her to him. "I can think of better things at the moment."

He did not notice the sudden tight look on her lovely face, or sense the frustration in her. There was no tangible reason to. Their relationship so far had proved to be completely satisfactory, from the first night when he'd taken her in a wave of sensual bemusement and hot, all-consuming desire. He had made an effort at first to be tender, believing with her naked form in his arms that such beauty, such exquisite delicacy of flowering proportions, warranted above all things consideration and gentleness. To his surprise she had quickly proved otherwise. Every trick known to woman had seemed induced to inflame him. Her lilylike limbs had arched and received him with the expert artistry of a qualified seductress. As his hands caressed her body, her soft lips seemed everywhere on his. The pounding of his heart became thunder in his ears, and the harder, crueler he was in possessing her, the wilder was her demand.

It was only later he'd said in the aftermath of consummation, "You were quite an expert, my darling," and she'd answered, ignoring the hint of suspicion in his voice, "Only because I love you, Justin."

He had forced himself to be content. But when he saw her in the hall that day, looking out toward the moors with that veiled expression in her eyes, he felt desire in him deepening to aggressive need.

"I don't wish you to go out at the moment," he said. "I wish—other things."

"But, Justin—" She attempted to draw away, and as she did so a servant appeared at the far end of the hall. Justin lifted Mara's hand to his lips, dispelling any suggestion of a rift between them. She allowed herself to accompany him to their bedroom, and by the time his hands were expertly removing the constricting frilly clothes, she had successfully disguised any show of opposition by one of physical desire.

There was no way for him to realize that while he claimed and possessed her, her mind was elsewhere —flying and racing through the hinterland of deepest need and dream to a dark house on a shadowed shore where Rohan waited—forever her lord and master.

8

Olivia was more than shocked when she received Justin's letter. She was acutely hurt, and at first tried to believe it was some monstrous joke. He was teasing. He must be—trying to see how she'd react. Perhaps he wanted her back at Penraven and was trying to get her home quickly in a fit of anger.

But when she read the note a second time, she knew he meant it. Such a carefully worded, cool letter—even kind in a way—suggesting she might leave school if she wished, sooner than had been intended.

But why? Why should she want to return, with that —that Mara girl—the gypsy's daughter taking the place that should have been hers, Olivia's, as the daughter of the house?

Justin, of all people, to get involved with such a person! The thought of Annabella as her brother's wife had been hard enough to bear. But Mara, that strange, beautiful, catlike creature with her secret smile and winning ways! Goodness, how furious her father would have been!

For a few moments a lump of emotion rose in her throat when she recalled Christin, his passion for Penraven and having heirs to follow after him. He had wanted the Fearnley connection just because of that. Then as she remembered other things, emotion died in her. She herself had never really mattered to him at all. He had patted her head vaguely when she was little, given presents sometimes at Christmas and for birthdays, but when she'd thanked him, he'd hardly noticed. Only Justin and Justin's future had been of any account.

And now, so soon after her father's death, he had done this stupid thing. Why? Why? The answer was not hard to find; it was Mara's beauty of course, and because Justin had been lonely with Christin gone and Elaine being such a silly weak creature.

Well, she told herself resolutely a little later, setting her chin firmly, it was his own fault; when he discovered his mistake—as he would one day—he'd have only himself to blame. She wouldn't be able to help him, no one would, because she, anyway, would not be there. Watching him and Mara together would be intolerable. She'd have to find a husband for herself just as soon as possible—as soon as she was old enough—and then she'd leave Penraven for good.

Even this decision did not appear entirely practical following the first miserable reaction. Who was there to marry that she could bear near her, from the acceptable family circle of friends? Sir William Porterrin's son, Godwin? But he was a stupid stout foppish character with clammy hands and a stutter. Someone like Mr. Bosallin perhaps? Oldish, and rich,

but oh, so terribly unattractive. Then Claude Ferris
—he was good-looking and fun to be with, but quite
brainless, and anyway he'd want a dowry.

Her mind traveled quickly over possibles, and
found none. The future really did appear a drab
affair. It wasn't as though she was beautiful like Mara.
No man would be enchanted by her fiery coloring
and proud temper. Her features and hair were good.
Her eyes were bright and large, and her cheeks rich
with a carnation glow. But there was nothing haunting or ethereal about her.

"You're a wild one, Livvy," Justin had said more
than once, and it was true. Wild and defiant, or she
would never have fought the horrible Miss Cobbet as
she had, facing whippings rather than giving in. Justin was like that too—or rather she'd thought he was.
But now she wondered. Wondered how he could
have been so weak as to be ensnared by the Mara girl.
It wouldn't have been like that with Cousin Rohan.
Rohan wasn't at all nice, but she sensed with uncanny
insight that no woman on earth would possess the
power to enslave him as Mara had enslaved Justin.

Because pondering over Rohan helped a little in
easing the pain of thinking about Justin, Olivia forced
her mind back to the day her cousin had rescued her
from her fall and taken her to Boscarrion. What a
strange house it had been—how unreal yet curiously
vivid the impression remained of the mirrored room
with its many candles flickering on the rich furniture
and crystal—and mosaic floors. The stag's head on
the wall—the tall monastic windows, and the heavy
scent of wine and lingering perfume of Rohan's guest
—mistress, it was said—Lady Something-or-other—
Lefrougé, yes, that was it.

As she thought back, the picture intensified with
uncanny clarity. Just for a second or two Olivia was

there again, and the tall figure of Melusina was coming to meet her, ordering the great dog Brutus to lie
down. The rustle of purple silk echoed weirdly
through Olivia's brain; she could see as one glimpsing
through a mirage the extended white arms, hear
again the murmur of the low voice above the crack-
ling of logs and brush of wind from outside. There
were dots of lights where diamonds sprinkled the
very black piled-up hair. Then, suddenly, the impression of that strange dream out-of-time was ended,
and Olivia was brought back to the real world by her
school roommate.

"Here, what are you brooding about, Livvy? You
look—" She broke off as Olivia tore her face from the
ordinary square mirror on the mahogany school
dressing table.

"Nothing," she answered airily. "I was thinking of
my cousin's house."

"Well, the bell's already gone for lunch, and your
hair's a sight."

Olivia started tidying immediately, although the
uniformed dress had little about it to get out of place.

"I had a letter from home this morning," she explained. "You know that my father died recently—"

"Yes, you told me."

"Well, my brother's got married suddenly—"

"Do you mean—"

"No. Don't you dare suggest it." Olivia's cheeks
flushed. "It's just that Justin doesn't seem to want me
to go home for Easter—and I was wondering—"

"Good. Then you can join me. I did ask you, remember?"

"Yes. Thank you," Olivia agreed. "I've never been
to Bath. It will be nice."

The matter was settled between the two girls there
and then, and, helpfully for Olivia, the second lunch-

eon bell rang immediately afterward, delaying any
further probing from her friend concerning Justin's
marriage.

From time to time during the day, however,
Olivia's thoughts were never far from Penraven, and
at times strayed back to Rohan. She wondered if his
lady friend was still at Boscarrion, and if they would
ever meet again.

The latter, had she but known it, was extremely
doubtful; for Rohan Tregallis was concerned with no
woman at that period except Mara.

And Mara was imparting some very important
news indeed.

"How long is your devoted new husband likely to
be away?" he was asking, eyeing her enigmatically
from under half-closed lids. She was looking extremely elegant in a deep-blue velvet riding habit
and plumed hat—a very different character indeed
from the windblown wayward nymph of previous
visits. Her cheeks were faintly flushed from the ride,
her eyes sparkled. The jacket she wore was perfectly
designed to enhance the tiny waist below the firm
young breasts. At her neck was a jabot of lace, and
lace edged tightly fitting sleeves above the wrists. An
alluring creature indeed, Rohan thought apprecia-
tively. Beautiful she had always been, but the fashionable attire combined with her new status made
her all the more desirable and worthy as a mistress.
He himself was attired all in gray, including a calf-
length frac over pale gray knee breeches, silk stockings, and buckled shoes. His black hair was unpow-
dered, his lean face dark above the frilled white
cravat and long yellow silk waistcoat.

They sat opposite each other, with a rosewood
table between them containing a decanter and two
glasses.

"Tell me, how long is he away?" he repeated. "You were unwise coming at this hour, and against my express commands."

She lifted her chin, smiling faintly. "Now I'm Justin's wife—" she began, but was interrupted by a savage gesture of contempt as he sprang to his feet and with one arm swept his glass to the floor. "Don't throw your airs about here, madam," he said. "Remember who I am, and what I can do. Under those frills and graces your pretty body is still mine. To me you are still the slut I ravished and will do so whenever I feel inclined. Or are you thinking to trick me? Are you, madam?"

He grasped her shoulder and pulled her up to face him. She flinched. Suddenly defiance left her. Her lips trembled childishly while resistance died into desire.

He laughed, and pressed her close. The plumed hat toppled and fell from her head. As his fingers caressed her skull through the silky mass of her hair, his breath was hot on her cheeks. "Tell me, you little minx," he whispered against her ear. "Remember what I promised if you ever played me false."

"Rohan—Rohan—" Her voice, through its protest, was husky with longing. "Justin won't be back for a week." His grip slackened. "He's gone to Wales to see someone—some engineer about a mine. Crannick. And no one saw me ride here. I came by the high route, above the ridge."

"On a wild pony?"

"No. A mare—my own. She's tethered below, and no one saw me; believe me, it's true. I came in through the side door. There was only the boy about —the Negro."

"Hm." He walked to the door of the room and gave a sharp call to the housekeeper. She was a short

woman with shrewd eyes and a fanatical devotion to
her master.

"See all the servants are occupied in the kitchens
or upstairs," he said, "and after half an hour send
Nelson to me. Complete secrecy—nothing about a
visitor, you understand?"

The woman gave a little bob. "Yes, sir, of course,
sir. You can trust me, you know that." Her hard,
shrewd stare glittered on Mara a moment, then she
left, closing the door soundlessly behind her. Rohan
poured himself a drink and handed one to Mara.
"You'd better begin," he said. "Explain why madam
fly-by-night has come at noon instead of by moonlight."

He waited.

She smiled again—her slow sweet smile that held
so curious a mixture of innocence and seductive mischief.

"I have news for you, Rohan. I'm with child." She
paused before adding quietly, "Yours."

He stared. "Mine? How the devil do you know?"

"A woman does know these things. Dates, instinct.
Besides, it was conceived before I ever slept with
Justin."

There was a long pause in which his eyes never left
her face, nor hers his. Then he said, "How do I know
you've not lain with others? I don't, do I? A woman
who can cheat and pretend and steal at fairs could
have taken any Tom, Dick or Harry as lover, providing of course"—his lip curled—"he had sufficient in
his pocket."

The color ebbed from her face. She would have
rushed to the door, but he prevented her, standing
there with his back to it.

"Don't be a fool. You may have fine clothes and
marriage lines to flaunt—but only because I permit-
ted it. If I wish, and when—I could destroy your little

game with a few words. So don't act the fine madam before me, Mara."

He grasped the lacy jabot at her throat and jerked her forward so her chin was tilted upward close under his. They glared at each other until her eyes fell. He laughed again. She tried to speak; he silenced her. "Hold your tongue. I'm in no mood for lies or flattery, and I know very well what you're trying to say—'I love no one but you, Rohan—and I've not deceived you, I swear it—'" He broke off, adding after a pause, "Is that true? Could it possibly be—"

"You know it is."

He appeared to lose interest suddenly and released her. "Maybe. In any case—why should I care? I've tasted your charms enough. I know your body as well as any man could know a woman's, and with familiarity desire can become boring."

She winced.

"The child, of course, makes a difference."

"I thought it might."

"Not in the way you think, I imagine." Heavy sarcasm flooded his voice. "I have no feeling for it, no wish to see it when you so dutifully deliver an infant to the noble house of Tregallis. My lusty cousin Justin shall take full pride and responsibility. There will be celebrations and wine flowing that day, no doubt. An heir to Penraven. How very fitting. How extremely dutiful of you to oblige so soon. Oh, don't worry. I've no intention of putting the cat among the pigeons—yet, Mara. Perhaps the occasion will never arise. Perhaps fate itself will take charge."

"What do you mean?"

"Why the devil should I tell you?"

"No, of course not. Only—"

"Listen!" The cold lines of his mouth and narrowed eyes chilled her. "I wish for no more of this conversation. As far as I'm concerned, it never took place. You will return to Penraven and bear your gypsy bastard, playing the doting wife and mother with your usual talent. I will keep my mouth shut so long as it suits me, provided you do as you've been told and keep me informed of even the smallest detail concerning Tregallis affairs. You will watch, and listen, and manipulate that drunken fool of a matron—until every secret of her life spent with Uncle Christin is spilled into your pretty ear. You'll use your cunning with care, and on the day I get what I want, I'll—"

"Yes?" The question was little more than a breathless sigh, but it jerked Rohan to reality.

"I would not marry you," he said, "even if there were no Justin. Having tasted the fruit is sufficient. But I'll pay for my pleasures generously, and withhold the whip. You understand?"

A wild spurt of courage came to her. Her eyes blazed.

"Yes. And you are a boor—a bully, and a cruel one, Rohan Tregallis. Take your hand off my arm—" She shook herself from his sudden grasp. "Don't touch me. I'm no longer your—your—"

"Concubine?" He threw his head back. There was the harsh, grating sound of laughter, then a sudden silence before he continued. "But you are, you know, that's just what you are. Mistress, chattel, and whore of whores—the honored wife of Justin Tregallis."

She caught him a swinging blow across a cheek. What color he had ebbed from his face, leaving it ashy gray.

"If you ever dare to do that again," he said, "I'll kill you."

At that moment she believed him. She swept past him and plunged through the door, down the hall and out of the house, leaving him standing by the door feeling nothing for that short interim but a concentrated determination for revenge.

Hatred and desire warred within him. Presently he moved to the window. High against the moorland hills he saw the girl and horse galloping toward the bridge. Before crossing she turned, glancing down to Boscarrion. He did not move. The next moment her form was lost behind a fold in the landscape.

Rohan, walking stiffly, moved to a chest and unlocked a drawer mechanically. From it he took a small miniature painted on ivory in an oval gold frame. He carried it to the light. Delicate features stared up at him from highly dressed pale hair. The shoulders of the girl were bare above the blue, low-cut gown. The rosy lips were slightly parted in a half smile—the smile that had once tilted the lips of Elaine Tregallis.

"Damn you," he whispered. "If it hadn't been for you, things would have been quite different." He threw the memento back again, closed the drawer sharply, and glanced to the wall where portraits hung of his father, Ellis, and his wife, Clara—Rohan's mother. Clara was no beauty, but proud, dark, and haughty-looking. No wonder his father had rebelled.

Conjecturing no further at that point, Rohan poured himself a drink, and then another. Slowly a retrospective gleam of satisfaction spread from his eyes to lips.

Little vixen, he thought as his mind turned from Elaine to Mara. Spit and fight as she might, he knew she was his and always would be. Nothing would divide them—nothing in the world. He had only to command, and she would be there. A threat from him was as well an invitation.

And in the end it was Mara who would bring him to his birthright.

Olivia returned to Penraven in August. The coach journey from Plymouth had been wearying and tedious; there were so many stopping places from Bodmin to Redruth, the weather was hot, and too many people were traveling for comfort. Her only consolation was that she had left school for good—and that she would so soon be seeing Justin.

She had contrived so far to reduce the unpleasant idea of also having to face Mara to a minimum. It was only when the family chaise drew up near the inn yard where the coach stopped, that boredom and tiredness suddenly vanished. Justin was already waiting for her while passengers dismounted. She pushed between a stout man and woman and ran excitedly toward him. Her heart was pounding, her eyes bright and cheeks crimson.

He drew her to him, laughed, and said, "Livvy, Livvy, don't strangle me—" He put both hands on her shoulders and stared. "You've grown," he told her. "And altered . . ." His voice trailed off uncertainly.

The glint of white teeth shone between red lips. Then the thick black lashes fell over her eyes. She looked away. "Yes. It's been a long time, Justin."

"Six months. Just six months."

"I'm not a child anymore."

"No. Well—" He pulled himself together abruptly. "Where's that luggage? You've more than that small valise, surely?"

"The driver's got it—there. Look—the box with the rope around it." Justin followed her directions, and when her possessions were loaded at the back of the Tregallis chaise, they started off for Penraven.

An air of formality fell on their conversation following Olivia's first exuberance. Justin answered questions concerning her father's death and funeral with the minimum of detail, and did his best to put his marriage to Mara in perspective. "I'm sure you'll get on with her better than you would have with Annabella," he said. "Annabella might have overwhelmed you. Mara won't do that, I can assure you."

"Of course not." Olivia's tones were acid. "I wouldn't allow her to. And naturally having been a servant—"

Justin glanced at her warningly.

"None of that, Olivia. Mara's my wife now. See you're polite to her."

Olivia did not reply. Her eyes were on the passing vista of countryside—the sweep of moors and thread of road bearing always a little to their right where the main lane eventually met the rougher track winding toward the coast and Penraven. A thin fog was already creeping inland from the sea, shrouding the distant coastline into hazed uniformity. Land and water became merged into the furred shapes of bushes and windblown trees. Humped rocks rose at intervals from massed clumps of heather and gorse, giving the impression of great beasts sleeping in their primeval beds. As the thin wind freshened, coils of vaporous fog rolled and billowed around standing stones and menhirs from far-off centuries, giving a fleeting impression of movement. The air had a damp tang in it—heavy with moist greenery, foxgloves, and salty brine.

Through the open window Olivia drew a strong whiff of it deep into her lungs. Her heart leaped. During the long months at school she had forgotten how potent Cornwall itself was. Justin—yes; Justin had always been an image in her mind. But this—the strong sense of familiarity and magical elemental awareness—revived feelings in her that had lain dormant during the enforced period of discipline and learning manners and deportment, and of conducting herself as a young lady of her position was sup-

posed to, and acting with propriety in the best social
circles.

"Propriety!" "Social circles!" The phrases now
echoed in her memory meaninglessly. How ridiculous of those starchy, pompous schoolmistresses to
imagine she could ever really be molded to their own
stuffy pattern; she, Olivia Tregallis, who so often in
the past had longed to dance naked through the
heather and around the ancient dolmens—who had
done so as a child and been caught once and chas-
tised soundly for it.

A little laugh rippled from her throat as she
remembered. The adventure had been worth the
fleeting pain of the punishment, and although she'd
been careful for some time afterward, there had
been occasions when she'd bathed in her own secret
place—a moorland pool—and lain on a bed of thyme
until the warm sun left her flesh glowing and dry.
She'd wanted Justin to be there then. Justin, whom
she loved so much—to share things with. But she'd
only met him when she was dressed again and making her way home. His eyes had been filled with
suspicion. "What have you been up to?" he'd asked,
and she'd replied, "Dancing with—with—"

"Who?" The word had fallen harshly from his lips.

"Myself, and—the old ones."

"What old ones?"

"The gods," Olivia had whispered, "the old, old
gods from ancient times. Let's go back, Justin—
let's—"

But his eyes had darkened. He'd looked quite
angry and taken her hand, pulling her roughly down
the slope. "You behave, Livvy, you just behave," he'd
said, "or there'll be trouble."

She hadn't quite known what he'd meant; neither
had he. But she'd realized, deep down, that he'd

understood. Although they were so different, there
was something between them uniquely their own
that nothing or no one could ever entirely change.

And it was the same still. As the chaise rattled
down the steepest part of the lane to Penraven,
Olivia determined that not even Mara should spoil
things between them.

When she saw Mara just before dinner, however,
her self-confidence was dashed. Justin's wife had always been beautiful. Olivia well remembered the
lovely azure-blue eyes shadowed by thick dark
lashes, the delicate features and ethereal coloring,
the slender graceful neck and figure, but she had
never before seen Mara with her creamy shoulders
bare above blue silk, jewels gleaming from her ears
and at her breast—had never seen her face soften or
lips smile in that particular sweet way as she turned
to Justin, waiting to be kissed.

At first Olivia was too shocked by envy to notice
the faint but swelling lines of Mara's figure beneath
the cleverly designed gown. Her heart contracted in
physical pain as she noted Justin's expression, the
look of adoration in his eyes. He was entranced—
well, of course he was, she thought with a rush of
resentment. No man could fail to be. And yet Mara
was nothing, really—nothing but a tinker's daughter
who'd stolen into Penraven and spoiled everything
by beguiling them by her looks and manners. And
she would do Justin no good; Olivia was certain of it,
even in those quick few minutes of confrontation.
There was something strange about Mara—something elusive and unknowable, possessing secret
depths that could be dark and turbulent as a river's
hidden forces, beneath a clear and shining surface.

Yet her welcome was apparently warm; she insisted on Olivia sitting next to Justin at the table, and

placed herself farther down, opposite Elaine, who for once had decided to eat with them.

"Why don't you take the end chair and preside in your proper place, Mama?" Justin asked. "It's your right."

Elaine, looking haggard, elegant, and rather ridiculous in too much finery and wearing too many rings and bracelets, with far too many feathers and flowers in her faded hair, swayed slightly and answered, "I should—should miss everything, should I not? Is th-that what you want, Justin? For your mother to be pushed out? I'm a lonely woman. I haven't seen my darling daughter for so—so l-long."

Her speech slurred as she slumped into a chair. Justin eyed her distastefully. "Just as you like. If you're interested in listening to school gossip."

"School?" Elaine's voice quivered like discordant bells through the air. "But there's so much more, surely? The baby? Who t-talks of school, when th-there's a b-baby coming?"

Olivia glanced at her mother sharply, and caught a quick glance of malice in the older woman's eyes. Did Elaine mean what she'd said, she wondered, or were those shrill words merely an attempt to hurt her? Why was it that her mother seemed to dislike her so much?

Through a wave of conjecture Olivia's mind switched suddenly again to Elaine's remark about a baby. She tried not to believe it; but when she looked at Justin's face, she knew it was true. Confusion mounted in her. She could feel the warm blood staining her cheeks. It was natural, of course, she told herself, digging the fingers of both hands into her palms. Justin and Mara were married, and married people expected children. But so soon? Surely they could have waited a little? With questions and answers racing through her mind she heard herself saying lamely, "I didn't know. I thought—"

"What did you think my—d-dear?" Elaine's voice was mocking now. "That my strong son would wish t-to devote himself to his p-p-poor old mother, and g-gauche young sister only? Oh, no, no. Dear me, no." She reached for the decanter. Justin's hand drew it away firmly.

"Mama," he said coldly, "you have already had an aperitif. It's time to eat now."

"Eat?" Elaine's voice thickened with fury. She got up unsteadily, almost toppled over the chair, and faced Justin angrily. "Who are you to tell me wh-what to eat and drink, you—you big bully. I am a lady. I d-do what I choose. Why should I partake of your sickly soup and hog's food? Why should I demean myself by—by—" She turned and stumbled awkwardly to the door. Justin followed quickly and caught her arm. She leaned against him, and with her flash of rage suddenly over, allowed him to lead her from the room.

During the five minutes of his absence Mara made an effort to be friendly. "I know you didn't want me to marry Justin," she said, watching Olivia closely. "I can understand it. I never thought I would myself. But it happened, you see; like some things do."

"Why?" Olivia interrupted coldly. "Because you loved him? Or because you wanted to be mistress of Penraven?"

As soon as the question was out, she wished she'd not spoken, knowing she must appear childish and jealous.

"No," Mara answered coolly. "Neither, not completely."

"What do you mean?"

"I'm so very fond of Justin," Mara said truthfully.

"I'm sure I love him as much as it's possible for me to love anyone. And of course it's pleasant living in such a—such a large house. But if I hadn't thought I could make Justin happy, I'd never have done it. And I hope having the baby will please him, too." Her manner was restrained; her words apparently so carefully chosen to make goodwill between herself and her sister-in-law that Olivia was instantly suspicious.

It occurred to her in a flash that Mara was acting a part. Behind the lovely facade was a completely unknowable individual who was managing very skillfully to weave a web of illusion about them. She was pretending kindliness to Olivia because it was to her advantage, and unless she was very careful Olivia sensed Mara might soon cause a rift between her and Justin.

So Olivia did her best to be polite, and by the time Justin returned to the dining room, all appeared amicable between his wife and sister.

All the same, Olivia was discomforted. Mara obviously was not going to oppose or openly resent her. But she could not help wondering what her role in the household was going to be. Justin clearly doted on Mara. He would expect his sister to respond in friendship. Well, she'd have to try, of course, for peace and the coming child. For Justin too. But why? Why had he married Lillith's daughter? She wasn't their kind—she hadn't been brought up to their way of life. Her mother was a gypsy reputed to be a witch, and wouldn't be accepted by any of their friends. Not that that mattered, Olivia told herself later as she stood at her bedroom window staring out over the moorland hills. Most of the Tregallis friends were snobbish bores. And anyway—Mara had very fine ways about her. That was strange too. Where had she got her manners from? Her gracious airs and delicate looks?

With a sudden start of surprise—almost shock— Olivia realized how like Elaine she was. Not the tipsy eccentric creature of present times, but the one remembered from long ago when Olivia had been a tiny child trying to win her mother's affection. She had so longed to feel wanted. But Elaine, though seldom impatient, had generally been too tired or wearied by migraine to bother with the warm demands of the little girl. Her smile had always been sweet, but the lovely eyes more often than not had been chilly with fatigue, any words of endearment ending with "Run away now. Mama's needing a rest." Olivia's ardor, then, had died into a lump of disappointment. With her father it had been worse. He appeared definitely to dislike her. Only Justin had been kind.

Justin.

A warm glow stirred in her when she thought of him. In spite of Mara there would be times when they could be together. He wouldn't always want to be mooning about the house. They would have the chance to ride the moors again, and when the baby came, Mara would be too occupied with maternal duties to want Justin every moment at her side. She supposed there'd be a nurse, and nurses had to be watched; Mara would want to see everything was being attended to properly, wouldn't she? Or would she? Would she just be thankful to leave the bothersome business of looking after a young child to anyone else who was at hand?

Try as she would, Olivia could not conjure up any entirely satisfactory picture of the future. So instead she allowed herself to lapse into retrospection, remembering days before Christin had died, her stormy interludes with Miss Cobbet, who now, God be praised, had gone, and other happier times when she had been able to escape and wander the moors, either walking or riding Moonbeam.

She remembered in particular a certain evening after an angry scene with her governess when she had determined to run away forever and join the circus people at Camborne. But a mist had come down, and she'd lost the path in the thickening fog. Although she'd worn a cloak, she'd been very cold, and had crouched down by a large standing stone. The thin wind had whipped the heather and fronds of dripping fern against her damp cheeks. There was no sound but the creaking of undergrowth and moaning of the wind. When she'd gotten up and tried to find her way again, she'd come up against more granite.

She'd put out a hand and steadied herself against the rough surface. Through a momentary clearing of the air where the fog billowed, more tall stones had emerged fitfully and she'd known they were the "old ones"—the lordly relics of a lost race that had been turned to stones for disobeying the ancient gods. A strange sense of kinship had possessed her. She'd wandered from one to another through the gray light, thinking, "Perhaps it will happen to me too. Perhaps I'll stiffen and change and be one of them forever and ever—" The idea had been awesome, but she hadn't been frightened. She had been too cold to care.

And then, just ahead of her, something had moved —a distorted swaying shape that drew nearer with the hollow thudding of horses' hooves. Was this the king, she'd wondered, the high king of ancient Cornwall come to pronounce her doom? She'd crouched deeper into the tangled wet undergrowth, with a hand gone to her throat fearfully. Her heart had almost stopped beating.

Then, suddenly, the terrible strange dream had been broken by a voice saying, "What's this? Who—hells bells! Is it really you, Livvy?"

A little cry had left her throat. She'd tried to struggle to her feet, but there'd been no need. Justin had lifted her up and was holding her close against his strong young body.

"Thank heaven," he was saying. "You could catch your death. What do you mean by it, eh? You've been gone for hours. The whole house is in a furor."

"Is it, Justin? Is it? Why? Nobody minds about me —no one. I was—I was going to the circus. I was—"

"You little idiot. And what do you mean no one minds? I mind."

Her arms had reached up to his neck. She was sobbing and laughing all at once, as her senses thawed from the warmth of him. "Really, Justin? Do you really mind?"

He had not answered, but his hand fondling her hair and pressing her face close against his chest told enough.

"Why do you think I've been searching this barren place for hours?" he'd asked. "It's damned cold out here, and believe me, Livvy, there'll be all hell waiting when we get back."

"Need we go back, Justin? Couldn't we just gallop away forever and live together like—like—"

"Gypsies? Tinkers? Paupers? You don't know what you're talking about. And if you ever give me a fright like this again, I'll put you over my knee and give you a sound spanking myself to save Cobby the trouble."

She'd shivered.

"I expect she will be cross. Oh, Justin—if only Papa liked me." Tears of exhaustion had filled her eyes and started trickling down her round cheeks. He'd tried to comfort her then.

"It'll be all right, Livvy," he'd told her. "I'm not quite a man yet, but I'm strong enough to tackle any who threaten you, and I have a way with my father. I'll see there's no trouble this time, but you just be careful in future." He placed her on his horse before him, and a minute later they were cantering carefully toward the west.

She'd been asleep when they reached Penraven, and miraculously Justin had succeeded in keeping his word. There'd been no whipping, no punishment at all. Since that day they had been closer than ever.

From this incident Olivia's mind traveled to others, and she recalled once again her strange visit to Boscarrion, thinking how odd it was any family could be so divided—strange, but also mystifying and somehow exciting. She had not liked Cousin Rohan, of course—he was not the type anyone would choose for a friend. But still—the possibility of meeting him once more was intriguing, especially since Justin was obviously going to be so concerned with Mara, he'd probably have little time to go riding with her, his own sister.

She sighed. It had been so wonderful looking forward to leaving school during those last days at the Plymouth "Academy for Young Ladies." She'd managed effectively to reduce all thought of Mara to a mere shadow, just an obstacle to be overcome when she got back to Penraven. She'd forgotten that things were bound to be very different indeed. Not only had Justin a wife, but he had Christin's duties as well to shoulder, now that her father was dead.

Poor Papa. She tried to be sorry for him, but she could no longer look back with affection, and for her mother she had only pity tinged with contempt. So it was natural, she told herself, that Rohan should loom in her imagination from time to time. However wicked he might be, he was still her cousin, and perhaps if she managed things carefully, a chance would come to know him better and help solve the riddle of the feud started by her father and his dead brother, her uncle Ellis.

The opportunity came earlier than she'd thought.

Olivia was feeling fretful and rebellious on the day of the storm. Justin had insisted the previous evening that the following week she had to return to Fairclose for the autumn term.

"But why?" she'd asked obstinately. "You'd told me I could leave earlier. You know you did, Justin—"

"I said next year," he'd answered. "You've not been there long enough to complete your education. Good heavens, Livvy, do you expect me to waste money uselessly?"

"You haven't wasted it," she said with a flash of temper. "I've learned quite a lot, and stupid things, too. Anyway, it wasn't your money, was it, that sent me there? It was Papa's."

He regarded her coldly, forcing himself not to be softened by the willful set of her small chin, the glowing rose of her cheeks and fiery brilliance of her dark eyes. She was facing him defiantly, yet a perceptible quiver of her full underlip told him she was hurt. His feelings were mixed. He'd disliked making her unhappy; if he'd obeyed his instincts, he'd have capitulated, drawn her to him, stroking her luxurious dark hair, murmuring words of affection and endearment. But damnit! She was only a child, his sister. She had to learn not to throw her temper about, causing emotional scenes whenever she didn't get her way.

He'd looked away, refusing to be intimidated, and said sternly, "It's no use arguing, Olivia. You're going back to school, for this term anyway. If you behave we'll consider later about next year."

He was walking toward the door, but she'd followed and got there before him. With her back to it she'd cried rebelliously, "I may *not* behave at that awful place. I'll probably disgrace you terribly and make such a scandal even Cousin Rohan will be shocked."

"If you do," Justin had told her, "and if you mention Cousin Rohan's name just once more, I'll see Cobby returns to give you a good dose of her cane."

"Cobby wouldn't. She's got a place in Liskeard. Mrs. Broome told me."

"Then I'd have to do it myself, wouldn't I?" Justin had said. "Make no mistake, Livvy, I'm your brother, and master here now. And you're going to obey when I think fit. Understand?"

She'd turned and rushed away, seething with frustration and bitter resentment at Justin's obtuseness. She wasn't a child. Why had he to treat her like one? It was that Mara, of course. Only Mara mattered to him since their marriage. It was as if her own wishes didn't count anymore.

So when the clouds came up the following morning predicting one of those freak summer storms capable of distorting the coastline by one high tide, Olivia found her own mood responding to the stimulus of darkening yellow light, rising wind, and threat of approaching thunder.

The grooms were not about when she went to the stables; so she saddled Moonbeam herself and before anyone knew of it was cantering across a field bordering Penraven, following a track upward and to her right where the moorland hills rose bleak and clearly

defined against the lowering sky. Instinctively her
direction took her to the stretch of land above Red
River. She rode bareheaded and had not changed
into her habit but was wearing a long dark skirt covered by her brown woolen cape. The gale was from
the north, an evil gale that was already churning
thickening veils of sand toward the rocks and dunes
bordering Boscarrion below.

Soon the sting of rain was mingling ominously with
that of salty brine. Moonbeam snorted joyously in
defiance of the elements, galloping on with tail and
mane flying. Olivia headed her over the swelling
stream and then cut downward along a more sheltered track. She was close upon her cousin's house
when a shattering sound rose above the roar of wind
and tide, crashing thunderously on the shore to the
right of Boscarrion. Olivia reined her horse with difficulty, and rubbed her smarting eyes. Through the
blown sand and breaking of mountainous waves she
could see the dark shape of a ship foundering on a
stretch of beach to the west of the river's narrow
estuary.

Not thinking of her own safety, Olivia tethered her
horse to a tree and made her precarious way above
the cut to Boscarrion. As she reached the front door,
it opened to reveal Rohan's form in the drunken
swaying of an oil lamp. At the same moment the
screaming and shouting of many human beings—
surely a whole army of them, Olivia thought desperately—was carried piercingly on the gale.

"What the hell are you doing here?" Rohan
shouted. "You fool—you little fool—"

She gasped out her news, and as she ended with
"There'll be people there, Rohan—people dying and
drowned—"she broke off, struggling for air.

He pulled her inside and pushed her to the

kitchen. "Do you think I don't know?" he shouted. "What do you think I'm doing? The men are already off to give help. Now sit there and don't you dare move until I get back. Mrs. Trellis—" The woman appeared from a scullery adjoining the main kitchens. She wore a dour expression that day, her grim eyes watchful and hard under a mob cap. Olivia shivered. She was shocked, tense, and sensed that the woman could be a ruthless character.

"Ais?" The woman peered shrewdly at Olivia.

"See this young relative of mine does not stir from here until I return," Rohan told her curtly. "You understand? Feed her and give her something warming to drink, then get her to the fire. If she tries to leave, you know what to do."

Mrs. Trellis, cook, housekeeper, or whichever it was, nodded and put a hand on Olivia's shoulder. Olivia pulled herself free. "You needn't try and force me," she said. "I'm not stupid."

"Good," the woman remarked grimly.

Rohan laughed. "It's as well. We have no use for half-wits here."

He went out, slamming the door behind him, leaving Olivia alone with her jailer. She knew Rohan had meant what he said, and guessed the unpleasant Mrs. Trellis had help at hand in case she tried to escape. When she mentioned Moonbeam, the woman proved Olivia had been right.

"Who's Moonbeam?" she asked.

"My mare," Olivia explained. "She's tethered above the ravine. If she breaks free, she'll race straight back to Penraven and there'll be a fuss. My brother and servants will come looking. Still—never mind. Perhaps that would be as well—certainly for me."

Mrs. Trellis frowned. "Moses," she called, "where

are you, you good-for-nothing oaf?" A minute later
an immense, rather foolish-looking but belligerent
character came in, wearing an apron and smelling of
beer. The woman leaned forward with a fist raised.
"You just tell that boy of yours to get on up-over," she
snarled. "By the ravine there. There's a hoss waitin'!
Get 'en untied an' bring et to stables. An ef you doan
find en, you just search till you do or come tell me.
See? Got that in your thick head?"

The man's full underlip came out. His small eyes
contracted under a bulbous forehead.

"I'll get lad," he said, "I'll tell un. Doan' you fret,
missis. My Nick'll find th' beast."

"He's not a beast. It's a she, a mare," Olivia exclaimed sharply, "and she's a valuable, gentle horse.
Take care of her or I'll tell my cousin."

The man gave her a leering glance, and a moment
later had gone.

Time dragged as Olivia tried to relax and made an
effort to eat the food put before her. She and the
housekeeper hardly spoke, and when they did the
watchful old creature only answered in monosylla-
bles. As storm and wind heightened, Olivia had the
restricted, smothering feeling of being confined in a
prison of sand; sand blew in thick clouds against the
windows, was caught up by the waves and driven
against the walls of the house, creeping through
cracks and around windowpanes, even spreading an
insidious veil across the kitchen floor. And from
below, the moaning and crashing of waves and broken ship intensified, penetrated by intermittent
screaming.

"Is it often like this?" Olivia asked once.

The woman eyed her sullenly. "We've had wuss.
As you should know—being born hereabouts."

"I hope they don't drown—those poor men."

"Ha! Hopen' doan save lives. There'll be many go
this day, I'm thinkin'! You just thank your stars, girl,
you be safe an' warm in maister's house 'stead of out
wi' him on that theer beach."

Olivia did not ask the woman how long the rescue
attempt was likely to be or when she expected Rohan
to be back, knowing she'd receive no civil answer.
Several times she toyed with the idea of trying to
escape, but realizing it would be useless, she had to
ease her impatience by wandering to and fro about
the kitchen, from door to window and back again to
the table. The light seemed to grow worse as the
hours ticked by. It could have been night instead of
day. But from the clock she saw it was not yet twelve
thirty, nearing lunchtime at Penraven. By then she
knew she must have been missed, and that Justin was
already probably searching for her. Oh dear! What a
fuss there'd be when she arrived back, and a worse
scene if it was discovered where she'd been.

Meanwhile, Rohan below was directing and ac-
tively taking part in operations from the treacherous
stretch of shore. The vessel was a Cornish smuggler
returning from France containing two hundred ankers of spirit and some silk. But the ostensible rescue
attempt was double-edged. Under a show of public-
spirited enthusiasm, Rohan—who had backed the
venture—had already managed to inform the Revenue, knowing full well that he would otherwise be
suspect when investigations got under way. Failure
of a plan of this kind always exasperated him; but by
the time the law arrived, a certain amount of spirit
had been cunningly diverted to his own cellars. The
rest was either submerged in the sinking hold, taken
and swept out to sea as mere jetsam, or being plundered over by locals, mostly Gwyfna men, in angry
skirmish with the struggling crew.

Rohan's display of concern and bravery was one cleverly calculated to win approval of the king's men. The scene could have been one from a tragic play—with pale hands clawing uselessly for a moment to the air before submergence by the tide. Faces swam lifelessly near the water's surface, eyes vacant and glazed turned to the wild sky. Voices screeched, dark figures scrambled and plundered like greedy flies.

When the waters at last receded a little, it was found that several villagers had been drowned, and of the twenty crew only nine were rescued.

The nine lives saved caused Rohan little reason for jubilation. He had no ill will to them personally, but the fact that the Revenue cutter would most probably take them to Plymouth for service with a fleet of ships to bombard Algiers was a bitter pill to swallow. The government attack was to be for the purpose of quelling Barbary pirates who so cruelly and mercilessly seized men from British ships for slavery.

Rohan had considerable interest in many of such wretched dealings. That allies in smuggling should be pressed to the opposing side proved the futility of depending on any dubious scheme. In future he would have to be more careful—more cunning—and take no risks at all where the weather was concerned.

So while he made his way along the dunes to Boscarrion in the company of the officials followed by a little group assisting the injured and carrying the dead, determination filled him to cultivate a further measure of respectability. As a Tregallis, he wielded certain power. But power should be endorsed by approbation of family in order to provide its full potentials. He had none of his own anymore. Christin's household did not accept him. Mara was an ally. But Mara was not sufficient. He needed someone with no blot on her character or heritage. Someone who could in all innocence be his helpmate, and mate in the flesh. Olivia?

The flicker of a smile touched his mouth. If that watchdog of a housekeeper had done her job properly, his cousin would still be waiting for him at the house. Young she was, but maturing physically. He would see that she had a glass of wine with his unwanted visitors who would inform her no doubt of her kinsman's help and considerable courage through the disastrous morning. He had no doubts of her behavior at all under such circumstances.

Olivia Tregallis was certainly a young woman to be cultivated. The thought both titillated and amused him. To win her confidence was a challenge, and he would well know how to charm her once the first was accomplished.

After that? The future was unpredictable. But he did not doubt his capacity to deal with both Mara and Olivia effectively to his own advantage when the time came.

Olivia was surprised to find how agreeable Rohan could be, even following the dramatic and distressing hours of the rescue attempt. He appeared haggard and cold, naturally; there was a cut across his forehead, and his hands were bleeding. But after a quick wash and change of clothing, while the Revenue company were drying themselves before a log fire ablaze in the library, he behaved courteously as host, and the king's men were obviously impressed by his loyalty to the Crown. At the back of the house the injured were made as comfortable as possible until help arrived to get them to the hospital. Bodies retrieved from the sea were laid out respectably under tarpaulin near the porch to await removal to the mortuary.

Olivia was invited to take a glass of wine with the redcoats, and was flattered by their attention. She was aware of Rohan's dark eyes upon her, and though she could not yet completely like or trust him, she was not entirely immune from his magnetic power. It also seemed to her that her father might in some way have misjudged his nephew in the past, and she determined not to believe all the scandalous tales concerning Rohan Tregallis without good cause and proof.

Gradually the gale abated, and Rohan suggested it was time she was conducted safely back to Penraven.

"My Cousin Justin is overzealous concerning her welfare," he explained to the captain, a tall, very erect, and rather intimidating-looking character by the name of Rupert Cosgrave. "My Uncle Christin, her father, died recently, which you may have heard, so doubtless it's perfectly natural."

"Of course," Captain Cosgrave agreed, "and I will personally accompany the young lady to her home. I know Penraven, and dined there once or twice with the late squire." For a moment a hint of curiosity lit his eyes. Rohan's reputation was not without blemish, and he had heard many dubious stories concerning the feud between the two family houses. However, the day's events were in Rohan's favor; without his information none of the smugglers would have been caught, and the whole cargo would have been lost. So he kept any niggling suspicions to himself, well satisfied that he would be complimented from headquarters for providing useful men to serve with the fleet bound for Barbary.

When Olivia set off a little later with the handsome

captain and his lieutenant, she could hardly believe
that one wild gale could have so ruthlessly changed
that immediate line of coast. The dunes that before
had sloped gently toward Boscarrion had now been
swept in mountains of sand against the lower walls of
the house. Great chunks had been torn from the
beach adjoining the property on the other side, exposing massive granite boulders and a stretch of dark
stones and shingle.

It was easy, then, to accept the strange stories of a
complete village lying buried under the humped
sandhills. From time to time Olivia had heard that
utensils were found from primitive times, and that
under certain weather conditions bells from the lost
church still echoed from their ocean bed.

She shivered as Captain Cosgrave helped her into
her saddle. Suddenly she was wanting nothing more
but to be away from the place as soon as possible.
Moonbeam, too, was restive, pounding the ground
with her hooves.

With the change of tide the wind had quieted, and
by the time they reached Penraven, most of the rain
had abated.

The household, as she had anticipated, was in a
state of tense anxiety when they arrived. But the
officer's presence prevented a scene, and after the
two men left, Justin was strangely controlled and
quiet. He admonished her for going riding when the
weather was so uncertain, and commanded her to be
careful in future. There was only one allusion to
Rohan, which ended by Justin saying, "I'm not going
to curse him, since he gave you protection and apparently acted better than I'd have expected, in giving
full assistance to those needing it. But that doesn't
make him good company for a young girl; so behave
yourself and see you don't go that way in the future."

He did not look at her as he spoke.

Olivia knew the restrained speech from him had not been easy, and sensed with developing awareness that in some strange way he was jealous.

Her heart gave a little leap of pleasure; the blood was warm in her veins again.

"Yes, Justin," she said meekly.

He turned abruptly and left the room, closing the door with a slam.

Two days later, on a Friday, Olivia returned to school.

9

Mara's son was born at the beginning of October, slightly prematurely. He was small and puny, bearing no distinct likeness to anyone, except for the fluff of fine hair, almost white, inherited from his mother, and lively black eyes that could have been said to resemble Justin's, or equally Rohan's. Only Mara recognized Rohan's inquisitive brilliance in their darting glance—only she felt the pangs of gnawing guilt on Justin's behalf, because she knew this heir of his was no son but merely stepchild and of his name, and that in temperament they would most probably develop opposing characteristics.

During the early days Mara was passionately devoted and possessive of the tiny boy. She had a rich flow of milk on which he quickly thrived. Elaine at first had shuddered at the sight of the screaming wrinkled little creature. "He's not at all like my children were," she said fretfully. "And he seems already to hate me."

Mara had eyed her closely. "I thought you did not remember your own children being born," she'd said with the hint of a question in her voice.

"Neither do I. Not Justin—" Elaine had admitted. "I always thought—" Her voice became confused, puzzled. "Never mind. Small children are always obnoxious. When he is older, perhaps I shall be able to endure him." She had taken a draft from her small flask and departed on unsteady feet, leaving Mara staring after her enigmatically.

By the time Olivia returned from school in early December, Elaine, in her rare sober moments, found herself softening to the child. His monkeylike appearance had completely changed. The quick intelligence had intensified in the dark eyes. His features had assumed a distinct likeness to Mara's, and his moments with his grandmother were beamingly good-humored because she spoiled him badly with sweets and creamy lollypops. Out of her sight he could be willful and determined on having his own way.

Because he was Mara's son, Justin tried to be affectionate and like him. But young Lucien—Mara's choice of a name because it reminded her, she said, of starlight, speed, and wild night things—never aroused any deep feeling of fatherhood in him. His tempers could be excessive, and though lightly regarded by Mara as mere childish tantrums, Justin felt something peculiarly hostile in them. One day, he thought more than once, I'll have to take him in hand and teach him a lesson or two.

Justin did not look forward to the prospect and for

the time being allowed Mara full control of the child,
with a nurse. It was a relief to be able to do so. Crannick was needing most of his attention now that the
work upon the old site had started. Partridge insisted
on caution, and on frequent visits by an engineer
from the north who was in temporary residence—at
Tregallis expense—at a well-known coaching house
on the outskirts of Redruth. He had hired a horse and
rode over to the mine almost daily for inspection of
the works, making what appeared to Justin an unnecessary detailed survey and tests of the soil. Everyone knew by then the ore was there, Justin told himself irritably. Joe Pollard even had accepted the
evidence, and was beginning to resent the interfer-
ence of "furriners from up-country."

Justin, smothering any show of his own impatience, did his best to placate his mining manager's
rising belligerence.

"Have patience, Joe," he said. "While Watson's
here, he takes the rap with Partridge if anything goes
wrong—I'll see to that. You just hang on with me for
a bit. We'll soon have the nosey parker out."

But the nosey parker in question seemed to be
enjoying his spell of Cornish air, which meant that his
break from city life was extended, consequently
keeping Justin away from Mara's side for long periods of time.

"I don't know why you have to be at that old mine
so much," she complained fretfully one day. "There's
not much company for me with only your mother
and the servants. And I don't see why that man—that
engineer—couldn't have stayed here. There'd have
been company at mealtimes, and something going
on."

Justin studied her intently, noting the pout on the
pretty lips, the faint frown between the brows. She

was seated in the small parlor leading off the main drawing room, and was looking intriguingly charming in blue silk, the color of her eyes. By her feet the baby Lucien was lying, one small hand crumpled against his cheek.

Justin felt an unusual stirring of tenderness in him. "I'm sorry, my love," he said. "I'm afraid I have to go along with Partridge at the moment. His investments have made the Crannick project possible, and in the end it's all for you and our son. Another thing—you'd have found Joshua very boring and pompous company here. We'd have had no privacy together at all."

"We don't have much now," she said tartly. "Except at nights, and then you're always so late in . . ." Her voice trailed off—yes, too late, she was thinking, to enjoy his lovemaking; and too early for her to be able to slip out and see Rohan. Justin said nothing, just kissed her gently and presently went out. And Mara's impatience increased.

For some time the thought of Rohan had not particularly worried her; but as the days went by, his image once more began to invade her mind, and although she tried to be faithful in her heart to Justin, it was Rohan she longed for—Rohan who tormented her restless sleep and caused her to wake fitfully and pace the bedroom until she could no longer bear its luxurious warmth. The pink velvet curtains and exotic embroidered upholstery and hangings, the silver dadoed walls and ornate ceiling encrusted with baby angels, became a prison then. The pungent odor from burning logs in the immense grate filled her with a passionate despair and a desire for the real scent of moorland fires and distant woodsmoke. For the sting of wind, and gradual drift of brine on her cheek as she neared Boscarrion.

Yet she could do nothing. All nights were the same. She never knew when Justin would return, and a gradual feeling was developing in her that the baby no longer acutely needed her. He had his nurse and Dora, and his supposed grandmother, who spoiled him utterly.

It was while Elaine was fussing over the little boy one day that she suddenly exclaimed, "Why! It's there after all. The mark! He bears the stain—the Bennedick mark. Justin doesn't."

Mara stared.

"I have it the same. Only I always thought—Lillith called it something else."

"You?" Elaine automatically replaced the child in its crib and thrust her haggard face at Mara's. Azure-blue eyes held the faded blue light of her own. Her breathing quickened. When she spoke, her voice was no more than a rasping command—almost a whisper.

"Show me."

Mara lifted her wrap and lacy shift beneath, exposing the cream flesh of her thigh. The mark showed lurid and clear, as though it had been specifically inscribed there.

Elaine's mouth had dropped open. Her expression was shocked, almost frightened. She put a hand to her lips and then spoke.

"I always knew."

"What?"

"The wrong. The deceit. He lied to me. I always —" She took her bottle from its usual place at her side and drank without wisdom or restraint. When she replaced it in her reticule, the blood was bright on the high cheekbones. Then she said harshly, "Cover yourself up. I hate nudity."

"Certainly," Mara said coldly. "And I didn't ask to show you. It was at your request."

Elaine made an effort to pull herself together.

"Do you—d-d-you know what this means?" The spirit was already working. A strange bemusement was creeping over her.

"What are you trying to say?" Mara asked almost contemptuously.

Elaine got to her feet, clutching the chair for support. "Th-that mark. You have it, I have it and—and now this child—this precious grandson." Her tones became maudlin. "Do you not realize, M-Mara, how that lying boor deceived us? You and I, deprived and cheated? You are miné, after all—my d-daughter— my own flesh. Ah!" She raised her hands as her eyes rolled toward the ceiling.

Mara took her shoulder gently but firmly. "I don't quite know what you're talking about, Mother-in-law, although"—she hesitated as her quick mind began to piece things together—"I think I'm beginning to."

"Think? Think? There's no need for that. It's there —proof. I didn't dream after all. The girl child was real. And Justin, he's a—a bastard!" She threw back her head, breaking into peal after peal of hysterical laughter that ended as suddenly as it had started. Then she fell back, a crumpled heap, into the chair. Her face now bore the unhealthy pallor of yellowed paper. Tears of confusion and weakness trickled from her eyes.

"You b'lieve me, don't you?" she asked. "He is a bastard that Christin wished on me."

Mara felt her knees weakening. "Do go on," she said, "please tell me. About the wishing and—and Justin."

Elaine's features drooped. She looked pathetic, a sorry sight.

"He did it—that husband of mine, Christin. He never liked me y'know. Because of Ellis. Yes—that's it—Ellis." A secret, drunken little smile twisted her lips. She cocked her head sideways, smiling at Mara slyly. "But you don't know about Ellis, do you? Rohan's father, y'know—oh, dear me! What'm I talkin' about?" The thread of narrative disintegrated suddenly. She looked flustered, amiable, and woebegone at the same time, and very, very drunk.

Mara gave her a little shake. "Please try and remember. Please tell me what you were going to, about Ellis, and—and Rohan."

Elaine shook her head.

"No. No. Can't remember. Not 'member a thing," she muttered half incoherently. "Ellis? Who's Ellis? Nothing. Nobody. No good. Y-you jus 'member that, see?"

She tried to get up, but fell back again immediately. Her eyes closed, but opened when Mara said softly, cajolingly, "Mother-in-law, dear, you were trying to tell me something very important. We're friends, aren't we? We like each other, you and I. Please do say what it was about Ellis—and Rohan. You can trust me, I'm your friend."

For a moment Mara thought the older woman was going to confide in her. There was a flash of knowledge—or ironic comprehension—in the exhausted stare. A second later it had died, leaving only childish petulance and anger.

"You're *not* my friend," Elaine cried, thrusting her chin out. "Jus' a—a common servant, tha's all. You take care or—or—" Her hand went to her thin breast, the lips had a bluish tinge. Mara rushed for a glass of water and held it to the poor creature's lips. Most of it dribbled down her chin onto her wrap, but its chill revived her a little. Faint color tinged the leaden gray of her cheeks. Mara pulled a bell, and Dora soon came hurrying.

"Your mistress has had a turn," Mara said. "Perhaps you can help her to her room—get Thamsin. The two of you should manage."

By the time the other girl arrived, Elaine was asleep and snoring. Somehow they succeeded in getting Elaine to her own boudoir and onto her bed.

For some time after they'd gone, Mara moved about the room, doing things mechanically, straightening a cushion, smoothing the child's coverlets, and opening a window to let a wave of cool air dispel the heavy odor of spirits and perfume left behind by Elaine.

Her expression was veiled and enigmatic, slowly giving place to one of quiet satisfaction. She had much now to tell Rohan, she thought dreamily; whether that inebriated creature—Christin's widow —remembered or not what she had been talking about, didn't matter. Facts were slipping into place. One day she would be more powerful at Penraven than anyone before could have dreamed. And her son! Rohan's natural heir.

Rohan would forever be indebted to her. Thinking of him sent a wave of wild longing through her. All the pulses of her body seemed to leap and quicken.

As if sensing unrest, the little boy suddenly stirred and screamed.

Mara felt a rush of irritation. She turned quickly and touched the bell. A girl appeared to take the place of the nurse who had her afternoon off.

"Where is Miss Olivia?" Mara asked sharply. "She is needed here. Please call her immediately."

The girl's eyes narrowed. Stuck-up bitch, she thought, who does she think she is, playing the lady when she's nuthen' but tinker's spawn. Her cheeks were red. Somehow she managed to control the hot words on her lips, but her voice held smug satisfaction when she said, "I can't do that. Miss Olivia's away up at the mine, an' none here's got time to go all that way."

"Of course not," Mara said shortly. "Very well. That's all."

The girl left.

Mara moved to the crib and lifted her son up into her arms. His cries stopped immediately, leaving the mouth a small bud of solemnity. But the dark eyes had a wicked glint in them—brilliant, black, probing eyes, possessing a knowledge beyond the child's years—the eyes of Rohan or some small mischievous Pan.

10

Olivia was wearing breeches from the stables and against the cold sky appeared like a boy astride her horse, except for the rippling cascade of dark hair blown behind her. It was tied by a ribbon. Her cape was black. From the distance she appeared more as some youthful highwayman than the young lady of Penraven—Christin Tregallis's daughter.

The air was fine but fresh. Against the line of cliffs and sea the workings of Crannick were already rising bleakly intimidating—a symbol, it seemed to Olivia, of man's defiance and determination to conquer the elements.

She reined her horse on the ridge, at a wild spot above the gentle slope down toward the mine. From below she could hear the crash of waves pounding against Hell's Gap, which had claimed many ships and victims in past storms. The gap was bordered by precipitous rocks of dark, red-stained granite stretching hundreds of feet in parts, at a sheer angle to the sea. In certain lights their surface appeared black. Olivia on one or two escapades of childhood, and against stern adult warnings, had managed nevertheless to peer over the abrupt cliff edge by lying on her stomach and staring into the swirling depths of water. She had been frightened, but fascinated. Did sea witches and the great Demon himself live there, she'd wondered? Was Hell's Gap a prison for the dead, as country folk said? Did their ghosts haunt the green twilight on dark evenings? And their master ride the wanton clouds?

She had never stayed long, and as she'd sped away over the short turf sprinkled with thyme and pink wild thrift, her heart had sung joyously because it was good to be alive, and young, with all the years ahead waiting for her. And Justin.

Justin. Her mind swung back to the present.

Screwing up her eyes, she saw several figures emerge above the cliff face, just beyond the gap where Crannick was to be explored and worked. Already a great chimney stack was rising from the rough earth. A shaft of fifty fathoms was being sunk very near the site of the first one, which had been abandoned at the depth of only twenty. Nothing of this was really important to Olivia. The earth was living, and mines were not—except by the energy put into them by human beings. But she could understand Justin wanting to put his stamp on Tregallis country. He was a man, and men had to prove themselves. When once he had got over the first exhilaration of the project, perhaps he'd have more time for her.

For a few moments she had managed to forget Mara. When she remembered, it was like a slap in the face.

Botheration! she thought. Why had he got married so soon, before she'd left school and been able to argue him out of it?

With sudden decision she kicked Moonbeam into a sharp canter that quickly became a gallop, and had soon skirted a slight bend in the land and arrived at the Crannick site.

The small group of men turned for an instant as she jerked the filly to a halt.

Justin broke away from his companions and came toward her. His face lit up, then darkened.

"Livvy! What are you doing here?"

Her lips and eyes flashed impudently.

"Taking note of things," she answered. "I'm interested too, you know."

Her manner had a mocking grown-up quality that irritated and amused him at the same time.

"Is that why you arrive here looking like something out of a masquerade?"

Olivia's smile died instantly.

"No. I just wanted to see you, Justin."

He gave her a hand and she swung herself from the saddle.

"This is my young sister," Justin explained, leading her forward to the little group of men. "Apparently she has a dedicated interest in shaft-sinking, adits, and the potentials of levels. This is Mr. Partridge, Livvy, and of course you know my mine manager, Joe Pollard."

Feeling her cheeks crimson, Olivia allowed her

hand to be taken, and after her introduction to the
engineer from the north, she had recovered sufficient poise to say cheerfully, "I don't know a thing
about adits—my brother was just teasing, of course—
but I'm very pleased to meet you."

There were a few more interchanges of polite conversation, after which Justin suggested it was time to
be getting back to Penraven before she was missed,
a hint she was only too relieved to take.

Justin was always so preoccupied when anything
concerning Crannick was discussed, she thought
moodily as she cantered away. It was as if people no
longer existed—only copper and tin, and making
great scars on the landscape. Seeing Justin that day
hadn't really been very rewarding. But the ride itself
had helped, and for once she found herself mildly
pitying Mara. Mara was bound to the house now. For
whole days at a time—weeks perhaps when Justin
was away up north on business—she would be on her
own and missing his companionship. If she complained or tried to bind him too closely, something of
the young wife's fascination would inevitably fade in
his eyes.

Young in experience of life Olivia might be, but
she knew Justin. In some ways almost as well as she
knew herself. Duty might inflict obligations, but obligations too strictly enforced could slowly but surely
change passion and desire into sterile habit lacking
wonder or lasting enchantment.

Olivia didn't consciously wish this to happen. To
see Justin's buoyancy turn sour and old before its
time would sadden her. But it would be pleasant, she
decided, if Mara herself could realize the mistake
she'd made and go away somewhere—somewhere
with her gypsy mother out of range of Penraven or
Boscarrion country. Justin would probably want to

keep the baby. That could be arranged; if Crannick proved as good an investment as he anticipated, there should be sufficient gold to bribe Mara and Lillith into acceding to some tempting proposition. Perhaps Justin would agree to providing an establishment for them both up-country somewhere—Bodmin way, or even Plymouth.

The plan seemed so feasible, Olivia found herself already envisaging a future in which she and Justin could be alone together at Penraven, with Elaine as their only tribulation. She could even picture the family feud with Rohan being ended at last. During that gallop ride home astride Moonbeam, no obstacle seemed insurmountable.

But when she reached the house, everything changed; she was suddenly downcast again. After leading Moonbeam to the stables, she took the side way through the conservatory, and before entering the hall paused, hearing an unfamiliar voice—harsh, rather thick—talking with Mara.

Olivia hesitated only a few seconds, but the words were quite clear.

"Don't you go expectin' forever to have me in the background, girl. A proud one you always was, but a mother has rights. I could make trouble for you ef I wanted, you just remember that."

Olivia took a step forward, and as she did so she caught Mara's reply in clear, cool tones.

"You can make no trouble for me. You don't own me any more. And if you spread lies about me, it's only you who'll suffer."

"And what about the rich one? The fine proud one of Boscarrion?"

Mara's voice changed, became a subdued yet distinct hiss.

"You can do nothing there—nothing, nothing. And

don't you try. You're paid well from both, and if you
dare upset Rohan—"

At this point Olivia, who detested eavesdropping,
gave a loud cough, went through the door into the
hall, and saw who she'd expected standing near the
front entrance—Lillith. The spreading figure was
gaudily dressed in a crimson skirt overspread by a
heavy brightly colored tartan cape. A feathered
black bonnet-hat was perched on her black hair,
which was either a wig or had been recently dyed.
Large gilt rings swung from her ears. Even over the
cape, glass beads and jewels glittered. Although rice
powder had been liberally applied to her stout
cheeks, the mottled dark complexion was crudely
visible. Her black eyes glittered angrily. It was obvious she had been badly upset and in some way humiliated.

Olivia felt a swift stab of sympathy. In spite of the
woman's effort at smartness, her gypsy origin was so
very apparent. It was hard to believe any true relationship existed between her and the ethereal-look-
ing Mara. Her hands, though beringed, were stubby-
fingered and roughened by work. Any looks she had
once possessed had coarsened and sagged. She was
breathing heavily.

Olivia flashed a look of inquiry at Mara.

"I didn't know your mother was calling," she said
calmly.

"Neither did she," the woman snapped. "She's far
too good for the likes of me, these days. So I thought
I'd come without word or patrin. Most grannies have
a right to a peek at their grandchilder, I said to myself. So I set off with a few bits and pieces for the
chavi, even though he's diddikai."

She bent down to a handmade rush basket, produced an amulet, a coral bead on a string, a soft cap

made of rabbit skin, a small woolen jacket, and a green brooch shaped like a four-leafed clover.

"My son has no need of such," Mara told her coldly.

"They're presents," Olivia interceded quickly. "How do you know?" She held out a hand to Lillith. "Come, and thank you. I'm sure my"—she struggled for the word—"my little nephew will treasure them when he's older."

Mara laughed. "A Tregallis?"

"And more," Lillith snapped. "Does he bear the mark, girl?" She eyed Mara fiercely. "Does he?"

Olivia was confused.

"What mark?"

"Oh, nothing," Mara answered impatiently. "She's just trying her stupid tricks on us. Please don't—" she added to the woman more quietly. "One day when it's time, you shall see my son. But he's sleeping now. About the other business, I'll talk to my husband. But don't expect too much."

"Nothing but what's my right," Lillith replied, setting her chin determinedly. "My roof has a leak, an' some gorgio fool threw stones at my window th' other night. That hovel isn't right for the grannie of such a fine lady an' gentleman's chavi. Mochardi it is —unclean. There's that cottage up under the ridge. Empty it's bin, since old Bengy took off. With a bit more in my pocket it could be made neat and nice. An' et's on Tregallis land. So you talk to your young squire, girl, an' be quick about et."

"I'll do it when I think fit," Mara said coldly.

Lillith drew herself up to her full height. The earrings shook; Olivia noticed one brown hand was clenched.

"In the past you wouldn' have dared speak so," she said. "Brought up to respect your elders, you was. A smart beatin' you'd have had for such words. But then—" She sniffed. "As I said—nuthen' *I* am now. But you beware, rackli." She moved forward with remarkable speed for one of her bulk and thrust her hard face close to Mara's. "The gavvers are prowlin', an' there's things I could tell would do harm to you an' yours—things that would bring your folk soon crashin'. Respectable, that's all I want, to live respectable like what's my due."

Thinking it high time to end the argument, Olivia touched the woman's cape.

"I'll talk to my brother," she said soothingly. "I'm sure he wouldn't want you to live in bad conditions. Don't worry." Sensing Mara's hostility, she continued, "Something should have been done before if things are so poor with you. And I know the cottage. It belonged to the old shepherd, didn't it? I always thought it could be made nice."

Lillith's expression, at first suspicious, slowly softened. "That's right, miss. And so it could be—it could be a pretty home for an aging wumman like me. I know what folks say of me—gyppo, tinker, an', what's worse, witch. But I've worked hard all my life. My baskets an' pegs are best in all Cornwall, an' ef I have the sight, et's my true heritage, and one that's used only for the good. There's no true ill-wishing in me, miss. Mumper-born I may be. But mumpers edn' no devil's spawn."

Wondering what "mumper" meant, Olivia nodded in agreement. "Of course not. I understand."

"Very well, then," Lillith made a movement toward the door. "I won't intrude no further where I'm not wanted. Good day to you then, miss."

Suddenly Mara bent down, reached the basket and thrust it at the retreating figure.

"Take this with you," she cried rather shrilly. The

large face looked around. The dark eyes now were
flashing again. She pushed the gifts away, muttering
something unintelligible under her breath.

Olivia bent down hastily to retrieve the gifts. The
woman stood staring at her. Mara rushed away
quickly, retreating into the drawing room.

As Lillith's bright color faded to dull brownish-red,
Olivia got up and smiled.

"I'll see the little boy has his presents," she said. "It
was kind of you to think of him. One day you must
come again." What prompted the invitation she
could not have said. Her mind was a confusion of
outrage at Mara's behavior and a certain subtle sense
of achievement in having put Mara in her place. She
had no liking for Lillith, but a sense of justice told her
that the woman was entitled to a little family recognition, being Mara's mother.

Her mother.

How odd, she thought, watching the stout figure
retreating down the drive a few minutes later. Nature indeed had played a strange trick in delivering
such a beautiful daughter to so flamboyant a creature.

At the end of the drive Lillith turned, lifted her
hand, and wove a sign in the air. Remembering the
stories of witchcraft, Olivia felt a fleeting spasm of
fear. Then the colorful figure bowed, looking like
some gaudy monstrous macaw in the distance, doing
homage to its alien ancient deity.

Olivia smiled secretly to herself. Whatever strange
powers Lillith might possess—if any—quite clearly
she bore no ill will to Olivia, but to the contrary had
wished her well.

Mara was hovering by the drawing room when the
front door closed.

Her eyes were narrowed, her lips tight.

"How *could* you?" she said. "Interfering in my affairs. You know nothing about—"

"Your mother?"

"Lillith," Mara emphasized, shortly. "I don't want her here."

"I don't suppose you do; neither do I," Olivia retaliated with her temper rising. "But sometimes we have to accept people we don't care about."

"I suppose by that you're referring to me? You've never liked me, have you? You hated it when Justin married me—"

"Yes," Olivia agreed. "I didn't think you were right for him. I still don't. I'm not sure you really love him either. But"—her lip quivered—"he loves you. And I can understand it. You're so beautiful."

The coldness vanished from Mara's face. Her lips softened. "It's nice of you to say that. You're very—young, Olivia."

"No." Olivia turned away. "In years, perhaps. But not deep down, not really. I do love Justin, you see. So much I almost want to die sometimes."

"But he's your brother—"

"I know. That's the trouble."

Mara's eyes watched Olivia musingly as the younger girl shrugged and walked away toward the stairs. Her head drooped a little. The dejected curve of her shoulders sent a momentary stab of sympathy through Mara's nerves. Olivia's confession was disturbing. Mara had not expected to find such depth of feeling in Christin's daughter. Through her own passion for Rohan, Mara accepted what wild torture the emotions could arouse. In her own case she had found certain fulfillment. But Olivia and Justin! The picture was a somber one. They'd been brought up as brother and sister, after all. But Justin—never. She doubted that he had the slightest inkling of his sister's true feeling.

Anyway, she reasoned when pondering over the matter later, Olivia was a child still in many ways. Sooner or later she would be jerked out of her stupid sentimentalizing when a suitable young man strong enough to take her in hand turned up. The sooner this happened, the better. Olivia had already become an upsetting influence at Penraven; if Justin had decided definitely to allow her to leave school for good, then he should see about producing a suitor. The girl might so easily prove an obstacle in her own —Mara's—future meetings with Rohan.

And this she would not tolerate.

That evening the wind intensified and a gale sprang up. Olivia could not sleep, and at two o'clock went down to the library for a book.

When she had found one, she opened the door quietly and, with her hand still on the knob, stopped, ears and eyes alert. Above the fitful creaking, moaning, and tapping of twigs against windows, above the rustling and scuttling and patter of rats and mice somewhere behind boards and rafters, was another sound, like cautious footsteps approaching overhead. Olivia lifted her head and saw a circle of light wavering and spreading from the landing above, followed by the dark shape of a shrouded figure emerging toward the stairs. Olivia's heart lurched. She blew her candle out, but it was too late. The figure had seen. It halted a moment and then very slowly turned, disappearing again into the shadows.

Olivia waited until all light had finally died, and her own tense nerves had relaxed. What was it? Who had it been? Penraven was very old, dating from Tudor times. Its exterior with ornate flying buttresses and high-domed towers, though overimpressive for only a medium-size mansion, had given rise to many legends through the centuries. The interior could be equally awe-inspiring with its pointed arches and decorative niches where carved figures loomed, grotesquely shadowed through uncertain light.

As a child, Olivia had found the great passages awesome and subtly terrifying, especially at night, when she'd fancied soft feet padded past her door. Sometimes she'd peeped out and quickly snapped the latch again, creeping back to hide in bed with her face under the sheets. There had been rumors of ghosts ever since she remembered.

So could it be some phantom shape she'd just seen? Some restless spirit doomed to pace the centuries for some past misdeeds?

The next moment she quickly dispelled the idea. She did not believe in ghosts, she told herself stubbornly, except the natural lingering presence haunting dolmens and great primeval tracts of pools, bog, and windswept hills outside.

No. What she had just seen was real. Someone was prowling about the house as wakeful and restless as she herself was.

Then who?

Her first thought was Mara. But then Mara was with Justin. In his arms, probably—lying with her head close against his body, her pale hair a silken cloak over his strong chest.

The picture was so upsetting, so vividly clear, she forgot all about ghosts and hauntings, and lighted the lamp always kept by her bedside.

From outside a spatter of rain beat against the window.

Meanwhile, in the great bedroom Justin shared with his wife, Mara stood at the window, frustrated and alone, watching the rain-swollen angry clouds race across the face of a thin moon. Her eyes searched the landscape with hungry, hopeless longing, not for Justin—who had suddenly thought fit, earlier, to ride back to Crannick in search of plans he'd left at the office—but for a darker more potent lover, the Rohan of her nightmares and dreams, both the demon and the king of her tempestuous deepest nature. She did not wish it to be so. Peace and the fulfillment Justin could give her were, she knew, more worthy and enduring. But in his absence Rohan ruled, and always would.

The knowledge caused a bitter anger to rise in her. Why should her husband neglect and leave her at a time when his presence was so necessary? And why must that watchful, probing young sister always be about, ready to thwart her when her whole being so longed for an hour's escape?

Half an hour later when Justin arrived back at Penraven, she realized grudgingly that to have visited Rohan at such an hour would have meant inevitable disaster to her marriage. Rohan, too, might have been angered.

She should, then, be grateful to Olivia for intercepting her wild action.

But it was a long time before she slept, and when she woke in the morning, she felt bored and tired, with a dull headache thumping at her temples.

She wondered, as she had more than once, how she was going to bear the restrictions of her married life. It was not as though Justin really loved her. She knew now he didn't. Her beauty alone was what had ensnared him—and a kind of pity, in the beginning. Pity—as if she wanted that.

I must see Rohan, she thought. If I don't, I'll go mad—or die.

As it happened, she did not have to wait long, because shortly after Christmas, Justin set off for the Midlands, where he expected to stay for a fortnight.

He had been gone three days when Mara, staring despondently over the winter landscape, saw Nelson from her window. He was some distance away to her right, up the moor—a small dark figure with a basket, gathering either mushrooms or berries.

She slipped on a cape and managed to leave the house unseen except for a new kitchenmaid, from whom she exacted a vow to keep her mouth shut in fear of dread reprisals. The girl was a miner's daughter from Camborne who had a great terror of the evil eye, snails, white hares, toads, and rabbit's paws. She had heard also that the new young mistress of Penraven was reputed to be the daughter of a witch, with the capacity to work dark spells against any who offended her. Had it not been that her family so needed money and that her father, Will Tregorse, had threatened to "take the skin off her back" if she refused to work at the big house, she would never have gone there. As it was, she did her best at the menial tasks laid on her and kept her mouth shut, hardly saying a word during the long working day.

So when Mara left by the dairy door and cut toward the moor, keeping well in the shadow of the high granite walls, she knew her word would be respected. She followed the track upward between thick clumps of undergrowth and gorse.

Nelson scrambled to his feet, startled, as she appeared suddenly from behind a rock. The flash of white teeth gleamed in his dark face. "Yes, missie, yes?" He pushed a basket containing a few small mushrooms toward her.

She waved a hand. "I don't want those. Keep them.

It's your master, Nelson. Do you understand? I"—she pointed to her breast—"wish to see him."

The boy stared at her for a minute, then nodded excitedly several times. "Yes—yes, me understan'. Nelson do what lady want."

"Very well." Mara took a small notebook and silver pencil from her pockette. The notebook was leather covered and bore the words "as used by Lord Byron." It had been plundered by her from a gentleman of high quality during one of her adventurous pranks at a fair. She wrote a few words hastily: "At the Indian Rose tonight. Sunset. Mara." Then she tore the page out and thrust it into the boy's hand. "Quick now, off with you. I'll see you have a shiny coin if you're a good boy."

With the speed of a fox, he darted through the bushes, and her last sight of him was with head bent forward, racing against the moors like some black bird about to soar the skies. At a point nearing Red River he disappeared abruptly, taking a downward plunge in the direction of Boscarrion.

Mara's heart lifted. Her blood raced joyously in anticipation of her meeting with Rohan. He would come, she knew. He wanted her as much as she needed him. Not entirely because of sensuous gratification, but because of his overwhelming curiosity concerning Penraven. She had much to tell him, she thought musingly as she made her way back to the house, about the Bennedick mark primarily. But for a time she was going to hold that back. She would merely titillate and suggest for a time, until desire for her made him forget other things. After that? There was no way of forming a clear plan, only that never, never would she give him up.

There was a mist that evening, which made her

assignation with Rohan easier. Olivia, generally so watchful, was in the library writing letters to her school friends. Mara had told her she was tired and going to bed early. The nurse, as usual, was reading Richardson's *Clarissa Harlowe* in the night nursery she now shared with the baby. The servants were all occupied in gossiping or a routine of evening tasks. Elaine was blissfully asleep with a brandy flask beside her. So there was no problem in escaping household vigilance.

The Indian Rose, unlike its name, was a small dark kiddley-wink hidden in a dip in a fold of the moors, halfway toward Hell's Gap. It was a considerable walk, even taking the shortest route, but Mara was agile and knew the district by heart. The building that evening appeared a mere lump of rock through the thickening air—an outthrust giant fist of granite that any moment might go toppling in the Atlantic below. But as she drew close, the pale of gray curdled into the rosy blur of an oil lamp swinging from a porch.

It had not a good name. Many ill deeds had been hatched there. It was an illicit meeting place for smugglers, vagrants, seamen, and rich and poor alike who were out to defraud and benefit from honest men's pockets. Yet in the daytime it wore an appearance of respectability, and the Law kept away, preferring safety rather than murder, and choosing to turn a blind eye and ear where dubious stories were concerned.

Mara had been there once or twice in her younger days, but only when she and Lillith had been in need. Her air of childlike innocence had been a worthy pawn in earning a living. Her naive tricks had amused and warmed the hardest hearts.

Once she had stayed the night in the cellars, following a chase by the police from Redruth. She had been wearing boy's clothes then, and her rough pockets were filled with stolen gold.

The memory chilled her a little now as she entered through the low porch; but with her hair hidden by her hood, the cape firmly round her, she went into the taproom, head held high in the manner of a great lady. Her brows were darkened, a beauty patch had been applied to one cheek near the temple, and her lips were painted. She approached the counter bravely, saying in clear tones, "Have you a private room please? I'm awaiting a friend."

The landlord eyed her shrewdly. He was a burly-faced black-eyed man with a hawk nose, half Spanish, as many were in those parts. Whether he recognized Mara or not, she did not know. There was no flicker of acknowledgment between them. But she was aware of a sudden silence and concentrated interest from the rest of those drinking there. As usual, they were a mixed crowd—a black-bearded seaman, an unsavory-looking character wearing a long, tattered coat over knee breeches and high boots with a patch over one eye; a round-faced blue-eyed youth who looked like a farmer and had an arm round a yellow-haired girl; and a tall figure of more highly bred appearance in a black frac.

An ancient crone sat on a bench in the shadows. She was slumped forward and every few seconds put a bottle to her mouth. One or two more moved furtively in the fitful light. A large woman with painted cheeks, garishly red hair, and an expanse of flesh bulging over her low neckline nudged the seaman as Mara entered. She had a raucous laugh and a lewd tongue, and was obviously a prostitute.

"Hark at her," she shrieked. "Waiting for a friend." She paused, then added, sticking her full underlip out maliciously, "Let you down, as 'e luv? Shame."

There was a bellow of sound, followed by a sharp snap that sounded like the crack of a pistol. The jibes died suddenly. All eyes turned. Rohan entered, and the woman and her companion instinctively moved and let him pass. He had a fine air about him. His gray cloak swung back from his shoulders. His bold features for a second were arrogantly clear in the rosy glow of lamp and candlelight.

There was a muttering and interchange of glances between those present. Most recognized him, and those who didn't knew that here was one of power and influence.

The landlord flung him a quick glance of acknowledgment and gave a slight bow. Mara, with her cloak drawn half over her face, said quietly, "I've demanded a room. Or shall we leave and go elsewhere?"

"There's room at back, surr," the man said hurriedly. "This way, surr—"

Mara and Rohan passed before him into a small parlor where a couple sat playing cards near a fire. The woman's profession was again obvious. Black ringlets straggled loose over a shoulder. One breast was bare. The man had a furtive cadaverous appearance with quick bright eyes and the dark skin of a Spaniard or Basque.

They gave one look at the intruders, got up, and at a word from the landlord collected the cards and the woman's few accessories. "Get out," Nick Boaze, the innkeeper, said shortly. "Room's wanted."

The other man gave a contemptuous snort. Neither looked at the other.

"Oh *deagh!*" the woman said, drawing herself up and flinging something thick and furlike around her neck. "We are in great comp'ny so't seems."

Her tawdry jewelry flashed as she moved to the door. The man's expression was truculent. But a moment later the latch had shut, and Rohan and Mara were left together by the fire while Boaze said, "You want refreshment, Mr. Tregallis, surr? Sorry 'bout them theer. Didn' know you was comin', see."

"Well, you know now," Rohan answered. "So you just be quick about it and bring the best you have of wine and victuals. And remember this—"

The man, who was already on the way out, paused and turned. "Yes surr?"

"I happen to know what you've got."

"O' course, surr."

When he'd gone, Rohan turned to Mara impatiently. "What's this all about? Why that sudden message from Nelson? What are you playing at?"

Mara let the hood fall from her face. As always, her beauty, against his will, inflamed him.

"There's no game, Rohan," she said softly. "I wanted to see you. There was no other way. I daren't ride—I could have been seen. So I came on foot. Boscarrion was too far. Oh, Rohan, I needed you so."

"And because you fancy a taste of my male presence you think you've the right to call on me at any hour, day or night, to some dissolute meeting place likely to be raided by the Revenue at any moment?"

She shook her head. "No. No rights, Rohan. My duty now is only to Justin; and that was your doing. I wouldn't have married him if—"

He drew her to him and put a hand over her mouth. "Shut up," he whispered. "Hold your tongue before I make you." She closed her eyes and sighed, feeling a hand travel insidiously from her thighs to her buttocks.

"My God! I've missed you," he continued. "You sly slut of a tinker's wench. What do you think—"

"No, no, Rohan," she murmured. "I'm not, I'm not."

Her denial took him by surprise. He let her go abruptly. Then, with eyes narrowed under his heavy brows, he said, "What do you mean—*not?*"

She smiled sweetly. "I'm not Lillith's child," she replied quietly, but with such conviction he could think of no scathing comment to fling at her. "I'm—I'm Elaine's daughter—a Bennedick, and I'm certain, as sure as I can be at the moment, that Christin was my father."

"*Christin?*"

She nodded.

"But what the devil do you mean? Is this a trick, Mara? Another of your playacting parts?" He put his hands on her shoulders with such force she winced.

"No, no, it's true. I'll prove it—later."

"Later? Why not now?"

"Because I need time. More proof. I'll get it, I swear I will, if you'll only wait."

He was debating how to treat this last remark when Nick Boaze entered with wine, and glasses on a tray.

A frowzy-looking girl followed him carrying a platter containing cutlery, plates, a dish of lammy pie and other victuals.

When the performance of setting the table and uncorking the bottles was over, the man and servant left. By then Rohan had decided to treat Mara's revelation with a certain amused incredulity. After all, he told himself shrewdly, she seldom missed a chance to impress. Later, if there was anything in her wild story, she would be bound to unfold more of it.

But, strangely, she did not.

When they'd drunk the wine and had a taste of the pie, Mara suddenly said she should leave.

"I don't want anyone to find me missing," she said. "I only came because I promised I would, if anything happened. And this—this is only the beginning, Rohan."

A suggestive smile curved the saturnine lines of his mouth.

"Beginning? I'd hardly say that." His arm encircled her waist possessively. "Don't imagine one moment of the past can be erased," he told her, and the words held an insidious quality that in spite of the threat thrilled every nerve of her body. "Don't dare let your mind wander or forget for one instant to whom you really belong. In name you may be a Tregallis—what the hell does a name matter? However daintily you prance and preen before your lusty young squire, although his flesh claims yours, your spirit flinches, doesn't it? And your womb rejects him? Tell me it is so! Tell me—you—you queen of whores—"

Mara's face blanched.

"You have no right—"

"I have every right, damn you—"

His hand hardened on her wrist. "Yes, yes," she murmured. "Oh, yes, Rohan."

Minutes later they were outside in the cold night. The fog had thickened into a dark shroud over land and sea. Rohan led her to the tree where his horse was tethered. He was about to take the bridle when he changed his mind. "I shall see you to—your home," he said, "but first of all—" He lifted her up and strode cautiously but decisively through the dripping furze. In a clearing sheltered by boulders and an arched windblown sloe, he laid her down and claimed her with the ruthless strength she longed for and knew so well. There was no world anymore but the dark vortex of passion released, of her spirit and

flesh united with his. There were no words of love—
no gentleness or tender flowering—only a wild and
terrible commitment holding the deep, elemental
awareness of the earth's first waking; of thunder and
light, of torment that was both birth and death, and
a pulsing drawn-out sweetness beyond the understanding of mentality or reason.

When all was over, he fastened her clothes and
pulled her to her feet. Through the drowning dusk
she could sense his smile. On her lips the bittersweet-
ness of his kisses mingled with that of brine and the
faint suggestion of blood on her mouth. Then she
lifted a hand to her cheek. There were tears there.

"Take me back, Rohan," she whispered, and, she
was thinking, to Justin. Poor Justin.

He placed her on his mount before him and they
rode away—phantom shapes through the sea of fog,
with only the gulls crying and soft thud of horses'
hooves to indicate substance or reality.

Rohan's thoughts were reflective when he reached
Boscarrion. With his passion appeased, Mara's out-
burst was forced into clearer perspective. If what she
said was true, that she was Christin's daughter, then
his deep resentment concerning Justin—the sneak-
ing suspicion that he'd so far failed completely to
acknowledge or understand—could very well have a
logical foundation. Elaine, his uncle's widow, had
surely not bred twins—and if she had not, then
where did Justin fit in? He, Rohan, had never felt
Justin to be a true Tregallis. There was something too
obvious about him—too bold and free, set in too wild
and honest a mold.

If Justin had not inherited Penraven Rohan might
even have liked the young fellow—educated him
into a subtler role than playing the hale-fellow-well-

met young squire with boring notions of working his fingers to the bone for copper and tin. But Justin was too direct, and in that way formidable. There wasn't a single characteristic about him that could really be applied to his so-called late father. Christin had been shrewd and devious. An honorable man, of course—oh, so honorable. But Rohan's lip curled when he remembered what his own father, Ellis, had told him of the past. Of Elaine, who had been young and trusting when Christin had bargained for her hand with powerful Sir Charles Bennedick. Rohan had been only a child then, but quick in mind and understanding.

For how long Ellis had been enamored of the young woman, Rohan had never known. His own mother had been dead for seven years, and Ellis had been lonely. But the Boscarrion estate was already impoverished through poor land, lack of labor in the fields owing to bad wages that had sent workers to the cotton mills of the north, and a love of indulgence and dubious gambling deals on Ellis's part. So he could neither bribe nor inveigle.

He had seen Christin bring the girl as his bride to Penraven, and during the first year had seduced her on the earliest opportunity. If Christin, knowing of the infatuation, had not made it his business to catch the lovers out, much bitterness could have been spared. But the aging master of Penraven had been cunning, and had trapped them in a gazebo near the dip bordering Red River.

None had known of the incident but Christin and Ellis, and later, Rohan. There had been no duel—no spectacular show of force—only a curse from Christin so concentrated with hatred and ill will that Ellis had sickened from that day, and matters at Boscarrion had gone from bad to worse.

Ellis's child had been conceived, but was never born. Why, Rohan could guess. The frail Elaine would have been no match for her ruthless husband's demands, and if the seed had flourished in her, means would soon have been found to destroy it. It was ironic, Rohan had thought frequently, that in killing Ellis's potential child, Christin had also, it seemed, effectively destroyed her capacity for bearing sons in wedlock. Only girls. Ironic, but just. And Justin—well, there was something fishy there. Rohan secretly had never accepted him, and if what Mara said could be proved, then that young upstart could go to the devil for all he cared.

On that evening following his meeting with Mara, Rohan's objective reasoning gradually turned to ruthless decision. It would have been pleasant to woo and win through passion and love alone. But passion he had already savored to the full, and the act of possessing with such abandon what Justin now felt to be his gave an added zest. He had no conscience, not a qualm of feeling concerning the rights and wrongs of the situation. Mara was his, and always had been. And eventually he'd have Olivia, too. Rebellious hoyden she might be, but already her dark eyes softened at his approach. He'd win and tame her and in this way strike at Justin's pride and heart, and the heritage of Penraven.

Love her? The idea was highly amusing. For too long he'd been treated with contempt by his uncle's household. Let one of them, at least, suffer for a change.

He went to the chest and had more whiskey than was wise at such an hour—or any hour, for that matter. Then once more he took the little miniature of Elaine from its box. The one keepsake left by Ellis.

"Fool," he muttered, staring at the pale features swimming before his eyes. He threw it down, but it did not break, just lay like the uncertain quivering of some phantom's visage in a pool of light on the floor.

Now what did it remind him of? What? Another woman? A face once seen in a hole on the moor? What hole—where?

He put a hand to his head. It was damp with sweat. He was trembling all over. He knew now he had gone too far ever to turn back.

Perhaps Olivia—even though he'd no great liking for her—would be able at least to subdue some of the terrors that were never far from his mind those days.

She must, he thought. She must, and would.

Presently, unable to stand properly, he managed to half crawl up to his bed.

The mist was clearing, but the soughing of a rising wind was gathering strength, and in its hollow moaning brought the inevitable brushing and stinging sigh of sand from the sea.

11

Joshua Partridge was standing on the ridge overlooking Crannick one April day, when Rohan cantered down from the moor above. Tregallis appeared elegant in pale gray, his saturnine features emphasized by early sunlight from the east. He reined near Partridge and said coolly, "I can see you're admiring our Cornish scenery, sir, or is it those abominable earth workings?"

Joshua stared at the intruder with a hint of annoyance.

"Earth workings, sir? Before you is a remarkable piece of engineering. A new mine of great potentials rising from an old site."

"Are you sure?" Rohan's tones were so suggestively intimidating that the other man bristled; his color heightened.

"What d'ye mean, sir? Of course I'm sure. I wouldn't be investing otherwise. I've been told by the best authorities on mine ore that Crannick's a valuable project likely to swell the pockets of any who put a handful of gold into it."

"Glad to hear it," Rohan said. "And if you're only thinking of a sovereign or two's outlay, then there's no harm done. Sorry to have seemed interfering." He jerked the horse's reins. "On, boy—"

"Hey!" Joshua called as the man and horse turned. "D'you mind telling me exactly what you were talking about? I know better, mind you, but I like to know where rumors start."

Rohan headed the stallion around and paused again. "I've a feeling it's no rumor, sir," he said. "Crannick's been in our family for centuries. Mined once, as you must know. But it was always a white elephant. There's soil subsidence in these parts. And though the granite's hard, the earth isn't—in parts. If you take a tip from me, you'll listen to my cousin's fairy tale with a pinch of salt."

"Cousin, sir?"

Rohan touched his forehead. "Justin Tregallis. I'm his uncle's son—his late uncle's, I should say—Rohan.

Uncle Christin was a smart man. If Crannick held anything but fool's gold, he'd have had it out long ago. Sorry to depress you, but I have no liking for seeing a knowledgeable man throw good money after bad. The ground's treacherous, sir, and levels will sink. That's my opinion and the opinion of others about here who know the way of mining. Good day to you."

Before Partridge had the chance to answer, Rohan's gray figure was already galloping toward the high lane and over it to the moors above. Partridge, looking after him, took his chin between a finger and thumb. Now what had got into the fellow? he wondered. Clear as day it was that Justin's elegant-looking connection with the malicious tongue was affronted at not having a finger in the pie. Still, for the sake of all concerned, he'd have to question the young man about things. No smart partner in any enterprise—and Joshua complimented himself on his considerable business acumen—allowed a single derogatory innuendo to pass without being fully tested.

So later when Justin arrived at the site, Joshua's manner was forthright, his words blunt.

"You've a relation living around here. Cousin, is it?" he said, continuing without waiting for a reply. "Thinks we're on to fool's gold, or fool's copper, if you like. Something about land subsidence. Is that true?"

Justin's jaw came out truculently. "You must be alluding to Rohan," he said.

"Aye. That's the name."

"He was trespassing," Justin continued. "This is Tregallis land. He knows nothing whatever about mining and is simply trying to make trouble. Heavens, man, haven't the experts given you proof enough?"

"You can never have enough proof until it's properly in your hand," Partridge stated. "And I didn't like the way he sniggered to himself."

"Very few people like Rohan at all," Justin said coldly. "He and his father have always been at loggerheads with the rest of the family. We don't mix, we never have. It's an accepted state of affairs."

"Why?"

Justin reddened. The blunt question took him aback. "I couldn't say. It all started before I was born, and we've had no cause to reestablish any relationship."

"Not you, perhaps," Partridge emphasized. "What about the rest of you, though?"

"What do you mean?"

"Your young sister."

"Olivia?" Justin frowned. "Well—what about her?"

"They were out riding the other day," Partridge told him in even tones. "Saw them myself. And I've heard it's not the first time."

Justin managed to control any show of temper. But later that day when he was back at Penraven, he found Olivia by the stables and started questioning. None of the grooms were about. The air was tangy with mingled animal scents, hay, and the lush sweet smell of growing things from the garden beyond. Olivia was nuzzling Moonbeam when he got there. Her hair in the dewy sunlight shone glossy and sleek as the mare's coat.

"Olivia!" he said sharply.

She turned, smiling. Her face was morning-flushed with rose and gold, her teeth gleamed. Happiness and longing intensified by innocence emanated a radiance that clutched his heart with almost physical pain. But he showed no softening or betrayal of emotion. His voice was hard when he asked, "Is it true that you've been out with Rohan?"

Her smile died into defiance.

"Yes."

He took a step toward her. "How dare you?"

Her lips parted, not in surprise but in shock. She'd known that sometime Justin was bound to discover about her occasional meetings with his cousin. But she had not expected such unmitigated and, it seemed to her, quite unwarranted anger. Annoyance? Yes. A lecture no doubt. But this! It was too ridiculous.

"It did not take much courage, Justin," she said coolly. "He can be very pleasant when he tries. And it's quite stupid of you to go so—so frenzied. You have no right."

He took a quick step forward and seized her by her shoulders. "I have every right. I'm your sole guardian. You will behave and promise never to speak to that reprobate again or I'll send you straight back to boarding school for another year."

"And if you do," she cried, shaking herself free, "I will run away at the first possible moment and bring terrible disgrace on you by marrying a—a tinker or something, or having a bastard baby. You wouldn't like that, Justin, would you?" She stood defiantly facing him, brilliant eyes swimming with unshed tears. But he did not notice them—only the determined set of her jaw and the proud lift of her head above the tight bodice of her dress. The gown was far too tight now, he realized irrelevantly; a gleam of white lace and flesh showed fleetingly between the buttons under the stress of her breathing. Suddenly he felt defeated—not by her rebellion but through his very love of her. Nevertheless his tones remained unrelenting when he spoke sternly.

"Perhaps it would be better to reinstate Cobby and give her my full blessing to beat you."

Her eyes flashed then.

"Don't be a fool. Cobby! That puerile creature. No —" Her expression changed. There was an assessing half-frightened look on her face when she continued, "If I must be beaten, do it yourself, Justin. But you won't, will you?"

He turned away abruptly. "I might. If I have to."

She ran toward him, put both arms to his shoulders and said, "Oh, Justin, dear Justin, need we quarrel? Was it so really awful? Just a ride with Rohan? There aren't many people around here to mix with, you know. If it weren't for Mara—"

"Please leave Mara out of it," he said shortly.

"Why should I?"

"She's my wife. This is her home. It's no use you saying 'if it weren't for Mara.' She's here to stay, Olivia, and it might be a good idea if you spent more time with her. She doesn't have much company either. And I'm sure you could be of more help than you are with the baby."

"Can you see me as someone else's baby-sitter?" Olivia asked bitterly. "I like babies—but not necessarily all of them."

She placed her face once more against Moonbeam's neck, drawing the nearness of the animal deep into her lungs for comfort.

Before he walked away, Justin said curtly, "Well, remember what I've said, or you'll be sorry."

As he went into the house he was seething with a sense of his own ineptitude; also a curious sense of loss.

For the very first time he felt a reluctance to see Mara, although he knew that her beauty would disturb him as it always did. The truth was that apart from the excitement of possessing her, she still remained to him an unknown quality; understanding between them—any contact of mind and shared interests—was practically nonexistent. Even the first tenderness he'd felt for her was now abating gradually into an irritating awareness that she did not deep down wish for tenderness at all. Then, had becoming "Mistress of Penraven" been her sole reason for marrying him?

No, he thought, when he considered the question honestly. Ambition only played a part in her life when there was amusement in the challenge. There was something in her he had yet to plumb; something that was demanding day by day more of his energy and dedication than he was prepared to give. He had thought when he married her she would be satisfied by security and life at Penraven. But she was not. Her expression was frequently evasive; her smile, when he approached, superficial.

The warmth he expected was not there, except in the purely sexual and physical expression of bodily passion. Occasionally her aptitude—her expert mastery of the seductive act—mildly dismayed him. Not because he did not respond, but because he was beginning to know every move—every wile—by heart. She was the unfailing mistress of her art; and though he had known, when he took her for wife, of her outrageous beginnings, he had believed her wild pranks had been nothing more than the innocent pranks of youth and necessity—of the eternal Eve, the temptress.

Now a faint core of disillusionment and unbelief was slowly beginning to stir in him. He had no practical complaint, except of her resentment concerning Crannick—her eyes were narrow and condemning every day he set off, and he knew she would have

prevented him going if she could. But he would not
be henpecked in such a way. On the nights he left
her alone he apologized and tried to make her understand; it was his work, his ambition for both of them,
and when the mine was working, many men now
unemployed would be taken on. Later, things would
change. At present he had to be on the site as much
as possible for the sake of his reputation—and to keep
Pollard properly in the picture.

"It will be different once the pumping rod and
engines are going," he told her more than once, "I
shall be more free then."

"For what? Taking me about a little? To Plymouth
or Truro? For a few days away—in London, perhaps?" She was smiling, but her voice was shrill. "Or
to go galloping the moors with your madcap sister?"

He looked uncomfortable.

"I didn't know you had ambitions for London,
Mara."

"I haven't really." Her tones had died into boredom. "I'm sorry, Justin. And if you want to slip off
with Olivia, there's no reason why you shouldn't."

"What's all this about Olivia? Who said I wanted to
ride with her?"

"You don't have to," she said quietly. "It's obvious
you're devoted to each other."

He laughed and touched her chin. "Jealous? My
beautiful Mara? Of your own young sister-in-law?"

"And don't call me 'your Mara.' I'm not. I—" She
broke off, staring at him from eyes suddenly wide
and so brilliantly blue he was dazzled.

"Aren't you? Then whose? Do you mind telling
me—"

Once again she had won. An irrational upsurge of
resentment filled him. He pulled her to him roughly.
"Explain, if you please, Mrs. Tregallis."

Her tilted elfin lips and wayward rebellious glance taunted him.

"You'd like to know, wouldn't you, Justin, darling?" she mocked. Already the stimulus of her own defiance and ability to discomfort him was rousing the old impish instincts in her. She lifted a hand to his cheek—a delicate touch now, flowerlike in its softness—so different from those months ago when the slim fingers had been scratched and worn at the nails through carrying wood.

With a gurgle of light laughter she broke from him and sped up the stairs. Justin followed, angry but already hot with a conflict of emotions. From an alcove in the hall Olivia watched. How could he, she wondered? Mara was simply playing with him. And he didn't really love her. She knew Justin. From being a little girl she had learned to study his every mood; and she was grown up now. Sixteen—old enough to recognize it was not love she'd seen in his eyes lately. There had been no quality of compassion or sympathy—no melting awareness or true adoration between them. Only—lust.

The thought sickened her, and she dismissed it immediately. Justin was not that kind of man. She knew him better than anyone else in the world. High-spirited and hot-tempered he might be, frequently arrogant, sometimes even hard. But his true nature was honest and good, whereas Mara's was—what?

Hearing a door close on the landing overhead, Olivia turned and went slowly toward the kitchens. She needed someone desperately to talk to, and decided on the spur of the moment to visit Rohan.

The afternoon, though fine and warm, was filmed with thin glittering haze. Silver light quivered above the line of sea and sky. As she walked toward the

coast in her high-necked blue day dress, the glint of
birds' wings shone brilliantly for a moment until the
soaring shapes were taken into the general uncertainty of shrouded sunlight. Rocks and bracken were
grouped into iridescent stillness. At moments the
delicate filaments of spiders' webs quivered where
she walked, shaking with a shower of dew.

Olivia felt alone and free, cut off from the real
world. She did not, as usual, take a path along the
high moors, but turned steeply downward to the left
in the direction of Red River's mouth. By some it was
called an estuary. But at high tide it was little more
than a wide gap between dunes and rock—an inlet
carved through the centuries by freak storms and the
persistent onslaught of the great Atlantic.

When the tide was low and the river merely a
trickle, it was possible for those who knew the district
to cross the inlet on foot—in this way avoiding a
tedious moorland detour—and climb over the hills
from one point of the coast to the other. The route
was not without danger. There were quicksands at
the lower end of the beach. Ships had foundered and
been sucked down there, and in the past several
human beings had been taken. But Olivia knew that
by keeping well above waterline it was comparatively simple to crawl round the sandy promontory.

Once safely on the soft dunes she could make her
way without mishap to Boscarrion. So she hitched
her long skirts above her ankles and started the descent down the cut cautiously, supporting herself by
clumps of bent trees and furze bushes, as she half
jumped, half climbed, and swung herself along the
tricky goat path. She knew it by heart. As a child
she'd ventured there when none had known of her
whereabouts, and had somehow managed to elude
detection.

The area was out of bounds, of course; but the fact had only stimulated her. Now, whether or not the route was forbidden, did not affect her at all. Her driving urge was to see Rohan. To have some man's attention and interest, instead of Justin's hurtful and eternal scolding.

Oh, bother Justin, she thought as she waited for a moment to get her breath. Botheration! And botheration.

How angry he'd be if he could see her now. But perhaps it wouldn't worry him much after all. Mara and the mine—Mara—Mara—copper and tin. They were his life. And she had nothing of her own. Nothing at all. He could turn her out of Penraven if he wished. Not that he'd be likely to. But still, having Rohan as an ally in a secret kind of way would be a sort of refuge, someone to turn to if everything else went wrong.

So determination strengthened in her, as, rounding the bend safely, she came to the gentler ground sloping gradually to Boscarrion. Glancing down once, she noticed the remains of wreckage ahead only half seen in the cove where lumpy mounds of sand covered great hunks of timber scarred by relics of broken masts. She shivered, remembering the day of the storm, and as she walked on her mind went further back, to the occasion when Rohan had rescued her from a fall and she'd met Melusina, his mistress.

The scene still registered as no more than a queer kind of mirage or dream in her mind. Looking back, it was almost as though she had imagined the incident—the glinting glass and all the mirrors shining that gave the exotic interior such an odd impression of a room reflected through water.

And Melusina herself—the dark, luscious, full-bosomed creature in her rustling draperies who had quietened the massive dog—would she have returned there, Olivia wondered absently? Or had she left Rohan and Boscarrion for good?

She was still pondering over the problem of Rohan's mistress when she reached the seaside of the house. On the far right, the suggestion of what had once been a rock garden above a sloping lawn struggled bravely through layers of thin sand. But any clear design had long been lost to the covetous shore. A few plants still clung to life at haphazard intervals, waving tired leaves in the salty air. A drift of scarlet splashed the cold gray of granite steps where poppies quivered on their delicate stems, mingled with a touch of cornflower blue. But everywhere else held the muted shadowed quality of a place already claimed by encroaching sand. The gothic porch was cracked. The pointed windows immediately overlooking the beach were shuttered and filmed with the silvered yellow particles of countless millions of shattered minute shells and rock.

Olivia hesitated, peering upward at rusted gables and towers stretching indiscriminately through the mist. They could have been those of some ancient fairy-tale illustration having no true substance or reality. Boscarrion was considerably smaller than Penraven; but through the curdling light no boundaries were clear from the shadowed gray of sky and shore and sea below.

There was a constant dripping and hollow pounding of waves from the distance, and on Olivia's left the plunging continual ripple of Red River's race toward the Atlantic. A sense of deepening, elemental loneliness seized her. She forced herself to move and, clutching a tuft of sea grass, pulled herself to the steps. She tried the iron latch of the door, but did not rap. It was icy cold. The wood looked greenish-black and sodden with weed. No one could have used that particular entrance for a very long time.

She turned and plunged quickly along the path to the side of the house. The way from there was more clearly defined, though the flagstones were cracked and slippery underfoot. Poppies spattered with a few moon daisies nodded their frail ghost faces as she passed. She felt as though she were in a dream.

But as she neared a corner, everything changed. Light streamed in a fitful flow from a window above, and as she continued on her way a rosier, more comforting gleam lit the eerie atmosphere to an illusion of welcome from within.

She put a hand tentatively against a door. It gave a little, and the steamy scent of a greenhouse drifted through. But there was no light there, so she went on and presently, rounding a bend, came to the front of the house. The curtains were not yet drawn across the windows, and as she stood quite still again, pressed close to the wall, she saw a dark squat figure cross the interior carrying an oil lamp.

This was not a room Olivia had seen before. It was heavily furnished in mahogany, including a refectory table in the center and a tall grandfather clock with its pendulum swinging in one corner. The shapes were dim, dark, and forbidding, and in character with the woman's form moving so ponderously about. She was instantly recognizable.

The housekeeper.

Olivia, with her head bent a little, hurried on, and at last was encompassed by a sudden radiance of mellowed, misted light from a ground-floor window at the far end of the building. The sound of her footsteps on the flagstones must have been heard, for a moment later there was the grinding sound of wood grating on sand, and the misted air lifted as a door opened spilling a pool of quivering gold down the steps and over the damp ground.

Olivia stared and smiled tentatively as the features of Rohan Tregallis registered above her.

There was silence between them—a moment of surprise while her visit gathered meaning and significance in his mind. Then he stepped back, with his back against the carved woodwork, one arm motioning her in.

She passed through. Lamps hung at intervals down the hall, but their glow was hazy—the light diffused and distorted by the wafting mist and a strange impression of a million molecules of silvered sand blown in by a thin rising breeze from outside.

She tried to explain, but it was not until he'd ushered her into the same room of her former visit that any words came. And it was he who spoke first.

"Come to the fire, Cousin Olivia. The mist makes everything cold." He paused, adding almost instantly, "What's the matter? Don't be afraid. You look—"

"I'm not afraid," she interrupted. "I was just—"

"Yes?"

"Wondering what you must think of me."

He smiled. For a second her attention was held hypnotically by the dark flame of his eyes, his slow smile and air of courteous gentility.

"I'm extremely pleased to see you," he told her. "And do sit down. Here—" He indicated a carved chair upholstered in green brocade material. "This is comfortable, and you must have had a long walk. Or did you ride?" His eyes slid over the soiled hem of her dress and the sand clinging to the toes of her slippers. "No, I can see you came on foot."

"Yes. It was simpler," she admitted.

"Ah." He poured her a glass of wine and handed

it to her, saying, "I understand. If you were seen on that filly of yours—Moonbeam, wasn't it?—you'd have been stopped visiting your reprobate relative. So you made the dangerous quick cut around the point. Very tricky."

"I've done it before," Olivia answered. She was becoming more at ease and used to the reflected lights of candles and glass through the mirrored interior. "Many times. No one knows, of course."

"Naturally."

"Not even Justin," she continued.

"Most important he shouldn't," she heard Rohan saying.

Olivia could feel her cheeks flushing. "I don't generally keep anything from Justin. We've always been so close, you see. But—"

"It's different now. Yes, it must be. Marriage is bound to change things."

Her eyes widened. "You knew?"

"Of course. I'm not quite a hermit; and you'd be surprised how quickly gossip travels."

"Oh."

"Still—" He smiled again. "You're not here just to talk of my lusting young cousin, I hope." His tones were bright, but his eyes had narrowed. She was uneasily aware he was watching her closely. "Is there anything I can do for you, Olivia?"

She gave a short uncomfortable laugh.

"I'm not sure now. I don't think there is, really. At least—nothing positively." She glanced down, then faced him very deliberately and admitted, "I just wanted to see someone and get away from Penraven for a bit. Mara has a baby now, but I expect you've heard that too. The trouble is, I'm always expected to be a sort of—of extra nursemaid—" She broke off breathlessly.

"And you don't appreciate that? Naturally not.

Why should you?" He added a little more wine to her glass. "You're a young lady now. And a very charming one too. I'm flattered to know you thought of me. I was rather afraid after your last visit you'd keep rigidly away. A miserable affair, wasn't it?"

"Yes. For those poor men," Olivia answered. "But exciting. I mean—" She searched for the right words and ended by concluding, "You were very brave, Cousin Rohan. I don't know why—"

"I'm such a bête noir to my respected relatives at Penraven? Oh, they can be a stuffy crowd. Pity, isn't it? They miss such a lot. But of course there's only Justin now, isn't there—Justin and my esteemed aunt-in-law Elaine, apart from Mara and her—offspring."

"She's very beautiful, you know—Mara," Olivia said reflectively.

"So I've heard, and a tinker's wench into the bargain." Rohan quaffed his wine at a single gulp. "Still" —pouring another—"quite fitting, I imagine."

"No." A wave of quick anger pricked Olivia's spine. "It's not fitting at all. They have different ideas over everything. And Mara hasn't the slightest understanding with him over Crannick."

"The old mine. Well, I can understand that. Beautiful women and copper are not always compatible, and probably your brother is the down-to-earth practical type?"

Olivia did not answer.

With a start she saw Rohan get up and come toward her. He bent his head and drew her hand up to his lips. The pressure of his mouth was cool and gentle, and in a subtle way disturbing. She pulled her palm away firmly.

"Oh, Cousin Rohan—"

"Let it be Rohan, please—"

"Rohan, then. You shouldn't. I mean—"

"Why shouldn't I? And what do you mean, Olivia? You gave me the impression when you came in that you were no longer a child—"

"I'm not. But—"

"There's no need to be afraid of me," he said quietly. "I'm asking nothing of you, forcing no confidences, but obviously you're unhappy."

Feeling her underlip quiver, she turned away.

A hand touched her shoulder gently.

"My dear girl, forgive me if I've been too—forthcoming. First of all I want to be a friend. My reputation may not be very commendable, I don't pretend to be a saint. But if you ever want help—of any kind whatever, you've only to ask and I'll do all in my power to assist. Another thing—"

"Yes?"

The brilliance of her eyes, the proud lift of her chin, for a moment stirred emotions in him that had no place in his scheme.

"Don't let your family override you," he told her firmly. "Remember, you have a right to your own future, Olivia—and if you ever decide it might lie alongside mine—" He waited for a fraction of time before ending, "then I'm quite sure it can be arranged—one way or another."

He waited for the significance of his words to sink in, then turned the conversation to more practical matters.

When she left an hour later, the tide was already flowing quickly toward the shore. Rohan insisted on a groom leading her on one of his mares up a track to the top of the moors, and from there along a path toward the north on the other side of the ridge. At a certain point behind a clump of sloes, she dismounted and made her way down to Penraven.

She arrived at the house with her visit to Boscarrion quite unsuspected. When Justin returned from Crannick later, he gave her only a quick glance before hurrying to Mara's side. Olivia had not the slightest knowledge of the bitterness and longing in that short look—of the thwarted emotions in him as he tore his eyes away. Only his brusqueness registered, chilling and wounding her so acutely she knew that somehow she'd have to end the painful relationship between them in the best way that presented itself.

Rohan?

During the weeks that followed she contrived to see him many times, and gradually trust and warmth replaced her early faint fears and suspicion. His compliments and capacity to charm when it suited him were effective balm to her loneliness and hurt pride, and when on an October day he suggested marriage, she agreed, feeling it to be the one answer to her need and escape from her passionate yearning for her brother's undivided devotion.

Owing to her youth and the dangerous family situation, the marriage was a secret affair, held in Penjust. Olivia's age was falsified, and a note from Rohan was later delivered at Penraven, telling Justin of the event.

Sickened and furious, Justin rode to Boscarrion the same day, demanding confrontation with Rohan. But Rohan was in Gwynfa on a hurried business appointment, and when Justin saw Olivia's white and strained face blazing at him, all his intentions of carrying her back immediately were stilled into momentary shock. She hates me, he thought. My own sister hates me.

"Go back to your wife, Justin," Olivia was saying in shrill, cold tones. "I'm married now too. For months, years now, you've hardly noticed me. All you've wanted is riches, and power, and—Mara. Well, they're all yours, aren't they? So leave me alone. I don't want you here, or to see you again, ever, until you can behave properly to Rohan. Take things to law if you like. The marriage is legal, whatever my age says. And if you fight, you'll drag everything into the mud, and I'll inform against you and the witch you married. She *is* a witch, isn't she? Oh, Justin—" For a moment the anger left her voice. "I was so happy with you once, when Papa was alive. I would have done anything in the world for you. But now— it's all over. I belong to Rohan. He's"—her tones quietened—"very kind, you know."

But he wasn't.

That was the trouble.

Later that same night Olivia discovered many qualities in Rohan Tregallis she had not even contemplated before.

12

She stood alone in the large room, looking down on the bed, which was canopied and ornately carved, with a lace-spread covering the sheets. The air was faintly musty with the hint of lavender and smell of camphor. The carpet that had once been thick was now worn in parts, pinkish showing a faded pattern of roses. Heavy maroon-shaded velvet hangings had been drawn against the window curtains of yellow-

ing lace; there was a slight creaking coming from
shuttered panes outside, one of which had half broken from its hinges. The furniture was of heavy walnut, and must once have appeared rich and elegant.
But the impression remaining now was of neglect
and forgotten things left to decay in their own
memories. A fire had been lighted in the grate and
burned fitfully, spitting ash and coils of smoke around
the marble surround. Shadows leaped up the pan-
eled walls, and Olivia had an impulse to rush to the
windows and fling them wide so the cleansing smells
of sea and moorland winds could penetrate the interior.

She ran across the room and tugged at the drapes.
There was the rattle of curtain rings, and a streak of
greenish twilight snaking across the floor. Steeling
her fears—which after all, she told herself resolutely,
were quite ridiculous—she parted the lace curtains
and peered across the fading evening sky. The room
faced east over the river. To the north and west she
could distinguish only the gray of dunes and cliffs
against the blurred darker gray of the sea. And even
as she watched for those few moments a thin shower
of sand was blown against the glass.

Shivering a little, although it was not really cold,
Olivia pulled the velvet hangings close again and
went back to the bed. She smoothed the lace, staring
at the fine threadwork, wondering idly how many
other girls had come as brides to wait there for their
husbands? Had any been as young as she—seventeen
—and so desperately in need of comfort and compassion? In the last hour her defiance and anger caused
by Justin's neglect had crumbled into a sudden cold
assessment of reality. She was married to Rohan, and
she hardly knew him. The distressing scene with
Justin, his anger, the cold contempt on his face,

and the whiplash of his voice before he finally
left for Penraven without seeing Rohan, had left
her weakened, feeling frighteningly young and vul-
nerable.

No one would know it, though, she told herself as
she went to the oval cheval mirror and regarded her
stony young face with unchildlike objectivity. In the
sophisticated green dress she'd purchased secretly a
week before along with other essentials, on a jaunt to
Truro, she looked a young woman in her twenties at
least. The yoke was of cream lace, the neck high,
reaching to just under her chin. The lines of the skirt
flowed out from a pinched waist to a wide frilled
hemline. Bouffant sleeves from the shoulders were
gathered in at the elbows to tightly fitting lines taper-
ing to the wrists. Her dark hair was taken from a
center parting to coils nestling at both ears.

She would have liked to wear earrings as befitting
her married status. But Rohan had not supplied her
with sufficient money.

"Buy what is essential to make you attractive as a
wife," he'd said. "But don't waste money. You will
belong to a proud but somewhat impoverished
branch of the Tregallis family. So don't expect to be
able to squander my filthy lucre as braggart Justin
does."

A hot retort had been on the tip of her tongue.

"He's not—" Then the narrowing glint of Rohan's
eyes had stopped her.

"He's not what, my love?"

"A braggart," she'd said definitely. "And I wish you
wouldn't always be so quick to criticize him, Rohan.
It's not kind—or true, anyway."

"Isn't it? Isn't it indeed?" His hand had itched to
slap her, although he'd mastered the inclination.
"Well, if you don't mind I'd rather not hear his

praises sung, and in future please don't contradict. No woman has ever tried to put me in my place, Olivia, and I don't intend it should start now. Do you understand?"

"Yes," she had snapped, "and perhaps I'm not really the proper wife for you. Cobby always said I had a temper, and—"

"Who's Cobby?"

"My governess. I mean, she was once."

"Then Cobby must have known," he'd said shortly. "The thing is, she didn't know me. And apparently neither do you—very well."

"No."

He'd suddenly laughed and pulled her to him.

"Oh, Olivia, smile."

But she hadn't, and his lips had suddenly been on her mouth. She had struggled faintly, then resistance had died in her as she'd made herself believe it was Justin kissing her.

He'd released her abruptly and turned away, so the expression on his face had escaped her. When he'd come back and touched her hand, he was smiling, and her fit of nerves had died.

"If you're a good girl," he'd said, lifting a finger to her pert chin, "I'm sure we shall get on admirably. If you're not—I'll have to tame you, won't I?"

She'd frowned doubtfully. "Are you sure—?"

"Whatever you're asking—yes, I'm sure," he'd told her. "I give you my name, security, and all else that goes with it, which is more preferable to you, I'm sure, than playing nursemaid to a gypsy's brat, and spinster sister to Justin Tregallis. I can hardly see you as dependent maiden aunt for your lifetime."

The reminder of her true position at Penraven and in Justin's life if she turned from marriage with

Rohan had swept away any lingering hesitation; and
the mild difference between them had been thrust to
the back of her mind.

Now, waiting for Rohan, following the brief wedding ceremony, she steeled herself to have common
sense and be practical. In the daylight, she thought,
the room could be quite pleasant. It would surely be
possible to have brighter, fresh curtains at the windows, flowers on the dressing table, and lighter
upholstery for the gilded armchair and chaise
longue.

One wall, at least, which was free of the dark woodwork, could be covered in wallpaper to give a happier atmosphere—a gold and white design, perhaps,
with a pattern of small pink roses somewhere. The
forbidding-looking portrait hanging near the window and almost facing the bed could be moved somewhere else and replaced by a woodland scene or a
painting with animals grazing under blue skies.
Surely Rohan would not mind that?

The idea of lying in that great bed under the condemning gaze of the woman in the heavy oak frame
was already disconcerting. She had a foreign look and
appeared not at all handsome or kindly. Her features
were pronounced—thin lips over a determined chin,
bony large nose, cold eyes under very thick brows
and a high forehead from which the dark hair was
drawn back severely in a knot. Her dress showed no
vestige of flesh and was of deep purple, high-necked
and reaching tightly to each wrist where her mittened hands were spread one over the other in her
broad lap.

If this was Rohan's mother, Olivia thought with a
shudder of distaste, then she would have pitied him
in his youth. But then, perhaps it wasn't—perhaps

she was some relative—an aunt, or even a housekeeper or some family retainer.

She tore her eyes away from the unattractive countenance, lifted her light valise onto the bed, and unpacked the few clothes chosen to start her married life. They were simple and not costly, in accordance with Rohan's instructions. She would have liked to spend wildly on the rich ravishing garments most brides expected. Being extravagant over clothes would have helped her adjust to the strange new circumstances of life at Boscarrion. As it was, the green satin gown she had brought with her from Penraven was the most attractive she possessed, and her nightwear had been chosen for use rather than allure. She had wondered whether to wear the green at dinner after their return from Penzance, but before going out, Rohan had insisted on there being no show.

"You're all right as you are," he had said, throwing a cursory glance at her gray everyday dress. "When you've had a wash, we'll eat, and then you can retire early. After all the excitement, both of us I'm sure, will appreciate an early night. In the meantime, Mrs. Trellis will be at hand if you need anything. I should not be away from the house for more than half an hour."

So they had taken their meal later in a small parlor attended by the girl and the disapproving housekeeper. Olivia had drunk a little wine, but not much, and after that had been dismissed by Rohan to the bedroom.

"I will be up presently," he'd said. "Make yourself comfortable. If you want anything, ring."

Depressed by the cool dismissal, she'd nevertheless managed not to show it, and had left him standing by the table watching her enigmatically with an assessing wry look on his face.

Mrs. Trellis had been hovering about outside. She had insisted on seeing Olivia to the bedroom again, although she'd already been up once immediately following her arrival.

"This is a very special room," the housekeeper had said meaningfully. "See you doan' knock anythin' over or pull that spread—real lace it is an' old, the maister values et. So be careful now."

Olivia, flushing, had answered coldly, "I'm not a child, you know. I'm used to good things."

"Hm!" The woman had given a short cough that could have meant anything—either a laugh or a sneer—and had then departed.

That had been over half an hour ago, and Olivia had still made no move to undress or prepare herself for what was expected to be a bride's first initiation into the mysteries of the married state. Instead she had changed into the green, to feel beautiful and give confidence. Marriage, after all, was a great step to take.

She was not frightened at the idea—she would not allow herself to be—merely chilled and uncertain, because after all, she knew Rohan so little. Until the moment she started to unfasten her gown and properly disrobe, she had not realized the true implications of what she'd done. She knew she would never have acted so rashly if it had not been for Justin; and she blamed him for having left her to such an embarrassing situation.

He could have been nicer—kinder, she told herself stubbornly. Instead of flying into such a cold rage when she told him of the marriage, he could have eased matters by being reasonable and giving her

understanding. More than that—if he'd not thrust
her out of his life so cruelly she would probably never
have married Rohan at all. Now, of course, it was too
late. Even if Justin realized his own mistake, he
would never forgive her. In his mind, she would always be a traitor to the family name, have sacrificed
all right to his trust and consideration.

She set her chin suddenly and sat on the bed, bend-
ing to unlace her pointed best boots. Then she pulled
off her dress, unbuttoned her three petticoats,
slipped out of them, and determinedly unlaced her
tight stays. The relief was considerable. She got up,
let the constricting things fall to her feet, stepped out
of them; then she walked, head held high, to the
mirror and took the combs and pins from her hair.
The black masses fell over her shoulders; her breasts
were firm and round and tilted under the cotton
bodice.

In spite of the occasion a little burst of humor escaped her as she stared at her reflection. Like a
clown, she thought, hands on hips above the frilled
pantalettes. Or a ballet dancer, perhaps? But no. As
she lifted one leg at right angles to her rounded slim
body, it occurred to her she could easily have been
one of those poster girls advertised for the Ballet
Rouge. So she really must be a bit wicked. Instantly
she sobered, sped back to the bed, sat down again,
and removed the rest of the underwear including
stockings and garters. Then she quickly took her
long-sleeved cotton nightshift from a chair and
pulled it over her head.

She shook it down, and with her nakedness covered, felt a great wave of relief sweep over her.

She was only just in time.

A minute afterward, there was a slight tap on the

door. It opened and Rohan came in. He was carrying a candle, and wore a black wrap over his shift, reaching almost to his ankles. The garment was of shiny satin material, and his feet were encased in pointed black embroidered slippers. He looked exciting and somehow strange, like a figure out of some exotic fairy tale, she thought, and was instantly confused.

He did not smile, just walked toward her slowly, yet with such deliberation she moved involuntarily backward to the other side of the bed.

She clutched the cotton gown tightly to her neck, with a wild impulse in her to run away; but there was nowhere to run to.

He followed her, came close, and touched her shoulder. He was perfumed, and his dark eyes were pinpointed with tiny lights like black stars.

"Afraid?" he murmured, almost in a whisper.

She stiffened.

He laughed, letting a hand stray down her spine to the buttocks. Then he pushed her down. She stared up at him wide-eyed, with her heart pounding. He jerked his head up and laughed. She edged away. He caught her by the collar of the nightdress and pulled her up.

"Take that odious thing off, my dear wife," he said coldly. "Or would you prefer me to assist—" There was a rip of the material as he wrenched it from her shivering form. She made a wild instinctive attempt to hide under the bedclothes, but he was somehow on top of her, his hard body half smothering hers while she prayed inwardly, "Oh, don't let it happen —dear God, help me—"

But no deity seemed to hear her prayers, and it did happen—ruthlessly, with no word of love between them, no gesture of gentleness.

A terrible pain seared her as her virginal slim thighs were wrenched apart. She felt she was bleeding, and moaned. She closed her eyes, wanting to faint but refusing to. When it was all over, he sprang up and went to the window. "A clear evening," he remarked in aloof practical tones.

She lay unsmiling and unmoving. He returned to the bed, stood looking down on her for a few moments, then sharply slapped her face.

"Sit up," he said.

She faced him, biting her lip, two spots of crimson burning against the dead white of her cheeks.

"You could have been a little more subtle in your response," he said coldly. "A little show of warmth—even though it was only playacting, would have been rewarding for both of us, I think—especially yourself."

When she said nothing, he continued, "However, have no fear. It's hardly likely I shall trespass on your boring chastity again. But let there be one thing quite clear between us. You will remain faithful to me in word and deed, and never on any account go visiting or tale-telling to your upstart would-be protector at Penraven. If you do—he will suffer for it, and you, my love, will wish you'd never been born. I have a hard hand, and a worthy switch, and am well used to dealing with slaves and recalcitrant women. It's a pity there have to be such revelations together on our first night. But you should have been more careful in not so quickly betraying how you'd used me."

She tried to protest. "I didn't—"

"Oh, yes, you did. You're a liar and a cheat."

He went to the door, turned, and said, "I knew it, of course. I'm not a fool. But I expected you to behave with more artistry and appreciation of your position. In future I advise you to at least make the effort."

A moment later he had gone, leaving her to wonder miserably how she was going to bear life at Boscarrion.

13

During most of the night following Justin's stormy scene with Olivia and his unsuccessful attempt to confront Rohan after the marriage, he had paced the library debating what to do. Olivia was underage, and that devious scheming bastard Rohan, therefore, had somehow contracted an unlawful union. Justin's first instinct was to ride over to Boscarrion again early the next day and face the fellow with pistols or swords—maybe wring the truth out of him by getting his hands around the hated neck and squeezing it like a chicken's until he swore to right the wrong. But as early dawn gradually lightened the gray sky, the first fury of Justin's rage had abated into colder calm. He recalled the passion in Olivia's eyes, her stinging avowal that he could do nothing—nothing could alter the fact that she was legally married to Rohan.

Well, he thought more reasoningly, he'd soon see about that. If the ceremony had been performed legally and correctly—even despite misrepresentation in age—she had probably spoken truly. He could make trouble for them both, of course. A matter of perjury might come into it, but Rohan would somehow contrive to put the blame on Olivia, and whatever the penalty, she would still remain married to that unscrupulous villain.

The position, regarded objectively, was a distasteful one indeed. More than that—acutely painful.

Justin was shocked and surprised at the wild sensation of loss, the ache that swept over him. It had been inevitable that one day Olivia would marry, of course.

But Rohan, of all men.

Rohan!

The thought of her lying in Rohan's arms tortured him. His nerves and muscles ached with a frustration that was beyond all sense. She was only his sister, after all. One day, somehow, sometime, she would have left the family home. The halls and corridors would no more have resounded with her clear voice and laughter, or the swift rush of light feet. The trouble was, he had never cared to contemplate such a time. And in the meantime there had been Mara.

Mara.

In the turmoil of his emotions over Olivia he had almost forgotten he had a wife. Odd.

He had an early breakfast, then went into see her. A smell of flowers and perfume from the dressing table drifted to meet him. She was sitting up in bed, beautiful as ever, wearing a lacy negligée over her pale pink shift. Her fair hair fell in a cloud over her shoulders. Her azure-blue eyes held a cold condemning look.

"Well?" she said. "Where have you been, Justin? I've waited all night—wanting you."

Her perfect lips pouted petulantly, but beneath the gently reproachful exterior he sensed the hidden tiger lurking, ever watchful.

"I couldn't sleep," he said. "And I didn't want to disturb you."

"I see."

But you don't, he thought. You know nothing, and for a moment the idea of informing her of Rohan's marriage to Olivia—the shock it would be—gave him brief satisfaction. He was by then under no delusion concerning her weakness for Rohan—she had protested far too much when he'd questioned her, and the deliberate way she'd changed the conversation whenever his name was mentioned had not deceived him for one moment.

However, he said nothing to her curt comment, deciding it would be better to unfold the full story later when he knew exactly what the legal position was between his sister and cousin. He merely kissed Mara lightly, managing to draw himself away before her insidious feminine enchantment caught him unawares, weakening his resolve.

She stared at him, then said, "Something's wrong, isn't it? What's happened?"

"I have to go out immediately," he answered glibly.

"Why?"

"Mara, my love, that's my affair. I have business in Penjust, and on my way back I shall call at Crannick."

"Rather a long way round, isn't it?"

"Yes. But after a sleepless night the fresh air will do me good."

She shrugged and looked away. A moment later he left.

He took the high moorland track to Penjust, and reached the small town by ten o'clock. It was market day and the main street leading to the Corn Market was busy with stallholders and visitors. A butter market had recently been added to the main circular building. Nearby, shrill bidding was going on for a woman put up for auction by her husband. She was a strong-looking, plain female attached by a halter round her waist. The husband, grim-mouthed, with a sour mean face, kept a firm grip on his spouse until the sum of eightpence was offered and accepted. She was led away to shouts of approval and laughter.

Justin winced. He had seen many shady and unpleasant deals concocted on market day, but the sale of a woman—any woman—as so much cattle fodder was offensive in the extreme to him. He had a mind suddenly to follow the purchaser and outbid him sufficiently highly to take the woman himself back to Penraven for service, in the kitchens or dairy. But pressure of time and impatience to have the business of Olivia settled in his mind deterred him. He hurried on his way, unceremoniously pushing through crowds and stalls until he reached the cobbled byway leading to the Rectory.

He learned there that details concerning the binding in legal matrimony between one Rohan Tregallis of Boscarrion, and Olivia Tregallis of Penraven, were in perfect order. Her age, he discovered, had been given as twenty-one. Sick at heart, Justin did not openly contest the fact.

What was the use?

Olivia was lost to him.

But God help Rohan, he thought savagely as he walked away, if he in any way treated her ill. Sooner or later, he, Justin, would be bound to hear. And then Rohan would wish he had never seen the light of day.

When he arrived back at Penraven, he was surprised to find Annabella Fearnley waiting for him in the drawing room. Accompanying her was a smallish, rather stout man, pink-cheeked and already balding, who after the first formal introductions informed Justin he was a friend of Joshua Partridge's, Horace Lee, from Halifax.

As conversation progressed other salient facts became obvious, that he was rich, with a considerable financial interest in cotton mills and certain mining companies, and that it was through Partridge himself that he had met Annabella's father, with whom he was staying for the weekend.

Justin felt amused irony at the news. How quickly that fellow Partridge had taken advantage of the Tregallis connection, he thought. And how cunningly Annabella must have set out to entrap him. She wanted a husband, of course, and Fearnley, though so aristocratically well endowed with worldly goods, was ever one to be wanting more. No doubt unless Lee had a wife tucked away up north, an engagement was taking shape for the near future. Annabella had that complacent, mildly fatuous look about her that suggested she had already nicely netted her fish. Well, she might have taken on more than she'd bargained for, he thought wryly. In her own way Annabella was a good sort, but that pink-faced dumpling of a man could be devious. He had cunning, round blue eyes and the primped-up button type of mouth that denoted an iron will beneath the baby-smooth countenance.

Annabella was half a head taller than he, but he in no way seemed overshadowed. For one thing she half slouched toward him in an effort to reduce her height. This gave her a placating air.

"Horace—Mr. Lee—knows so much about mines and things," she said when they were seated drinking madeira a little later. "That's why we called at Crannick. I thought he'd be interested."

"Oh? Why?" Justin demanded abruptly.

"Well"—Annabella smiled sweetly, and for a moment Justin wondered whether she was quite so friendly and forgiving as he'd supposed— "with Mr. Partridge being so involved, you see, and their being such old friends, it's natural, isn't it?" She turned to the stranger. "That's right, isn't it—Horace"—the name came out with coy shyness —"you were impressed by it—Crannick, I mean?"

Lee twirled the stem of his glass between finger and thumb before replying. Then he remarked slowly, without commitment, "The idea's got possibilities, and Ah can see thee's a good lot of work done already. Thee might pull it off, lad. But on the other hand it looks risky to me."

Justin stared.

"Risky? We've had the best engineering brains from the north to give an opinion."

"And they gave it no doubt," the other man said. "But an opinion's only an opinion. Thee can never tell, so near the sea, with rock erosion and soil subsidence. Ninety-nine and a half percent's possible, but it's the half left thee'll have to watch And that's what I shall tell Josh—'be sure to keep an eye on that unknown half.' "

Justin felt himself stiffen with anger. Why the devil had the cocky little stranger come to poke his nose into Crannick affairs just at that point? he wondered. He felt a sudden rush of hostility toward Annabella. He glanced at her sharply. She was smiling ambiguously. But her eyes were cold. So she hadn't overlooked the past, as he'd hoped and imagined. She still held his rejection of her against him.

Only half aware of what he was saying, he heard himself commenting shortly, "I hardly think my partner needs advice from an outsider. We have complete confidence in our own engineering experts."

He was too annoyed to notice the swift deepening of color above the other man's cravat—the upthrust of the fleshy chin below the small tight mouth. Diver-

sion was caused at that moment by the entrance of
Mara, who, hearing from Jenny they had visitors, had
left a little tête-à-tête with Elaine to play a welcoming short part as hostess. She generally managed to
absent herself from Justin's boring business meetings, but titillated by the news of Annabella's presence, encouraged by Elaine, and remembering her
promise to Rohan, she had decided to make an ex-
ception on this occasion.

"You go, my dear," Elaine had urged, with a secret
sly look of satisfaction in her china-blue eyes. "The
Fearnleys were always so very c-condescending.
Shame that horsey big-footed creature Annabella
with your—your beauty. The Bennedicks always had
breeding an-and beauty. And that's what—what—
we are, isn't it, my love?" She peered at Mara closely
with tipsy intentness. "—Two Bennedicks as like as
two peas—" she had gulped, and started to laugh.
With underlying faint derision Mara had said socth-
ingly, "I'm sure you're right. But keep things to yourself. Have a little of your tonic and a sleep. I'll do
what you say."

"And—don't forget to tell me afterward," Elaine
had said, going to the bed. "You 'member to tell me
—yes? Everything that b-bumshious creature says."

"Of course."

"Send that girl to me," Elaine had commanded
then with a sudden change of mood. "I want my
maid. Do you—hear? My maid. Quick—quick."

She had half stumbled over the quilt. Mara had
helped her onto the bed, put a glass on the small
table with the brandy nearby, and hurried away before any further commands were forthcoming. By
the time the door was closed, Elaine had already
forgotten what the conversation was all about.

Everyone in the drawing room stared, looking mo-

mentarily startled as Mara entered. She was wearing
pale lilac—a shade that emphasized the lucid blue of
her eyes and wild-rose coloring of her skin. She had
hastily pinned her pale golden hair to the top of her
head. A few tendrils touched her soft cheeks below
the ears. She looked enchanting—more like a character from some legend than a woman of flesh and
blood.

Justin, as usual, was taken aback by her beauty. But
there was no softening in him anymore; the sense of
worship had gone. Lovely she might be, but he knew
her sufficiently well by then to recognize she was up
to something. She wished to have a hand in what was
going on, for some secret reason of her own. The
knowledge frustrated him. He introduced her formally to Horace Lee, who gave a little bow and
touched her hand with his stubby fingers. His small
eyes were admiring but without respect; and for a
quick angry moment Mara was disconcerted. It was
as though with his shrewd business acumen he was
probing through the fair facade to the very depths of
her concealed and all-consuming desires.

Rohan.

She steeled herself to be polite, and said with a
show of proud sweetness, "I hope you and Miss
Fearnley will stay to lunch?"

Annabella smiled brightly back.

"I'm so sorry, we haven't the time. Mr. Lee has to
be in Falmouth by one o'clock. We only called to see
your—to see Justin—just in passing. Mutual interests,
you could say." Her lips were still amicable, but her
eyes were hard.

Mara, relieved but annoyed, said coolly, "I quite
understand. Still, it's very pleasant to have met you."

When the visitors had left, she turned to Justin
with a steely glint in her eyes.

"I should be very careful, if I were you, Justin," she told him insinuatingly.

"What do you mean?"

She paused before answering.

"They wish you ill."

He laughed, trying to dispel a lingering sense of discomfort left behind by Lee and the domineering Annabella.

"You imagine things, my love."

He put a finger under her chin, and tilted her face to meet his. Her eyes by then were wide and very clear. His vulnerability, combined with his strength and rugged honesty, momentarily completely disarmed her. She wished she could be equally honest with him. At such moments her own deviousness genuinely distressed her. If it were not for Rohan, how she could have cared for him! A little later he told her of Olivia's elopement. She showed no undue shock, although her face was a degree paler when she said, "I'm not really surprised—she's been after him ever since she left school."

"No. I won't have that. I don't believe it."

"Oh, Justin," she murmured, "you're so trusting."

He kissed her lips gently.

"Of my friends I am—I have to be," he said, "and of you. Though I never completely feel sure."

She pulled herself away.

"I'm glad of that."

"Good heavens, why?"

She turned and once more stared him straight in the eyes. "Because you're too good for me, Justin. I've always known it, and so have you. You should have married someone quite different, like—more *like* Olivia perhaps."

He laughed shortly, uneasily.

"Please don't mention her name in front of me.

Olivia's cut herself completely off through this last wild act. In the end Rohan will destroy her. And when he does—"

"Yes?" The word was a whisper.

"Then I'll destroy him," Justin answered.

He turned and walked away abruptly, with such pain gnawing him he could not bear the intensity of Mara's gaze.

14

Autumn gradually turned toward approaching winter. The Cornish moors, from purple and the bright gold of flaming gorse, took on the deepening browns and grays of dried heather and leafless undergrowth. On fine days scudding shadows streaked from pale sunlight down the slopes, to fade suddenly as massed clouds rose against the sky. The sea, calm one day, could be wild the next, flinging its fury savagely at cliffs and dunes, sweeping great showers of sand and shingle against the granite coast.

On stormy days the moan of wind and crashing of waves beat in ceaseless cacophony round Boscarrion's walls, rising to a shrill screaming where the gulls flew, dipping and wheeling above the tide's thrust.

Even when the calm came, nothing was quite silent. There was always the rhythmic lapping and breaking of water on sand, and from the gap the monotonous distant gurgling of Red River to the sea. Hardly a moment passed without some sigh or brushing of wind around windows or under doors. It seemed to Olivia sometimes that the house belonged to the elements rather than human beings. She found it hard to adapt in any way to her new life.

Rohan, who could be harsh when it suited him, was at other times unconcerned and forbearing with her moods. Following the stormy beginning of their marriage he appeared frequently not to notice her presence at all. They did not sleep together. He had his own room at the end of the long corridor, and seldom visited hers. Her flinching from any lovemaking induced instinctive hostility on his part, and a quick retreat from her presence. Very occasionally he asserted "his rights," but eventually, following a number of such unrewarding and bitter incidents, he dismissed their connubial relationship as a mere waste of time, although he was quick to threaten her, and once, in a mood of rejection—humiliated and enraged by the contempt on her young face—he bent her over the bed and smartly slapped her.

She did not cry. The pain, though sharp, had been brief. But when she turned around, her eyes and cheeks blazed.

"You beast, Rohan Tregallis," she said. "How dare you? You horrible creature—"

He laughed, and, surveying her with his hands on his hips, said coldly, "If you behave like an ill-mannered boy, Olivia, expect to be treated like one. But don't fear I shall ever trespass on your sexual sensibilities again. I have far better ways of spending my time."

"With Melusina, I suppose?" she said bitterly on the spur of the moment, and at the sudden whitening of his face, put a hand quickly to her mouth.

He took an involuntary step forward, then turned and went to the door. Before leaving he gave her one hard, condemning look and said, "Never mention her name to me again, do you understand? And never, never consider you have the right to question me concerning my private affairs. You have no rights here—none—except as a chattel and slave, if I wish it. But I think that's extremely doubtful. Just see you don't provoke me again, or what you've had will be child's play compared to what you'll get."

A moment later he was gone, and shivering, she sat down on the bed with her head in her hands.

After this he kept strictly at his distance, although ever watchful upon her activities outside the house. She had the use of a mare, Speedwell, from his stables. But unlike the name, the horse had a leisurely temperament, was getting on in years, and at a soft call from Rohan would refuse stubbornly to obey any other. Olivia tried several times to lure the animal around the Red River route to Penraven, hoping to seize Moonbeam, and somehow make peace with Justin. But she was always intercepted by Rohan, who ordered her immediately back to Boscarrion. And gradually, as the first frosts came, physical initiative died in her, except for lonely walks down the dunes, where she stood staring toward the north hoping and longing for a glimpse of Justin. But he did not come that way; or if he did, she never knew. It seemed that her old life and contacts were cut off forever.

Christmas came and went with very little festivity at Boscarrion, although Rohan made a brief uneasy attempt to soften the atmosphere by conferring presents on the household—including perfume and other feminine accessories meant to bring a smile to Olivia's stony face. The effort was futile. Olivia's stubborn mood persisted. She fretted for Justin, although she refused to admit it, even to herself.

Only the great dog Brutus appeared to touch any chord of affection in her. She discovered his growl and bark were generally mere show. He was by nature an amiable creature easily tamed by kindness, and Olivia made a point of secreting tidbits from the table, which she fed him at odd moments, despite Mrs. Trellis's watchful eye. Rohan was not bothered by the new bond between girl and dog. He was already becoming bored by his young wife's truculent moods.

The only satisfaction gleaned from his marriage was the knowledge of Justin's loss and hurt. Gossip from Penraven—spread by Nelson, whose quick ears and eyes were always on the alert for his master—said that the new master of Penraven was becoming frequently aggressive, and withdrawn at times. That if Miss Olivia's name was ever mentioned there was trouble "sure nuff" for the one who spoke it. It was also common talk that he was more often at Crannick than where he should be—at home—and that his "gypsy wife" had taken to nightly walks in his absence. Mrs. Broome had more to do with the baby than the young madam herself, it was said, with a certain malicious satisfaction. The marriage was a mockery and was turning out badly, just as had been expected.

Whatever the truth, there were still occasions when Justin, seeing Mara in a certain light and posture, marveled anew at her beauty. But his emotions at such moments were more those of a connoisseur or artist than a man of flesh and blood. Desire for her had already turned from physical longing to aesthetic appreciation. He toyed with the idea of commissioning some artist to paint her for perpetuity. At rare times when she played with her baby son or bent over his crib, he could imagine her in stained glass, or hanging in some great gallery depicting an etherealized version of a Madonna and child.

But when she looked up, the image quickly faded. Her strange blue feline eyes had a cold look now when she faced him—wary and secretive. Sometimes he was chilled—frustrated because he knew at heart she had never really belonged to him. In the beginning jealousy had gnawed him, but as the days passed he began to feel only resentment, blaming her for having entrapped him and even for driving Olivia away.

At the same time he was aware of being grossly unfair. It was he who had lured Mara to his bed, and no one else. He need not have married her; the whole affair, seen in retrospect, had been a challenge and means merely of fulfilling his physical desires and thwarted forbidden longing for Olivia.

So he steeled his thoughts from domestic problems and obligations to an ever-increasing involvement with Crannick.

He was not entirely happy about Joshua Partridge's attitude. The man's initial enthusiasm had become charged with faint but perceptible doubt of the mine's potentials.

"You've had a certain amount of backing from me already," he said to Justin one day, "but remember I'm not throwing more in unless the deal proves worth it."

"You've had the experts' opinion; what more do you want?" Justin asked sharply.

"Proof. Some sign we're getting somewhere. This land subsidence problem—from what I understood, there was no chance of any danger at this particular spot of coastline. Now I hear different."

"Who from?"

Partridge wagged a finger. "Never you mind that. Not from imagination anyhow."

Justin frowned.

He remembered Lee's barbed comments at Penraven on the morning of his visit with Annabella, and suspected the hand of a jealous woman somewhere in Crannick affairs.

Damn her, he thought. He hadn't expected it of the forthright Miss Fearnley. It just showed one couldn't be certain of any woman.

"Well?" he heard Joshua remark testily. "Is that all you've got to say?"

Justin eyed him fiercely for a moment, then he replied bluntly, "Yes. And if you have any doubts, then all I can say is 'get out if you want to.' I'm going ahead, and there are others in it with me. Your backing is a help, but if we have to do without it, we can, sir."

Partridge shook his head slowly, trying to assess the precise qualities and knowledge of the stubborn sturdy character facing him.

A defiant young buck, he thought, and one who wouldn't easily give up, once he'd set his mind to anything. Joshua couldn't help but admire him, and he'd have no liking for letting him down. Still, business was business, and it had never been his way to go for a pig in the poke. However, better let things go on as they were for a time, he decided, provided no unreasonable call was made on his pocket.

So he said in easier tones, "Don't work yourself up, young man. No one said I was throwing my hand in. Caution, that's all. Caution's always necessary in a tricky enterprise, and whether you admit it or not, Crannick's tricky, or it wouldn't have been left idle in the first place. What I want's perfectly reasonable

—to see quicker progress on the site, everything working in the expected time limit, and the first signs of reward coming for what's been put into it. Nothing wrong in that, is there?"

"Not wrong," Justin agreed. "But some things can't be cut to an exact pattern. Neither mines or men."

Partridge smiled benevolently. "Ha! Quite a philosopher."

On the verge of losing his temper Justin turned away, saying guardedly, "I don't know about that. But I'll have to be away now. Business—in Penjust."

He gave a nod, made a quick move toward Blackfire, untethered the horse, and was off almost immediately, with a brief farewell wave to his watchful partner.

But not to Penjust.

Instead, when he reached the summit of the moor, he took a direct turn to the right beyond the hill's edge, then rounded the far trickle of Red River, and cut down again to a point directly overlooking Boscarrion.

He reined for a minute, with his eyes on the roofs and towers below, then impulsively continued at a trot down the track to the house. The doors were slightly ajar when he got there, and as he swung himself from the saddle a sinister sense of place chilled him. So forgotten and benighted it appeared —doomed-looking, with filters of sand everywhere, and on the far side the humped dunes rising to lumpy patches of darkish soil with a red tinge. Graves of deserted dwellings, they said. Well, he could believe it—even that the reputed lost village lay beneath those looming mounds of time. "Blast the fellow," he said to himself; his cousin should be jailed for bringing a young girl—a Tregallis—to such a prison of a place. He was still holding Blackfire by the reins, when the door swung wider, and Rohan appeared at the entrance.

They met halfway up the steps. Rohan's face was expressionless except for the twitching of a muscle at the corner of his mouth. Justin felt the hot blood mount under his collar. His eyes, dark and unswerving as Rohan's, held an unblinking challenge in them.

"Well?" he heard the other man say in cold tones. "Cousin Justin, I see. How very surprising. Is this a social call?"

"No."

"I thought not. Then I won't ask you in." He paused, adding the next moment, "Do you mind telling me what *does* bring you here? Could it be on behalf of—Olivia, my wife?"

Justin's face flushed. His jaw came out. "Damn you, Rohan—you know it is. But your wife?" He gave a short, contemptuous laugh. "You may have said a few words before some ignorant unsuspecting official— but that doesn't make a marriage. Morally there was a crime. She's only a child, and I demand to see her —" He broke off, enraged by the contempt on Rohan's face, the imperious wave of his hand.

"Off with you, you young braggart, and keep away from this place in future or you'll regret it. Whether Olivia would wish to see you or not, I certainly don't. For years now—all your life—you've withheld your company, and I certainly want none of it now. As for the child—" He laughed contemptuously. "The child, as you term my uncle's daughter, is an extremely sophisticated and lustful one, with more than her share of sexual prowess—" A sudden blow on his jaw temporarily silenced him.

He fell backward, and slipped down the remaining steps to the ground. Justin, breathing heavily, stood looking as the other man got up, holding his temple. Blood coursed from a cut and through his fingers. His cravat was already spattered with crimson.

"You young devil," he said between his teeth. "If I had my crop, I'd give you such a thrashing you'd never forget it. Or pistols. What about it? Have you courage enough to pit your skill against mine? Or will you run like the scared rabbit you are at heart, before I set the dogs on you?"

Justin glared.

"I'm not moving one inch until I see my sister. And if you so much as turn to get any weapon you like, I'll kick you to hell before you get there."

They stood facing each other while the urge to murder grew and intensified in both of them. It was during this interim that Olivia appeared. Her dark hair was loose about her shoulders, her eyes blazed with condemnation.

"What is it? What's happening?"

Hearing her voice, Justin pushed by Rohan and rushed up the steps toward her. "Olivia," he said, "God forgive me for not returning earlier. My heaven, what has he done to you? Look at your arm —" He stared at a purplish bruise just below the elbow, where the loose wrap had fallen away.

"I fell," she said coldly, "and I don't have to answer your questions. Go away, Justin."

"I will when you're ready. Until you dress decently and get your belongings, I'm staying. Then we'll leave together—for home—Penraven."

She gave him a long look; and in that drawn-out pause everything that had been, and everything that under different circumstances could have been between them, seemed to blossom and grow with a dark, flowering passion.

He saw before him not a girl recently returned

from school but a young woman aching with the pain and longing of overburdened emotions. The full lips trembled, the eyes brimmed with unshed tears and an anguish that cut him to the heart. Though mute, her unspoken desire reached and stabbed him as though a sword pierced his mind and flesh.

A hand went out to her. "Olivia—oh, my dear—"

Then behind him he heard a man's harsh laugh. The hand fell to his side. He glanced back briefly, turning again to Olivia.

"Well?" he found himself whispering. "Well?"

When she spoke, her expression had changed. Her whole body was rigid. The eyes had narrowed, and the soft lips hardened. Two fiery spots of color blazed on the high cheekbones, leaving the rest of her face chalk-white.

Then she said in the clear icy tones of calculated hate, "I told you before to go away, Justin. I don't want you here. Never come or try to see me again. Never, never—do you understand? I'm Rohan's wife, and you're nothing to me. *Nothing.*"

"But—" He stared at her, unbelieving at first.

"I said, go away," she echoed harshly.

Rohan, still with a kerchief to his face, moved to her side.

"You heard what she said," he remarked with deadly precision. "Are you leaving? Or do you wish me to use your own boorish methods?"

Justin turned without answering, and in a few long savage strides reached the patch nearby where Blackfire grazed. Once in the saddle he looked again toward Olivia and before galloping away called, "I'm always waiting—Livvy—when you need me."

She never moved, but stood rigidly watching until the figures of horse and man were mere dots against the landscape.

Then Rohan seized her arm. "Come in now. You were most loyal, I must say."

She shook herself free.

"Don't touch me. I hate you, too—both of you."

There was a wry quirk of amusement about his thin lips as he followed her into the house.

"Don't say that too often, Olivia, my dear," he said very quietly, "or I shall have to teach you a lesson, shan't I?"

She didn't reply.

"Go upstairs and tidy yourself," he said with contempt. "You look a slut. Pin your hair, and put a little color on. See you wear your most seductive dress. Tonight we dine together, in celebration of Cousin Justin's defeat."

"You bully," she said.

He smiled. "Of course. But you've always known, haven't you? Strange how women respond to brutes like me."

"Even—"

"Yes, even Melusina," he said in even tones. "But as I said before, don't talk of her. She's—" It was on the tip of his tongue to say "she's dead and gone," but he remembered in time to keep the dreaded words back, and tried to delude himself that he wasn't shaking, although his hand was still quivering later when he tried to untie his cravat.

She sat before him, erect and pale, with her chin held high above the olive-shaded satin dress that Rohan had given to her in an unexpected mood of generosity. Her dark hair was piled high on her head. She appeared so composed and cool that until she moved to lift a glass or eat, she might easily have been a figure carved of wax. During the last few weeks the contours of her face had lost their plumpness, and this aged her. The green satin fitted her tilted breasts seductively. On her left hand she wore a single gold ring, the symbol of her bondage to Rohan; a large emerald glowed from the third finger of her right. The creamy shoulders were bare above the bunched line of her sleeves, washed to fitful gold from the candlelight. Yet no warmth lit her dark eyes. She had done as he asked, and with a feeling of self-contempt had applied color to her lips and placed a patch near one temple. Olive—despite her name—was not her true shade, and she knew it. For Justin she would have chosen rich deep golds and reds, soft heather purples or brilliant gorse—the colors of the moors. But Rohan preferred her in green. He frequently wore it himself—the muted tones of sea at twilight, or palest grays and silvers of newly washed sand.

Sand—sand, she thought as she toyed with her food. She could hear it now, driven on a sibilant whisper against the windows, threatening the very foundations of Boscarrion. One day it would claim them all, she was sure of it. And she remembered Melusina—her flamboyance and rich exotic presence, her earthy full-blooded beauty that had symbolized so much in opposition to the forces of sand and wind and flying tide.

What had happened to her?

Where had she gone so suddenly, and why did Rohan flinch each time her name was mentioned?

The question surfaced in her mind again as she ate mechanically. Rohan, looking broodingly and darkly handsome in a gray silk coat with a white cravat, and a richly embroidered green and gold waistcoat, glanced at her then.

"What's the matter?" he asked. "Why can't you smile for a change?"

She forced a semblance of the gesture to her lips. He gave a dry cough.

"Thank you for trying. You're not adept at deception, though. A pity you can't please me more."

"I'm sorry." She spoke stiffly.

He said nothing, simply bent over and poured more wine into her glass. "Drink it up. Maybe more liquor will warm you."

"I'm not cold."

"You certainly make a good show of it. Drink it, I said."

She lifted the glass to her lips, hating him.

He threw his head back against the carved chair and sighed heavily. Then he suddenly thrust his lean face nearer hers over the table.

"You are a damned insulting young madam," he said very clearly. "Why I ever took you into this house I don't know."

"Neither do I."

He got up suddenly and swept his glass to the floor. It smashed and shattered in a shower of crystal splinters, leaving a stream of red staining the rich carpet. Before ringing for a servant, he said to Olivia coldly, "Eat your food. Don't waste it. And when you've finished, you'd better take yourself to bed."

For a second her mouth opened slightly. She looked scared.

A flash of cold humor crossed his face.

"Don't worry," he said dryly. "You can rely on your privacy. I've no wish at all to savor your sterile charms tonight. You have no subtlety my dear, and your gaucheness bores me. Good night."

He made a mock bow, and without another glance at her left the room. Olivia heard a brief muttered conversation in the hall. The next moment Mrs. Trellis appeared. She eyed Olivia disagreeably, surveyed

the damage, returned to the door, and called on
Jenny. Then, before the girl came, she turned again
and faced Olivia belligerently. "My Lady Melusina
would never've caused such a scene. Pity things've
worked out as they have," she said meaningfully.

Olivia did not condescend to reply. She took a few
quick steps to the hall and, with her skirts held above
the ankles by both hands, went upstairs.

She slept very little that night.

True to his word, Rohan did not appear, and Olivia
wondered which was the worse—his hostile presence, or the mournful loneliness of the great room
echoing the sigh of the wind from outside and the
thunderous impact of the waves breaking on the winter shore.

15

February came, gray and windswept, bringing high
seas and sudden storms to the Cornish coast. Boscarrion crouched desolately in its hollow of the dunes,
swept by barricades of sand that as quickly were
taken away again at ebb tide. A Breton trader foundered and was lost with all hands to the west of Hell's
Gap at a point not far from Boscarrion. There was no
evidence to suggest that every effort was not made
by natives and the men in Rohan's service to save life
and cargo, but neither was there any proof otherwise.

A matter of deliberate "wrecking" was suggested by the uncharitable. Whispers even reached the ears of the Law. Rohan was interviewed twice by kings' men, and on each occasion they departed well satisfied concerning his integrity and well fortified by vintage brandy from his cellars. No one considered it necessary to investigate the cellars in question.

A service was held in Gwynfa Church to mourn the dead, which Rohan attended as a mark of respect. He wore a long black frac over a cream silk satin waistcoat and black silk stockings. After the sad ceremony the vicar joined him for refreshment at Boscarrion, an occasion at which he expressed grateful thanks for Rohan's liberal donation on behalf of the bereaved families. How, and whether or not, the relatives ever received the gold was uncertain. One material fact was indisputable: The brandy served was excellent—so excellent that the spiritually and physically well-satisfied vicar rode back to the Rectory that evening in a jovial mood, knowing a welcome keg would be delivered the following day for his own use.

Meanwhile, the cleverly concealed storage space under the floors of Boscarrion was jammed tight with ankers ready for disposal at discreet intervals. No one would question their origin. Lips were tight when trade was beneficial, and men of conscience in those hard times were rare. It was simple enough to know which they were and to avoid their company at crucial times.

If at odd intervals Rohan suffered qualms of regret, he proved himself an adept at self-vindication. He had not willfully ordered human extinction. Fate and the elements had determined it—he himself was but one man out of many involved. Only a fool would refuse the benefits of luck and his own quick mind.

So he shut the gloomy scene from his thoughts.

And Olivia tried to do so.

But as the days passed, her opinion of Rohan gradually darkened into acute suspicion. His hardness, his contempt, and his bitter comments, she had grown to accept. But there was something else—a mysterious undercurrent to his life—she secretly feared.

And it had nothing to do with smuggling.

At nights when she lay alone in the great bed, there were frequently whispers—a furtive murmuring and movement from below that was not connected with any dark "trade" or illicit contraband business. She would lie wakeful for hours listening to the faint throaty murmur of half-subdued laughter—a woman's. Not any servants, or Mrs. Trellis—Mrs. Trellis never laughed—but in familiar tones. Tones that affected her unpleasantly because they did not belong to Boscarrion. Or to Melusina either—but to the unhappy period at Penraven before she'd left; to Mara.

The idea seemed so outrageous at first, she tried hard to dismiss it, telling herself the chuckle was but an echo of the wind's soughing from the corridors below. Then one night she knew she was not mistaken. As usual these days, she'd gone to bed early; Rohan obviously preferred it to be so. The banging of a door had awakened her after hours of sleep, and set her mind alight and her heart beating heavily from the impact. She lay quite still and rigid upon her back until her pulse quieted; then she got up, slipped on her wrap, and crossed the floor. The soft sounds of faint footsteps were unmistakable from along the landing.

She opened the bedroom door a fraction and peeped out. There was the flickering glow of candlelight from the far end 'of the corridor, and as she watched, contorted elongated shadows leaped round

a corner up the walls, followed by the emerging
shapes of a man with a woman in his arms. He was
moving furtively, catlike and almost soundless. Her
form was pressed and clinging against him, leaving a
trail of silvery light where her long hair fell. Olivia,
hardly daring to breathe, waited rigidly until they
had crossed and turned into Rohan's sanctum. The
door closed behind them, and for a few moments all
was quiet.

Olivia retreated into the bedroom and looked at
the clock. It was already one thirty. Her first instinctive reaction was of shock, followed by a question.
Where was Justin? How could Mara have left the
house without his knowing? He must be away, she
thought, or at that old mine. Perhaps he'd gone up
north again. Bewilderment in her turned to anger as
Mara's duplicity registered. Olivia's frustration and
desperate unhappiness concerning Justin's marriage,
and his consequent rejection of her, were swept
away in a wave of loyalty and undiminished longing
for him. She knew in that moment of revelation that
she would always love him. Ill-starred they might be,
but no other man would ever be able to take his
place.

She paused only briefly before stealing barefooted
out of the bedroom, making her way to Rohan's
room. However dangerous her action might be—and
he would certainly see she suffered, as he'd so often
threatened if she was discovered—she had to know
what was going on, for Justin's sake. The house
seemed quiet, and the corridors and landings were
deserted. The servants, she knew, always tired from
their day's labor, slept heavily in their own quarters.
So there was little to fear there. She moved cautiously, on tiptoe, and secreted herself in a recess
quite close to Rohan's door. At first nothing was clear.

Nothing but the little moans, subdued shrieks, and then the sighs and fitful whispers of passion appeased.

She waited, listening, then ventured from the shadows and stood with an ear close against the crack of wall and door. Only the sound of her own breathing registered through the vibrant silence. Presently it started. A little cough from Rohan, followed by two sharp words. "Tell me."

"The mark—" Though so lowly spoken, the voice was obviously Mara's.

"What mark—what the devil—" The next few sentences were a jumble and seemed to make no sense. Then Olivia heard quite clearly. "I have it; the baby has too. And Elaine. I told you. I'm Elaine's child. And I don't believe—" The sense of the muffled words died there into a meaningless whisper again. There was a silence, followed by a sharp exclamation from Rohan. "You mean Justin really *is* a— my God! my God!—and all this time—"

"Yes—yes—" Mara's soft voice rose and fell insistently. "It's true."

Olivia could catch no more except odd words rising above incoherent phrases. Words that shook her with a terrible deepening implication, although she couldn't believe them. "Bastard," and "Lillith," intercepted by amazed comments from Rohan, "I'll get him—knew it—" followed by "proof," and further insidious encouragement in Mara's undertones. Then there was again silence. Olivia strained her ears to the door, but nothing came except a sudden creaking and shuffling intermingled by muttered oaths and the sound of swift heavy movement across the floor.

Olivia, jerked to sudden awareness of her position, moved quickly and raced lightly to her bedroom.

Once inside, she stood with her back to the door while the heavy bumping of her heart eased. There was the sound of a latch being turned and snapped to again. She blew the candle out, rushed to the bed quickly, and covered herself by the heavy quilt. It was hardly likely that in the excitement Rohan had heard her or noticed a faint creaking of wood from the floor. But if he looked in she would appear asleep. Please God, though, she inwardly prayed, he wouldn't.

He did not.

A little later her strained ears caught the cautious tread of footsteps moving toward the stairs—a hollow muffled sound that was almost inperceptible above the faint moaning of the wind and intermittent crying of the gulls outside. Soon the echo had died, leaving only a sense of desolation and dread behind.

Olivia got up and went to the window. The lumpy dunes were half obscured by rolling waves of milky mist. Far above, the moon was at moments veiled and hidden; then suddenly there would be brief clarity, revealing elongated shadows streaking from the distant standing stones. Boulders reared as black shapes from the undergrowth. The clawing branches of windswept bushes and the snakelike rushes assumed an eerie menace through the luminous green light.

A haunted, phantom place, Olivia thought as a chill draft of air penetrated the window, stirring the hair across her forehead. And she wondered, as she had many times recently, why she had allowed herself, through jealousy of Mara, to take such a rash step in marrying Rohan.

She did not care for him; she never had. His presence was becoming increasingly distasteful and terrifying to her. If she could have escaped from Boscarrion, she would have done so in the past month. But Rohan—or Rohan's spies—were always watching. And she had nowhere to go. Penraven was her only refuge. The idea of living humiliated and despised under Justin's protection was somehow so hurtful and distressing to her, she knew she'd rather die.

Well, perhaps not quite that, she decided honestly when she really considered the suggestion. Life could be sweet. There were lovely things—riding Moonbeam, poor Moonbeam who must be so lonely without her, the smell of heather and autumn woodsmoke, the sting of brine from foam-flecked seas, and spring days ahead when the rocks and moorland turf were sprinkled with pink thrift. There would be primroses peeping between the curled fronds of young bracken, and the thrusting speared heads of bluebells and foxgloves. Oh, there were so many beautiful things ahead.

If only Justin— She tore her mind from him as a sickening pain clutched her; not merely physical— more of her heart, a part of her that was older than her years and capable of giving so much he never dreamed of. If only he'd understood. If only he'd looked into her eyes absolutely clearly, and seen what was so blatantly there, and if he'd said, "Olivia, I love you. But because I'm your brother we mustn't talk of it, or dream of certain things. To be near you will mean a great deal, and will have to suffice. There are things we can still do together, like riding and laughing, and sharing Penraven. But Mara is my wife and to the world she will remain so. Underneath. though—always, you and I belong."

Oh, yes. If only he had said something like this, perhaps she could have come to terms. But he had not.

She knew now he never would.

She was about to turn bleakly away from the window when she saw far away to her left a horse and riders galloping above toward Red River. Their shapes were silhouetted for a brief second in a wash of moonlight. The next they had disappeared behind the pale of rolling mist.

Olivia went slowly back to bed.

She understood only too well.

She had heard, and now had proof from her own eyes.

They would cut down presently to Penraven, and when Mara was safely inside, Rohan would return to Boscarrion—until the next time.

She jumped up impulsively, turned the key in the lock of the door, and with an effort pushed a chest against it. It was not likely Rohan would seek her company after his amorous interlude with Mara, but if he did—her lips became a hard tight line in her face as she looked around wildly for some heavy weapon, and spotted the valuable French clock on the chest of drawers—she'd knock him on the head with that rather than have him ever touch her again. The trouble was, she knew if it came to the point, she wouldn't. It just wasn't in her nature really to harm another human being.

Somehow she'd have to get away. It was the only answer.

The next day was calm and windless. Mist still brooded in a gray veil over the sea and landscape. Quite early Rohan saddled his stallion and set off up the moors for an unexpected call on Lillith.

He passed Red River at a high point near the ridge and continued in a direct line ahead, keeping well clear of Pookswood below. When he reached the far end of the forestland, he took an abrupt curve downward and was soon at the door of Lillith's cottage.

He gave a sharp rap with his whip. At first there was no reply. He knocked again and heard a muttering response and furtive shuffle of feet.

A bolt was withdrawn. The door opened a few inches, revealing bright beady eyes peering from a raddled brownish-red face surrounded by thick grayish-black hair.

"Yes?" the mouth snapped.

Rohan kicked the wood and entered, sweeping past the bulky figure unceremoniously. She followed him aggressively, pulling the multicolored shawl tightly over her sagging breasts. Gold rings swung from her ears. Bracelets tinkled from her mottled wrists. Her hands were knotted and clawlike. Yet there was an air of sullen pride about her that suggested to Rohan he might have no easy task ahead.

"What do you want?" she demanded. "And what right have you to come breakin' into others' property?"

Rohan smiled sardonically.

"My cousin's property, I think—or shall we say my family's? Which makes a difference, doesn't it?"

Was it his imagination, or did a swift gleam of fear flicker across her face?

"I don't know what you mean."

"No?" Rohan took a pinch of snuff. "Then let me explain." He seated himself on a chair by the table—quite a good one, he noticed, carved antique—while she studied him belligerently.

"Sit down, for God's sake, woman," Rohan told her, irritated. "We may as well both be comfortable for our—little talk. It won't take long, I can assure you, providing you're reasonable."

Lillith took a chair opposite to him, eyeing him furtively all the time.

"Well, then? What's this all about?" she asked. "I s'pose someone's bin talking—is that it? Makin' mischief, or tryin' to?"

"Now, now!" Rohan's tones became velvety suave. "What could anyone say evil about a respectable woman—with no cause whatsoever? Unless"—he paused before continuing—"unless of course you have something to hide."

She got up amazingly quickly for one of her weight, chin outthrust, breathing heavily. "What do you mean? You just tell me, see, an' don't you go harassin' a poor old woman like me or I'll get protection, that's what I'll do, set the Law—"

Rohan laughed.

"I hardly think the Law would be charitable on your account. There's been much whispering lately, you know—and whispers travel."

"Whispers?" Her voice stirred the air in a hissing undertone. "What whispers?"

Rohan shrugged. "You know very well. And if I've a mind to, I can easily endorse them. What's that?" He pointed to an immense crystal ball standing on a carved mahogany sideboard. "And those," indicating a pack of cards on a small table. "And that stuff hanging through there?" He turned his eyes to a door leading to a further room where bunches of herbs were clearly visible suspended from the ceiling. "What do you use them for, Lillith? And that brew cooking on the fire. Is it good medicine? Or Devil's stuff? The smell's an abomination." He took out a handkerchief and held it to his nose. "Did Farmer Jago's cow sicken through it? And poor Betty Treves take the fits and die? Are you what they say, Lillith? One of the dark ones? A true full-blooded black witch? Do you sprout bats' wings at night to drain the blood of harmless villagers? Is that it? Tell me, you old hag."

He got up and grasped her by the shoulders, thrusting his face at hers fiercely. She gasped and would have toppled back if he had not jerked her forward. Her jaws shook and teeth rattled as his grip intensified. She tried to protest, but he gave her no chance.

"One word from me," he continued ruthlessly, "and you could be hanging at the crossroads in a matter of hours. Not a nice death, Lillith, a black corpse swinging for the crows to pick—"

She blanched. Her eyes closed as he released her and pushed her back on to a chair. Then he took his flask from a pocket and forced it to her lips. "Drink it, you old beldame. I'll not harm you so long as you're sensible." He watched her closely as she opened her eyes, greedily taking the spirit.

After a moment he said more quietly, "Well?"

"What d'you want to know?"

"Who is Mara? And who bore Justin Tregallis?"

At first she didn't answer. He eyed her shrewdly, wondering whether to use more force or subtler tactics. He decided on the latter.

"All right, if that's your choice, woman, I'll have no other course but to do my duty."

He got up purposefully, and had taken two steps to the door when her brown wrist shot out in protest.

"No, no. I'll tell ye. I'll speak—an' I'm no witch, as God's my judge. I'll talk, surr—I'll talk."

He appeared to hesitate at first, then moved back slowly into the room.

"You'd better begin, then," he said.

After one long mutinous look she told her tale, simply, and without embellishment, adding at the end, "I didn't see no harm in it, surr, nor my mother either. Th' old squire wanted a son, an' I'd just had one I didn't particularly want—not—" she added hastily, "that he wouldn've bin useful in later years.

But I had to think of his good, didn' I? An' then, me
and my mother Sarah being so poor, it was handy
havin' good gold for my service."

"What gold? And for what?"

"For givin' up my son and takin' that flyaway airy
girl child instead. A sly puss she's proved to be, you
take my word for et. A load on my shoulders an' that's
for sure—till that other—the one of my own womb
—took her into that grand fancy place." She broke
off, to sniff contemptuously. "A fine one *he's* turned
out to be—but don't think I've any regrets."

"I don't damned care whether you've regrets or
not," Rohan told her roughly. "All I'm concerned
with is the truth. Do you realize that your trick has
cost me my lawful rights and heritage for all these
years? That I'm the true heir to Penraven, and your
gypsy bastard an impostor?"

"I hadn' thought of it that way, surr," Lillith said,
appearing falsely contrite. "I'm sorry 'bout that. But
if it's real truth you're wantin', let me say something
else—that reel son o' mine edn' no common breed.
His father was high up, an' that's God's truth. A lord
he was—Lord Tallard. Oh, he was mad about me, I
can tell you. Come down for a holiday, an' I was
swep' off me feet. Then, would you b'lieve it? He was
drowned at sea. I wrote to the address he'd given so
soon as I did know about the babe comin', but there
was no one of that family left, nor isn't now o' course
—none but that big dark fellow of my own flesh."

"I have only one interest in that big dark fellow of
your flesh," Rohan interrupted scathingly, "to kick
him out of my life and have you sign a statement
saying what you've told me is true. Understand?"

Lillith threw him a suspicious glance. "What about
me? What proof do I have you'll keep your word,
mister? S'pose all's written an' signed an' you let

those lies go on? What about my neck? You just tell me that, surr."

"You shall have your own document signed by myself that none must harass you on Tregallis property, and that I've found no evidence whatsoever of illdoing or witchcraft by yourself."

Eventually Lillith was satisfied. Rohan produced paper, ink, and quill pen from his container, prepared the statements, and signed the necessary vindication on Lillith's behalf. Although she could not write, she had a smattering of reading, and declared herself satisfied.

After this she clarified her own statement concerning Justin's birth, and allowed her hand to be guided by Rohan in the signature of her name at the bottom of the page.

When all was concluded to Rohan's satisfaction, he left the cottage, untethered his stallion, and galloped back at full speed to Boscarrion.

The future of Penraven was moving to its true pattern.

Ellis Tregallis was at last to be avenged.

16

The day was fine, but oppressive for the time of year. The wind had dropped, leaving the skies overhung with sullen clouds that gave a brooding light to the landscape.

Rohan set off early to see his solicitor in Penzance. He had documents with him concerning the entail of Penraven and his right to the estate, including Lillith's signed confession of Christin's fraud and the unlawful deception practiced for so many years. Apart from the evidence from Lillith herself, Mara, he knew, would support him should the question of claim be raised in court. If she hesitated, through some misplaced sudden pity for Justin, the Bennedick mark would substantiate the line of legal descent.

Mara and Elaine could both be forced for examination on this point, also the child. So he had no qualm of uncertainty as he took the high moorland road westward. His solicitor, Thurston Carnick, was a shrewd man with a taste for a cut-and-dried case, especially one that through its dramatic potentials could only bring kudos and a tidy sum to his pocket.

From an upstairs window Olivia had watched his receding figure canter up the track toward the high lane astride his favorite stallion, until horse and rider disappeared around the bend. She did not know what his business was, but guessed it had something to do with his hushed conversation with Mara in the night.

She was uneasy, and presently went to the stables, hoping there was no one about except perhaps the boy, who might allow her to use the mare Rohan had previously given her for a canter when she felt like it. A wild plan was seething in her; somehow she would reach Penraven stables unseen. She was longing desperately for Moonbeam—the touch of her gentle nuzzle against her cheek, and the affectionate whinny of the animal's welcome. If she rode the elderly Boscarrion mare to the high point of Red River, she could dismount there and send the horse back, then make her own way on foot to Penraven.

The visit, with luck, could even serve a second purpose—an opportunity for seeing Justin and somehow making peace following her turbulent attack on him. He must understand, she told herself desperately—surely he must know that she had been driven to such harsh words only through her own terrible unhappiness and because she needed him so achingly. If he didn't—but he must, he must.

Spurred on by her own youthful stubborn optimism, she hurried through Boscarrion's conservatory door and down the side path to the box where the old mare was kept. As she'd expected, at that hour only the boy was about. But he was uncooperative and had a faintly furtive look in his eyes.

"Oh, no, miss—no, ma'am," he said obstinately. "I can't let 'ee have that one nor any other neither—not today I can't. Maister did say so, see? 'You jes kip all o' them theer animals safe in stables,' he said. 'An 'ef I do find you've forgit, then I'll have skin of yer back' —that's what he did say." He turned away, mumbling, "Sorry, ma'am."

Olivia had an impulse to push past him and invade the stable herself, but the youth was large and strong, and a scene, she knew, would only result in her own defeat and unpleasant repercussions from Rohan.

So she went back to the house, put on her sturdiest boots, changed into her plainest cotton day dress, and wearing a shoulder cape, with nothing on her head, set off down the dunes toward the inlet of Red River's estuary. The tide was low. She had traveled the route before on foot, and could do it again with luck. Once over the treacherous sands she could climb the rocky part and make her way up the winding wild sheep track to Penraven, and Moonbeam.

In her enthusiasm she did not notice a dark face

peering at her through a clump of rushes near a tumbled rock. She was aware only of the sudden shrill cry of a seabird as it flew upward, disturbed by the swift movement of Nelson's small nimble figure darting back toward the house.

Olivia glanced up at the sky, then continued to the edge of the gap. From there the drop appeared more abrupt than she remembered—half earth and sand, interspersed with boulders shiny from sea and weed. She would have to be careful—very sure the ground was firm beneath each step she took. The riverbed had a desolate hungry look under the drab sky. Memories of lives taken there flooded her mind with unpleasant foreboding.

She was making her way round a perilous bend when her senses froze suddenly. Looking up, from only a few yards down, was a face. A broad, pale, moonlike face crowned by a tuft of ginger hair. He had immense shoulders, and although his wide mouth was smiling, revealing yellowing broken teeth, the small eyes were screwed up under heavy brows. Olivia stopped, instinctively clutching her cape under the chin. She knew him. He was a man-of-all-work at Boscarrion—a hulking creature with a record of ill deeds behind him, who had been rescued, some said, by Rohan from a slaving venture and taken into service for the benefit of both. Mostly he worked outside at any manual labor needed. He slept in a barn, and the household recognized him as an unpleasant watch-guard of his master's interests.

"Well?" he said with a leer. "Travelin', missis? Not a good day for et—not at all. Ef I wus you, I'd tek off afore rain do come."

Although the words themselves held no threat, his manner did. Olivia thought hard for a moment, then, summoning all her courage, she drew herself up, and holding to a bent furze branch replied coldly, "Do you mind getting out of my way, please? I know this track very well."

The smile left his face.

"Ef you be wise, you do as I say," he told her, thickly. "Actin' on maister's orders I be—an' seein' as how I'm big an' strong, an' you but a slip of a wench, well—" He grinned again. "I tek it you're no fool, girl. So go on with 'ee—quick, 'fore I forgit you'm be maister's wumman an' lay you meself—here an' now."

His expression was so insultingly lascivious, Olivia took a quick step back and tripped. She lay for a moment in a bed of prickly undergrowth. He swung himself up and loomed above her, laughing lewdly. Then the laughter died into something else. He was breathing heavily, his eyes slits of sexual desire.

She jumped up, tearing her dress and hands on the massed thorns, and turned suddenly to scramble back the way she had come.

Whether he followed at all she did not know. All she heard was a string of oaths in his thick voice, followed by "Doan' you come back now. You kip 'way. Off with 'ee—off—off—"

And then silence.

She heaved herself over a particularly precarious lump of granite, then went on, climbing and dragging herself upward, with her heart jerking uncertainly each time a branch gave or shiny rushes slipped from her fingers.

Near the top, where the rough ground eased into gentler dunes, she sat down for a rest. Her hands were badly scratched and bleeding. She had a small cut on her left temple, where the dark hair was slightly matted. She rubbed her face with a scrap of lace handkerchief, and glanced around. There was no sign of the man; all was lonely. Even the gulls had flown, leaving the sky empty and leaden. Presently, feeling more composed, she made an attempt to tidy her hair and wiped her boots with dry sand. Mud clung to her fingers. She cleaned them with a handful of rushes and pinned up the torn hem of a petticoat with a brooch. Then she got up and started walking again. The uneven turrets of Boscarrion presently emerged round the bend. She must have taken far longer than she'd thought on her precarious venture, because by the time she neared the house, Rohan was already back from Penzance and standing on the verge of dunes and forsaken garden, watching.

Of course, she should have known, she thought despondently. A gallop over the moors to town did not take long, and probably his business had been brief. He did not trust her. She should have guessed he would be back as soon as possible to make sure she made no attempt to contact Justin. The man—his spy —had obviously been told to be on the watch, just in case. She realized that her plan had been futile and a complete waste of energy.

It would always be like that, she thought bitterly. While she remained at Boscarrion, there would be no freedom. Unwittingly she had become a prisoner.

Rohan came forward to meet her as she approached the house.

"Well!" he said derisively. "What a mess you got into while I'm away. Are you never going to grow up, Olivia? Or is it that you're so homesick for Penraven you have to risk your neck at every available opportunity for a glimpse of it?"

She did not answer. He smiled wryly. "Sulking? How stupid of you. There's no need, I can assure you." He gripped her arm. She flinched. "Come along now, Mrs. Tregallis, while you're here you'll obey me. But, believe me, I have good news—ex-

tremely good for you—" He broke off insinuatingly,
but did not release her arm. She looked up question-
ingly.

"What do you mean, Rohan?"

He forced her forward and continued watching
her closely. "In short—if you do nothing silly to prevent it, you will be able to reside as legal mistress at
your old home. In fact, I shall insist on it."

Olivia stared. Her face had blanched.

"What do you mean? You're teasing me. Why do
you have to be—to be so cruel? Why, Rohan?"

He laughed and gave her a push. "I've no alternative with you," he said coldly. "You just ask for punishment. And I consider myself at fault for not oblig-
ing far earlier—with a whip."

She jerked her arm free. "Don't threaten me," she
said in a whisper. "If Justin heard—"

He laughed.

"Justin? Justin has no say in anything anymore,
Olivia, nor will have."

She stopped, cold with fear.

"You mean—what? What's happened? Tell me—
tell me."

She lifted both arms; her hands were clenched. He
took her wrists and held them hard, shaking her.

"Stop it. Behave. Do you hear?"

The hard note in his voice, the cold stare of his
narrowed eyes, silenced her. They walked on a few
paces. Feeling her chill hand go limp under his, he
released her.

"That's better," he said. "Shouting and screaming
won't help you at all. Wildcat you may be. But wild-
cats have to be tamed. So hold your tongue and don't
make a scene for the servants' pleasure. Servants
talk; and a show of decorum before you return to
Penraven is in all our interests."

Her curiosity was so overpowering she could not

help asking breathlessly, "What do you mean about Penraven—and—and Justin? Oh, Rohan, please say—"

"If you'll contain yourself and allow me to speak in my own time, I shall certainly do so," he told her sharply. "In the meantime, go to your room and make yourself presentable." They were nearing the side door. "It's not my habit to converse with sluts and vagabonds, and you certainly appear one. Quite revolting."

Ignoring the insult, she hurried through the house to the main hall and rushed upstairs.

She dragged off her muddied boots, washed, and changed into her most somber and conventional brown cotton dress, which was trimmed only at the high neckline with a discreet suggestion of ribbon and lace. She powdered her face in an attempt to disguise the cut cheek, applied a touch of perfume behind each ear, and, when she felt sufficiently respectable, went downstairs.

Rohan, a fastidious figure in gray velvet and silk, was waiting for her in the library.

She went in tentatively.

"Sit down, Olivia," he said, after taking a pinch of snuff.

She did so, feeling awkward, ill at ease, and absurdly apprehensive.

Then he told her.

She sat in stony silence until the end. There was a long pause in which he eyed her wryly, waiting for her reaction.

At last it came.

"You're telling me Justin isn't my brother at all, that he's a—a—"

"A common ill-bred gypsy bastard, my dear, that's all," Rohan said. "So how lucky you were when I took

you for my wife. And how really philanthropic of me
to take the risk."

She flushed.

Shock, combined with disbelief, rendered her temporarily speechless. At first, when the import of
Rohan's highly melodramatic statement registered,
she could do nothing but stare, telling herself he
must be mad. Justin not her father's child! But that
was quite ridiculous. Justin had always been Christin's favorite. His only son. His pride and heir,
whereas she had not mattered at all. No one had
cared for her really, not even her mother, Elaine.
She'd always felt herself in the way, unwanted. Justin
had been the only one to show her any affection, and
that was probably through a sense of duty, because
he was her brother.

Her brother!

Suddenly she felt the wild color in her cheeks fade
to trembling pallor. If what Rohan said was true and
not just a trick to frighten her, then he wasn't her
brother at all. And if so—her heart raced, thumping
wildly against her ribs. Oh, Justin, she thought, Justin
—Justin—everything can be so different— Then, like
a stone falling, her spirits sank. How could it be?

Whatever the truth, he was still married to Mara,
and she herself was still Rohan's wife. Nothing in the
world could alter that. Just one fact was bleakly clear
—should Rohan's statement be proved, Justin would
be deprived of everything that mattered. Mara
might stand by him, but Olivia doubted it. She didn't
love him. She loved Rohan. And Rohan—at that
point a slow, creeping fear flooded in a dark tide
through her, temporarily dispelling all other emotions.

What would Rohan do? She knew now of his secret
wild obsession for Justin's wife—she had proof—and

when Rohan wanted anything, he took it. No obstacle would prevent him. He would simply override everything else and destroy it if necessary.

Herself?

She shivered, knowing that somehow she had to escape and get away from Boscarrion. She must break the news herself to Justin before Rohan shocked him into taking some wild action that would part them forever.

And for her own safety, too.

She closed her eyes, trying to get things into perspective, and trying hard to believe Rohan was playing some cruel cat-and-mouse game with her, simply because he was resentful of her affection for Justin. He was sadistic enough, and seemed to take a delight in tormenting her.

Why? Why? When she'd done nothing to harm him except being born the daughter of Christin and Elaine Tregallis? And that had been no choice of hers.

Her head started to swim. Unconsciously she grasped the arm of a chair.

"What's the matter with you?" she heard Rohan ask. "Are you ill? Or playing for time?" He took her arm, with his fingers biting cruelly into her flesh. "When I speak, I expect an answer. Look at me, Olivia."

She lifted her face obediently. Her eyes were stormy and defensive. "What do you expect me to say?"

He freed her, giving a contemptuous push. "Nothing," he remarked. "You have no manners, and very little common sense. If you were wise at all, you'd smile sweetly, curtsey perhaps, and say, 'Thank you, Rohan, for offering me the status and comfort of becoming mistress of Penraven.' You might even lift your luscious red lips in sweetness and gratitude for once." He paused, continuing after a few tense seconds, "But you never have been grateful, have you? All you've lusted for in your secret cunning little breast has been Justin the bastard—Lillith's gypsy by-blow. I could have made life pleasant for you, Olivia—but you have cheap taste and have played me false in your heart; well—in future you will have no chance." He took another pinch of snuff.

"What do you mean?"

"You'll find out. I haven't decided yet. There's much on my mind. But remember this—" He lifted a warning finger. "No more attempts at running off to Justin. When you return there, it will be lawfully, with me. That oaf will be gone. You understand? So in the meantime I advise you to learn a little self-control and befit yourself as adequately as possible to take your place in my rightful household—Penraven."

"And Mara? Melusina, too—will she be back?" In spite of herself the names left her lips.

"That's my affair," Rohan said, with such venom in his voice that she shivered. "And don't ever again dare to question me concerning my personal life, or I myself will tie you naked to a bedpost and give the thrashing you deserve."

She knew then in one horrified moment that he meant it.

Rohan Tregallis was insane. And Melusina was somehow involved.

For the rest of the day Olivia kept rigidly to the bedroom, only unlocking the door if any of the servants wished to know anything. On the pretext of a headache she asked for her food to be sent up to her. But before the evening meal a maid knocked with a message from Rohan asking for her presence at dinner.

Knowing there was no point in refusal, she forced herself to dress and appeared promptly at seven in the dining room, wearing her gray dress, which was neither too provocative to taunt him, nor too drab to cause contempt. Beneath the fitted bodice her heart beat quickly, but her manner was cool and composed. She could have been a decade older than her years.

Rohan was waiting for her and instantly offered an aperitif. He was wearing a fawn velvet coat with a gold embroidered waistcoat, fawn breeches, silk stockings, and buckled shoes. A single ruby glittered from his cravat. His appearance was impeccable.

He smiled slightly, indicating a chair. "Be seated, Olivia, and take your wine. To enjoy one's food is important for the digestion."

She obeyed him, and played with the cordial, wondering at his calmness and apparent good humor following the earlier scene.

"The weather has lifted a little," he continued when she didn't speak. "So much pleasanter than that thunderous heat."

"Yes."

"Is that all you can say?"

"Oh, Rohan . . ." She paused with a feeling of desperation growing in her. "I'm so afraid."

"Of me?" He smiled winningly, though his eyes were cold and hard as pebbles.

"Of annoying you," she answered bluntly. "Whatever I say or do never seems to please you."

"Ah! But perhaps you don't try hard enough; and perhaps I'm too hasty in my speech sometimes. Believe me, though—I wouldn't really hurt you. You surely don't think so?"

"I don't always know what to think, Rohan."

"No. Well, let us forget your childishness of this morning, and my own quick temper. There are good times ahead for us, Olivia, and when we're both at Penraven, everything will seem different for you. That fraudulent tinker's son will be gone, and only the lawful Tregallis family in possession. You asked about Mara earlier. She'll remain, of course, being a daughter of the household, and your own legal sister. So I shall expect you to live in harmony with her."

"When do you expect to move in, Rohan?" Olivia heard herself inquiring bleakly.

"Oh—in a few days; certainly within a week, as I believe I've already told you."

"And what about—?" She was going to say "Justin," but changed her intention quickly to "—Crannick? The mine?"

"The mine, I assume, will still be there!" Rohan said with heavy sarcasm.

"Yes, but—but Justin's put money into it. He has men working there, and—"

"Of course," Rohan interrupted, and although his voice was quiet, reasoning, Olivia noticed that his hand under the frilled lace cuff was already starting to shake. Small red sparks—the signal of danger—lit his eyes. She held her breath until he continued. "You're suggesting I should give him a job, my dear?" The cold lips tilted in a false smile. "Why not? As a miner or laborer, he might be worth his salt. We shall have to see, shan't we?"

Olivia steeled herself to hold her tongue and looked away. At that point, mercifully, a servant came in with the dinner.

The rest of the evening was a charade of politeness interspersed with veiled, cutting comments from Rohan that she did her best to ignore.

Shortly after nine o'clock she went to bed. Not to sleep, but to think and wonder desperately what to do. The frail wind had blown the clouds apart, and at intervals brilliant moonlight streaked through the curtains. She lay for hours restless with her key turned in the lock, fearful that Rohan might attempt to enter. But soon after twelve she heard him go to his own sanctum, and close and bolt his door. With relief she got up and went to the window.

Above the dunes dark shadows streaked the hillside, elongated from racing-galleon cloud shapes black against the moon. The moorland seemed alive with flying witchlike forms remembered from childhood. Fingers beckoned, and ragged locks blew intertwined with bush and tree. When she was a small girl, she had felt elated yet frightened by her own imaginings. But there was no fear now, only a longing to be out there somewhere—anywhere—away from Boscarrion.

Escape.

But how?

She thought hard. The lower route over the tricky sands was not practical at night. Besides, the tide was up. Her only chance was somehow to reach the ridge overlooking Penraven, and that was a very long way to go on foot. There was a derelict shepherd's hut, though, just over the rim on the other side. If she got there undetected she'd have shelter till morning, and in the early hours could make her way to her old home.

The idea was a rash one, but the more she considered it, the more possible it seemed. So presently, when she was certain the household was all abed, she dressed herself suitably, and with her boots in her hand made her way downstairs.

Each faint creak of wood or scuttle of a mouse

terrified her. She waited with ears and senses alert, her back held rigidly against the wall until she was certain no one had heard. Then she went on, tiptoe-ing through the shadowed corridors until she reached the kitchens. Once there, she pulled on her boots, slipped through to the dairy, and let herself through an outer door into the neglected vegetable garden. She made her way carefully along the side of the house, keeping close in the shadows of walls and encroaching dunes.

When at last she reached open ground and the track leading to the moor, she glanced back fearfully. All was dark. The black eyes of windows lifeless and empty showed no glimmer of lamp or candle flame from within. Yet somewhere behind the crouched walls Rohan slept, and might wake any moment with an impulse to make certain she was still imprisoned there.

She quickened her pace, and as she climbed the hill the moon was suddenly swept into darkness be-hind a threatening surge of mounting cloud. Then the rain started. She pulled the hood of her cape well over her head and pushed on unseeingly, taking her route by instinct alone, stumbling sometimes and waiting a moment to get her breath back. A rumble of thunder came from the distance, followed quickly by jagged lightning and another ominous roll. Rain dripped into her eyes and down her face. Stones loosened by the downpour toppled by her feet. Yet she would not give up, telling herself she must soon reach the rim of moor and the deserted hut. But time passed, and as the rain began to abate she realized with a shock that she must somehow have lost her sense of direction and taken the wrong way.

She stood breathless and exhausted against the trunk of a bent tree, rubbing the rain from her eyes,

trying to get accustomed to the darkness. As her
breathing eased, a rim of greenish light pierced the
sky to the west, and a large huddle of blackness fell
into shape below. No house—just trees. Trees spreading their branches into a tract of forest land lying like
some immense elemental creature in wait—Pookswood. It must be Pookswood. She'd wandered miles
out of her way. She turned and began climbing again.
But there was no proper path, not even a sheep
track. Briars and furze confronted her, tearing her
hands and cheeks, and clutching at her bedraggled
wet clothes. The ground underfoot was dark and slippery, and at moments sucked her boots, indicating
bog. She waited several times while the sky gradually
lifted.

At last the rain stopped. A sudden shaft of brilliant
light broke from behind the clouds, and the whole
scene was vivid once more—a panorama of black
shapes and luminous green, lit to eerie clarity beneath the stars.

She turned quickly to retrace her direction, realizing she'd lost quite a lot of time. She cut up the moor,
and seeing a dark pool ahead, took a sharp circle
around it. By then anxiety had made her careless.
She suddenly tripped, caught by a tangle of bramble,
and found herself lying facedown clutched in a maze
of furze, thorny branches, and weed. She reached for
a jutting spike of dead wood, and pulled herself forward on her stomach. When her feet were clear, she
dragged herself to her knees, paused, and with a
lurch of nerves found herself staring down into a
watery dank void of darkness.

But it wasn't an ordinary tarn. It couldn't be. Although half covered by straggling briars, the rest of
it yawned empty and hungry-looking in the moon-

light, revealing a rough enclosing half-circle of weather-beaten granite.

A derelict shaft.

Unable to look away, impelled by some macabre impulse stronger than reason, Olivia edged herself nearer, and as she did so, her right hand enclosed the shining surface of a small object glinting gold at the roots of a heather bush. Clutching it tightly, she absentmindedly put it into a pocket before taking a second look down.

And then she shuddered.

The shaft was long and deep and dank, the walls slimy green and black, going down—down—down— to a menacing glittering pool of water. The surface, though so dark, was ruffled slightly, catching intermittent beams of brightness that gave a watery impression of movement and light. Fascinated, held by an apprehension more dreadful than any material fear, Olivia watched; and as she did so something swam into view, disappeared, and returned again.

A face.

A green, wasted, swollen face with something floating around it like weed—then nothing anymore until the semblance of a hand came up, a clutching still hand with the flesh rotting away. Olivia's eyes widened in terror. But before she screamed, the face in all its obscene horror was visible once more. And she knew.

Melusina.

Suddenly a wild cry left Olivia's lips—shriller than the gulls' high squawking as they rose into the air from the moor nearby, clearer and more penetrating than any other sound of man or beast on that storm-ridden night.

She shuddered once, and then the macabre sight

was taken into a welcoming vortex of swirling darkness that mercifully brought oblivion.

She had fainted.

Consciousness returned slowly. She felt herself being lifted, and when she opened her eyes, she once more saw a face—hazily at first, swimming in a sea of gray. Gradually it came into focus—a triangular pale face, black-haired, narrow-eyed, with a scar near one temple.

Rohan.

She started to struggle, giving a faint cry.

A hand slapped her cheek.

"Be quiet. No hysterics." She was jerked unceremoniously to the back of a horse. Before he swung himself into the saddle behind her, he said harshly, "You little fool. You could have been killed."

"And if I had been, what then? What about Melusina?" Her exhausted whisper was more a condemnation than question.

"Hold your tongue. She doesn't come into it." His eyes blazed. The thin mouth was contorted through the fitful light. "Leave her out of it."

"But I saw her—"

"You're a liar!" he shouted, thrusting his lean jaw close to her face. "Unless you hold your tongue, you'll be sorry."

"But she was there—it's true—in the shaft—I saw her," she protested again, all wisdom forgotten and swamped by the memory of those few ghastly seconds. "I looked down, and—and she was staring up from the water. There was weed and—and—"

He slapped her again, straight across the mouth, bringing a trickle of blood from her lips.

"Shut up. You saw nothing. *Nothing*. And if you

make such wild statements I'll—by God—I'll have you shut up as a lunatic. Just thank your stars I'm a humane man with a streak of mercy in me."

He jerked the reins, and a second later they were off—dark shapes in the wild moonlight, taking the desolate path back to Boscarrion.

It was only later when she'd had food and a sleep in her room that she recalled the object she'd picked up from the heather before discovering the shaft with Melusina's dead face floating in the black water.

Her wet cape had been dried and was hanging in the dressing room. She got up, took it from the peg, and felt in the pocket. The shining knickknack was still there.

Under the oil lamp near her bed she examined it.

It was a snuffbox with the elaborately engraved name on the back—"Rohan Tregallis." The script was small but quite decipherable.

Everything then appeared frighteningly clear to Olivia. In some way Rohan must have been implicated in his lover's death.

She rushed to the door, turning the knob frenziedly. It would not move.

She was locked in.

Trembling, she walked to the window and pulled the curtains. The moon had gone, but it was not yet dawn. Only a thin beam of light lingered along the vague horizon. All else was dark—inky line of dunes emerging through a sullen creeping mist, and the stark walls of Boscarrion stretching below to the shadowed landscape.

She had never felt so alone before.

"Justin—" her heart cried, "—oh, Justin, why aren't you here?"

There was no answer, of course, there couldn't be.

Only the shrill high crying of a bird somewhere from the distance.

And then silence.

Breakfast was brought up by Mrs. Trellis in the morning. Her small eyes were hard, her voice grim, when she said, "You'd better eat et. Master's coming up to see you soon. I'm tellin' you for your own good."

She put the tray on the bed, lifted her chin, and went to the door. When she closed it, there was the grating sound of the key being turned, followed by the woman's heavy footsteps receding down the landing.

Olivia toyed with the meal, then got up restlessly and went to the window. The wind had dropped, but she guessed it would only be a temporary cessation. The sky once again had a sullen yellowish tinge. There was no sun, no touch of color anywhere except for the somber muted shades of sandy dunes tipped by dull green rushes, and misted moors under the clouds. All was overhung by an ominous oppressive suggestion of storm to come.

When she managed to open the window a fraction, the filter of air was heavy and damp, smelling, to her shocked fancy, of dank water and decay. She could not help remembering Melusina's face as she'd seen it last—the ghostly semblance of a human being at the bottom of the yawning shaft. The memory was so terrifying, she tried to convince herself it had been imagination, as Rohan had insisted. But she could not.

Besides—she had the snuffbox in her possession.

Of course, Rohan could have dropped it there at any time while riding, but it was unlikely. For one thing, that spot of ground was regarded as dangerous. She remembered Justin telling her when she was a child never to wander around the high moors above Pookswood.

"It's not safe," he'd said. "Riddled with old mine works and treacherous bog. Promise me, Olivia, or I'll have to put a halter around you."

He'd spoken with a smile, but she'd known he meant the warning. So she'd obeyed, and avoided that particular stretch of land. It was not attractive anyway. Black in parts, with very little heather growing there. Even bluebells—so thick in other parts—seldom blossomed there, and the flame of gorse was rare in the ugly dark tangle of bent thorn and furze. Horsemen had always steered clear of it; yet Rohan had been there.

Why?

She was still brooding over the question when there was a tap on the door and the sound of the key being turned, and he came in, stern-faced, cold-looking, and a little paler than usual.

She stood facing him, drawing her wrap close at her neck above her breasts.

He waved a hand.

"Sit down. I'm not going to molest you."

She did so without a word.

"I've no intention of going over last night," he said in level expressionless tones, "or of attempting to reiterate your stupidity—you must be well aware of it by now. Neither am I going to beat you as I threatened, or comment on your absurd hysteria. I shall not even keep you prisoner here against your will. But I can promise you one thing, Olivia—if you attempt to return to Penraven before I think fit to take you, Justin will suffer. He's going to have a hard time anyway. But I will see to it that he's disgraced and humiliated beyond bearing, should you disobey me. If you want to jeopardize his life, go to him. Justin is already doomed. It's within my power to see him writhe in his doom, and creep and crawl to me like the sly imposter he is. Gypsy spawn. Cheat and liar. I'll so hound him everywhere he goes, his life will be worse than that of any starving cat."

He paused, then asked, still with the deadpan expression on his face, "Do you understand?"

"You've made it quite clear, Rohan," she said, thinking, he's mad. Quite mad. I must humor him.

"Very well." He straightened himself up, shot out an arm, and grabbed her by the neck of her wrap. "See you remember. Next time I won't be so lenient."

His black eyes pierced hers. "If I can't have you as a woman I'll have you as a slave. And slaves get whipped." She did not flinch. Her direct stare seemed to quiet him. "Well, well, we will not presuppose such unpleasant circumstances. If you are a good girl, we may have quite an amiable time ahead. By the way, you owe quite a lot to Nelson. It was Nelson who told me of your ridiculous departure last night. Another thing—your habit of suffering strange nightmares is well known to the household. Mrs. Trellis and others have heard you shouting in your sleep many times. So if I were you, I would not repeat your hallucination of seeing something at the bottom of a mine shaft. I would so regret having to get you certified."

A strange smile creased his face.

"Cheer up, Mrs. Tregallis. In three days we shall be ensconced together at your old home, Penraven, with your dear mother, Elaine, although I've heard unfortunately she is quite likely to quit this life at any moment. So sad. But then, alcoholics generally are."

He made a short, theatrical bow, and a moment later had gone.

Olivia felt numbed.

What could she do?

For the moment there seemed no answer except to pretend compliance with Rohan's wishes until some chance came to escape and warn Justin of the threats against him, and his own doubtful position at Penraven.

17

The morning dragged by. Olivia stayed in the bedroom until about twelve o'clock, then she went downstairs, looking pale and exhausted in her gray dress, wearing no touch of artifice or color. Her eyes were ringed by fatigue and shock, casting shadows on the high cheekbones; even her lips had lost their usual rosy glow, showing tight lines of strain at the corners.

She wandered aimlessly from room to room, aware of a strange silence in the house. No clatter of pots or chatter from servants echoed from the kitchen—only a distant cough from one of the men and a cat crying somewhere outside.

She wondered if Rohan had gone out, had already left to confront Justin from Penraven. But he had said "in a few days." And she'd heard no clatter of hooves from the stables, seen no glimpse of him astride his horse galloping up the moor. She had been watching restlessly from her window most of the time since their conversation, so presumably he was still somewhere about Boscarrion.

By instinct she walked cautiously, almost creeping down the corridors, pausing at each door and listening for any sound before glancing into the silent reception rooms. When she reached the large lounge, the flickering of a light zigzagged from the interior across the hall floor, followed by shadow. She stood with her back against the paneling, then edged herself closer to the opening between wall and door. Very slowly the light emerged again, as a ball of dim yellow reflected through a mirror.

She moved her head forward, and saw Rohan's image take shape in the glass—haggard, greenish-white, black eyes searching his own countenance. He looked frightened, but the fear itself was menacing because it was not sane—and Olivia realized with quickening pulse he had all the curtains drawn. It was noon outside, yet in that one room—"the room of mirrors" she'd always thought of it—there was no chink of daylight or flicker of sun from behind the clouds, only the fitful flickering of candles and fireglow, and of the lamp swaying in Rohan's lean hand. And of sand, of course, the brush of sand blowing in thin clouds through cracks of window frames, filtering in thin gusts under the exotic rugs.

There was always the threat of sand there, Olivia thought dazedly, almost as though the hungry shore was seeking to claim the house, despite its exotic furnishings, the glass, crystal, ornate antiques, and wealth of silver. She recalled the first time she'd visited Boscarrion, how Melusina had reclined by the fire with the great dog Brutus at her feet, then drawn herself up majestically with her hand extended in false welcome.

Yes, false. Olivia knew that now. She had been a child at the time. But looking back, it was clear to her that Melusina from the start had intended she should never visit Boscarrion again.

And perhaps she wouldn't have, if Rohan's exotic mistress had still been there. She wasn't, though. She was lying dead in that terrible dark hole on the moor. The memory was suddenly so vivid, Olivia almost screamed. A hand went to her mouth, and gradually tension eased.

She waited as Rohan's face loomed nearer and larger to its own mirrored reflection. The thin lips parted. In a low voice he muttered something like "You were a fool—fool—fool—" but whether he spoke to himself or to his own contorted fancies, it was impossible to say; for at that moment Rohan's dreams were curiously intermingled with reality. He was speaking to a countenance that had no physical substance in the room but was an image so strong in his mind, he could never entirely erase it.

He was recalling and reliving an incident months ago, when Melusina had taunted him over Mara. Once more her sibilant tones hissed through the quiet room over the hissing and spitting of the logs. He saw her eyes again lit with fury as she whispered, "No, you will never get rid of me, Rohan Tregallis— never. Never. You may have your cheap whores for a night or a day, and cast them off like mud from your boots whenever you feel like it. But me—I'm different. I am of a great family, and if you desert me now I will shame and dishonor you and have your head in a noose. I know things, Rohan. So—be nice, my love, and all will be well, with you, and me—your Melusina."

Her red lips had become a scarlet smiling gash in her dead-white powdered face. Suddenly he had hated—loathed her. Hardly realizing it, he'd struck out and caught the side of her face.

She'd fallen. She was a heavy woman, and the

crack of her skull as it hit the cold marble had been as sharp as that of a pistol shot.

She must have died almost instantly.

That night, known only to Mrs. Trellis, who had done what she could to assist, he had wrapped the body in a cloak and ridden with the corpse slung before him on his stallion to the dreaded place above Pookswood.

The operation, once he was there, had been easy. He was untroubled by conscience or regrets. He hadn't meant to kill her. But her death had been a release. Then why was she always there? Haunting every shadow at twilight? Every corner of passage and rooms, staring from the numerous mirrors that had once given him such erotic pleasure—even looming as a dim watchful shape on the dunes above the sea? Or waiting by the standing stones against the sky when evening fell? Why, why?

His face writhed, becoming a mask of such trembling fear, Olivia closed her eyes momentarily, feeling the palms of her hands grow damp against the wall. When she looked up again, the reflection had gone, leaving just an impression of flames leaping and dying drunkenly, followed by the furtive sound of footsteps crossing the floor.

She forced herself to move, and sped along the corridor light-footed as any ghost to the stairs. But Rohan heard. As she turned around a corner at the top, his voice was a shrill cry from below.

"What is it? Who? Where are you?"

She reached the bedroom quickly, closed and locked the door, unaware of Mrs. Trellis padding to the lounge from the kitchen, or of her broad squat form cuddling Rohan's head against her, and her harsh voice softening as she murmured, "There, there! 'Tes no one, surr. You'm safe with me, my fine

son, my darlin'—an' always will be. 'Tes our secret,
yours an' mine. So doan 'ee fret, luv. A wicked one
that Melusina was—worse than that theer wumman
Ellis yor father did marry, the cruel sterile critter.
Never you mind now. You just rest an' be sure o' this
—'tes maister you'll be of Boscarrion an' Penraven.
An' on that day, my luv, justice'll be properly done."

Presently all was quiet.

Fear was temporarily dispelled, and Rohan, once
more in command of himself, prepared for an afternoon with his solicitor, who was arriving at three
o'clock from Penzance for the second meeting concerning the Penraven inheritance

18

Although the wind had died, the sky was ominous
still, the sea leaden as though conserving its fury for
attack later. Justin felt fear and trepidation in his
bones—a sense of "disaster to come" that in the past
had seldom proved to be wrong. His "sixth sense" he
called it, but in this particular case it was more than
that. Half his worry concerned the mine itself. During the last month energy and manpower had been
strained to the limit in order to get copper produc-
tion fully under way. A certain amount had been
worked, but not sufficient to satisfy Joshua's expecta-
tions, and Justin knew that Partridge was on the
point of quitting the project. The venture, it was

true, had taken a little longer to get started than had been bargained for; but there had been obstacles—delays that no one had expected in the initial stages.

The danger of land subsidence had been thoroughly assessed by experts, and discounted except for a mere half-percent risk. A ninety-nine percent safety assurance would have satisfied any but the most wary of Jonahs. It was unfortunate that Partridge, in the face of the first minor problem, had proved to be one of these.

The difficulty was not insurmountable, but it had meant delay in precious time, as the "greedy furriner" put it, and in his own words, "time was money."

"Men's safety comes first," Justin had commented.

"So you admit there's danger?"

"No. Not at this point. But the main level being explored at the moment runs a bit too close in the direction of old workings, according to Pollard. There's a possibility—only a slight one, I agree—that a wall there could collapse. If there was no water behind it, the risk would be small, but in a case of flooding there's no knowing what could happen."

"Then why the devil didn't all those clever-dicks of engineers spot it?" Partridge had demanded furiously. "When I agreed to go into things with you, it was on the understanding everything was a plain and straight bid for good copper—'rich with it, Crannick is,' you said—"

"And so it is," Justin had protested, growing hot under his cravat. "Damn it, man, you must have known there could be minor problems? That was put clear to you. The main drive was only made that way just because of it, because the ore was so rich there —but it's everywhere—to the south, too; it'll take a bit longer to reach, but—"

"Then why the hell didn't you go south first?"
Justin's lips had hardened.

"Because drilling hadn't happened to show any
weakness to the north. No one can tell until the working's properly started if there's soft earth about. Anyway—so far there's only an indication of it. But earth
and rabble can mean water near. For heaven's sake!"
—he'd mopped his brow—"speak to Pollard about it.
He knows more than me."

Joshua had; and the result, for Justin, had not been
encouraging. So he decided on the morning following to have an early breakfast and be on the site
before any disruption was caused by Partridge's wailing and upsetting the men. If it had to be, he'd do
that himself. He'd no intention whatever of allowing
men's lives to be jeopardized, even in the interests of
Crannick.

So he went in early to tell Mara he wouldn't be
back until evening.

She frowned. Sulkiness, Justin thought, did not suit
her. In a fit of temper with her azure eyes bright and
startling in her heart-shaped face, she could be irre-
sistibly lovely. But with her lips drooping and sullen
she had a petulant air that robbed her strangely of
her charm.

"Oh, well, that's nothing new," she said, turning
away. "All you care about's that old mine. I'm nothing."

For a second Justin fancied his mother was talking
—the shrug of the shoulders, the lift of the chin,
droop of the underlip and the timbre of voice were
so evocative of Christin's wife in her younger days,
when Justin had been a small child. The wealth of
fine silky hair was similar too, except that Mara's was
longer and more luxurious. But Mara's attitude was
more defiant than Elaine's had ever been. Elaine had

been quick to bow to her husband's moods. This had
been a sore point with the young boy, who had
sensed she was incapable of giving support to him in
any family crisis, and had therefore felt little respect
or confidence in her character.

After one hard quick look at his wife he turned
away, saying abruptly, "I'm sorry. I can understand
you find life rather dull here following your adventurous beginning. But you have the child—"

"Oh, yes." Her voice was a little shrill. "I have him.
Thank you for reminding me. I suppose I must oc-
cupy myself in studying baby talk for the day."

"You could take a trip out somewhere perhaps?
Penzance or Penjust—"

"So I could," she retorted, coldly sweet, "if I had
a little money for a humble shopping spree."

Justin took coins from his pocket and handed them
to her.

"There you are. It's more than I can afford, but if
it makes you happy—"

Contrition suddenly softened her face.

"Oh, Justin, thank you. I'm not very nice; I know
that. But it's being confined here—please understand. I know I'm not good enough for you—but I
never pretended, did I?"

He laughed.

"My dear girl, you've never done anything else.
Still, don't fret. Just try and cheer up and be your
own beautiful self when I return."

"When will that be?"

"I don't know," he said abruptly. "There really is
a lot to do at Crannick just now. Pollard and Partridge have a meeting with the engineers, and it's
important I'm in on any new decisions—in fact, I
have to be. If discussions go on late, I may stay on and
camp down there for the night. So don't wait up for
me."

"I see," she said coolly, with apparent acceptance. "Very well." She smiled mechanically. "You must do what you think right."

For some time after he'd left, she lay against the pillows, staring through the window across the sullen sky. The somber gray reminded her of autumn, though it was still summer. Autumn was her favorite season. At the fall of the leaf with damp earth smells and woodsmoke filling the air, the sap rose in her veins, and excitement filled her, urging her to run away—fly—anywhere that would take her at last to Rohan's arms.

The mere thought of him flooded her with a wild restlessness that too long now had been quelled and unappeased during the uneventful changeless days of summertime. Summer could be a rich and dreaming time if passion too was there. But without Rohan's lustful kisses—his savage heart beating against hers, his hands ravaging and bruising her hungry body—the lush flowering of nature had no meaning for her. Their need of each other might be lacking in virtue, but the darkness and wild sweetness of the bond between them was beyond the morality and dictates of man. She needed him.

Oh God! she thought, lying there lonely and unfulfilled—life was nothing without him. Their meetings had been so few lately, his touch so rare. Insult her he might, at times, but deep in his violent heart he hungered for her as she did for him. They had not been so much star-crossed—which he'd declared more than once—as misguided in believing they could forever live apart.

They couldn't.

And she, for one, was determined at last they should not, even if he killed her for it. Indeed, there could be worse things than dying in his arms. Hadn't she, in spirit, done so many times?—closed her eyes half swooning against him—feeling a dark river taking her to the ultimate mystery of universal birth and extinction.

Death. What was death but a final surrender to appeasement of desire?

She got up automatically and went to the window. Her eyes blazed with the wild fanaticism of a climber envisaging the impossible peaks of a far-off unknown world.

I must go to him, she thought, there's nothing for me here.

She started to dress, critically and carefully, sensing that this time her secret visit held a strange significance never before experienced.

She wore blue, the translucent blue of her eyes, covered by a long black lace shawl; and on her piled-up gleaming pale hair, a scrap of flowery millinery. She used no makeup except a touch of deep pink on her lips. In her reticule she placed the coins, and before going downstairs dabbed a touch of perfume behind each ear. She did not look in on Elaine, or at the child who was being crooned over by the nurse in their shared domain. She felt curiously free of any commitment to all at Penraven, and moved quietly, almost drifting to the hall and out of a door leading onto the drive. She took a turn to the left and hurried to the stables. Only the boy was about.

"Get the small carriage ready," she said in a voice that brooked no questioning. "I want you to take me to Tolcarne turn and leave me there. I'm calling on friends in Gwynfa."

The young groom looked uncertain.

"Hurry up," she added sharply, "I'm going shopping in Penzance later. We shall go in my friends' chaise, so you can get back quite quickly. I shall be given transport when the time comes. Don't worry, boy—my husband knows of the outing."

"I can get 'ee all way to the village, ma'am," the youth insisted. "The track down theer edn' bad—"

"I want a walk," she insisted peremptorily. "Do as I say, now, and don't argue." She pressed a coin into his hand. He took it, with the fresh color deepening in his face, and hurried to harness the horses and small vehicle. Five minutes later they were on their way.

Olivia was at a bend in the staircase when she saw Mara walking toward Boscarrion over the dunes. Her head was high. The way she moved had a purpose and precision about it that was compelling. No light radiated her blue form against the heavy sky. Already the clouds were mounting behind her. A thin drift of wind was sighing insidiously through the heather. In spite of the season, heavy chill stirred the air. It was as though Mara herself was some ethereal being bringing warning of ill omen, or news of great significance.

Olivia, from the narrow gothic-shaped window where the steps curved, waited until the slim form hesitated halfway down the path. She saw Mara unexpectedly pause and look toward the door. Then a flare of wan light zigzagged toward the sands, and Rohan's form was silhouetted as a dark shadow going to meet her. Mara did not move for a second. Olivia could feel her hand stiffening against the cold wall. With a terrible strange sense of inevitability about her, she saw Mara's arms suddenly reach toward him, and his own dart forward to enclose her in a hard embrace. There was no attempt at subterfuge, no indication of doubt or hesitation. They stood locked together in an embrace so fierce and ruthless, so filled with despair and terrible passion, Olivia felt shocked and defeated, almost ashamed—not of Mara and Rohan, but of herself, because she had settled for second best. In that instant of awareness self-delusion fell from her. She knew she had no right to judge either of them. Her hatred of Rohan became a mere shadow—something bred from her own refusal to face the truth.

No one, ever, could matter to her but Justin.

From the very beginning she must have known—sensed beneath the facade of human dictates and moral obligations—that she and Justin belonged. Sister? Brother? But all human beings were that. She should have probed far earlier and somehow fathomed the root of the mystery. So much then could have been saved.

She shivered. They thought her young—all of them. She'd believed so herself—yesterday, today, an hour, even five minutes ago. But in a few seconds she'd known herself in a certain way to be old, as old as the ancient stones standing on the moor above, with the experience of a thousand years—more—coursing deep and dark through her blood.

She bowed her head in her hands and shuddered.

What could the end of it be?

Such a short time ago she'd intended to taunt Justin with the truth, the proof of Mara's duplicity. Now all desire for revenge or to hurt had left her. Without forgiveness or understanding there was no love. Even Rohan had been betrayed as much as betraying.

She wiped the dampness from her eyes and turned her face to the window again.

They were no more to be seen. But the wind was rising, and the forbidding landscape already held the darkness of a winter's night.

She turned slowly and made her way back to the bedroom.

From the hall below she could hear the woman's voice mingling with the man's. Without seeing, she knew the intense fiery avowal of their eyes—the hungering desire of lips, hearts, and pressure of hands eager for passion delayed, for moments lost.

"I must get away now," Olivia told herself desperately. "Now—now. This is their place, not mine, I must be with Justin. Oh, Justin—Justin—"

She put on her cape automatically, and changed from slippers into her boots. She loosened her hair and let it flow from the mockery of her bondage, in its thick rippling stream over her shoulders. Her eyes were dark pools in her white face, blazing with purpose as she went downstairs, uncaring if anyone heard or not, sensing that if they did, she would not be stopped anymore. It seemed that Nemesis itself urged her and forced her ahead, out of a side door and up in the direction of Red River and Penraven.

She glanced back several times and noticed the sea lunging with fanatical onslaught to the house. Mountains of sand were thrown against the dunes, and yawning gulps of coastline swallowed by the waves. The wind that had been wild at first had now expanded into a raging elemental fury. This was one of the savage unpredictable storms that had swept Cornwall at rare periods during the centuries—that in the past, it was said, had buried Lyonesse itself, and taken villages to the ocean bed.

Defiance rose in Olivia, to combat her own rising terror. The slope toward Red River was already a holocaust of tumbling stones and lashing undergrowth. Her clothes and flesh were torn. Soon the rain started. When she reached the brow of the moor, the river was swollen to a rushing torrent. It was impossible to cross there. She bowed her head and plunged over the hill, unseeing of the broken trees and derelict shattered hut. There were wild ponies ahead of her, scattering downward to the far valley, manes and tails flying with the elements as the sound of hooves was lost in the moaning wind.

Olivia reached ahead blindly to a granite dolmen —one of the ancient standing stones. She clung to it desperately as the breath was torn from her lungs. I shall never get there, she thought. But I must—I *must*—and through bewilderment, exhaustion, and an overbearing desperate longing, it seemed to her that Justin called. With cloud and rain his features merged. The looming crags became his form. Her head fell back, her knees crumpled. One arm reached toward the sky and dropped exhausted to her side. She pulled herself up again, grazing her face against the streaming menhir. Her head felt thick, bemused with shock. Where were the "old ones," she wondered once, where was the Great One? The dark king of her childhood and monarch of the moors? Why did they not come now, those ancient figures of youth and legend? Or were they but dreams long drained of life and living love?

She knew suddenly that her survival depended only on her will for it—and faith in some purpose beyond any man-made ritual.

And so she prayed, although she was not sure what she prayed to.

Slowly, steadily, the storm began to lose its force. The sky lightened gradually, and with the first frail indication of calm, landmarks and locality penetrated her mind. She pulled herself up the sodden ground to the ridge and turning to the north saw the strong walls and towers of Penraven blurred and gray against the windswept sky. In the opposite direction, below the moor, there was nothing to be seen but a humped gigantic line of dunes with no indication of a house where the roofs of Boscarrion should have been.

She rubbed her eyes, as though to rub them free

of sand and rain and sea. When her sight focused, the emptiness was still there—gray and desolate, the dark glassy Atlantic stretching to a lonely vista of the lifting horizon.

Presently Olivia started to walk again, keeping to the ridge where Red River narrowed to a rockbound stream. She managed to cross, although the land on the other side still sucked at her boots and was streaming with rivulets of water to the valley below. Once a foot was dragged into a pool of bog, which she escaped by jumping to a nearby flat boulder. Her whole body ached, but she dared not stop again in case exhaustion overcame her and she was left alone to the treacherous elements.

How long she walked, and how far, before she reached Penraven, she never knew.

But at last she was there. She stood shivering before the arched door opened to receive her, and then she fell.

19

At first a golden spot like a small blurred moon spread and extended through the shadowed room, bringing wavering shapes that moved and faded again into misted unreality. Olivia closed her eyes again, remembering vaguely a confusion of events holding no true coherence or meaning. There was the darkness of the hill, and the rain beating. There

was a tremendous reaching—a clutching, for what?
She started to shiver, and heard someone saying from
far away, "You're all right. You just tek this—"

She looked up and saw a dark hard-boned face
staring down at her. Olivia didn't answer. She sought
her memory, trying to place it. A creature of the
moor, surely? Something born of former experience
from the past? She pushed the hand away, tearing
her eyes from those unfathomable black ones.

"No—no—"

"You tek it." The voice was insistent and rough-
edged, but not unkind. Olivia swallowed from a glass,
and the stinging liquid revived her. She glanced
around, blinking, and a flood of recognition swept
through her. Of course. Penraven. She was back at
Penraven, her old home. She remembered everything then—her flight from Boscarrion, Mara and
Rohan, and the storm.

And Justin.

Where was Justin? Why wasn't he here beside her,
instead of—who was it? Lillith? Yes, it must be. And
Lillith was standing by the chaise longue where
Olivia lay, as though she had all the right in the world
to be there.

"I want Justin," Olivia said automatically.

"You'll have to want then. Justin edn' here."

Olivia sat up quickly. "Why isn't he? What's happened?"

Then another voice spoke. Gentler, more cultured,
weak, yet sober for once.

"He'll be back, Olivia. Don't fret. He's at the mine.
Dear God, we've had enough worry today." Elaine
moved unsteadily from the shadows and stood looking down at her daughter. "Everything will be all
right," she continued. "In the end it will be—it will
be. We're safe here—being so high—"

"What do you mean?"

Lillith's face was grim when she said, "The sand—et was the sand. Took all, it did, below—"

"All?"

"Boscarrion's gone, they say, the whole of et—swallowed by the tide. Nuthen' there any more but great mountains of earth and stone and sand everywhere, mountains of et. Men've gone to help, but"—a cloud seemed to pass her face, leaving a shadowed veil over the stern coarse features—" 'tws inevitable. Their dukkerin—his an' hers. . . ." As her voice faded Olivia suddenly knew.

The whole terrible truth hit her with the impact of a gun fired. There was a jerk of her heart, a momentary roaring in her ears. She jumped up and ran first to one window, then another. After that, before they could stop her, she raced upstairs to the highest lookout of all, in the tall tower room overlooking the dunes. She waited, pressed against the wall, until her breath had eased and her sight registered. Then she stared out.

It was true.

The landscape had changed. The dunes to the west had extended and grown like great beasts of the elements during those last hours. Against the gray skyline small dots of men ran hither and thither, like hysterical insects trying desperately to salvage their own from the freak storm.

But it would be useless.

Olivia knew that—knew it with the inner conviction she'd had over the inevitability of Rohan and Mara's last meeting.

They had gone.

Already the elements had claimed what was mortal of them—their agony and desires, frustrations and weaknesses, the ugliness and beauty, and their ulti-

mate commitment, which had flowered at the very
last.

In the end they had won; they had been together.

Very slowly Olivia turned and went downstairs
again to the lounge.

Lillith and Elaine were waiting.

"Tell me everything," Olivia said.

"But you know et," Lillith answered. "You know
'bout Justin, doan' you? An' that girl, that Mara?"

Olivia paused before replying. When she spoke her
voice held a hint of accusation.

"You mean that he's your son?"

Lillith nodded.

"*I* didn't—until recently. If I had—everything
could have been so different. Mara, too—my sister.
That's right, isn't it?"

"She was," Lillith said. "And a rare, wild wanton
one to be sure. I know. I brought her up, didn' I?"

Olivia did not reply.

Presently Lillith's voice began again, and the
whole tale was unfolded.

When it was over, she added in strangely subdued
tones, "I came along this morning because I thought
et only right your brother—no, my son—should hear
the truth from my own lips. How he was born diddikai, of my own flesh, an' no Rawni's babe. An' how
a fine Raj—a gentleman—sired him. Gago I am, an'
there's honor still in gago folk. Let that devil Rohan
spurn him, I thought—no no, *no*. 'Tis from me he
shall learn his own true heritage. Then"—she paused
—"the rains and wind came, dordi, to avenge the
past—"

"And it is avenged," Elaine interrupted in a
strange remote voice, as though from far away. "Ellis
was denied me. But through Mara's son his seed shall
thrive. The child is Rohan's; Mara, who is of my own
flesh, told me. But I sensed it long before. Maybe—

who knows?—one day he will inherit. At present, perhaps"—turning to Olivia—"the estate is yours. But in the end the blood will tell."

"How does Ellis come into it?" Olivia demanded.

Elaine faced her with a strange, bemused look in her tired, once-lovely eyes. For a moment, lost in the past, the years slipped away from her, leaving a wraithlike elusive image of her daughter Mara, who had been born of Bennedick blood.

"I loved him," she said simply. "He had lost his wife, who had been a hard, warped character; Rohan was only a child at the time. We thought—I thought —marriage would be possible. But Christin and my father were too determined. Perhaps if I'd been stronger—but there was no way. I was married off to Christin—by connivance, a trick. I saw Ellis once afterward—and"—her lip trembled—"Christin found out. There was a child born dead; mine and Ellis's. It was hushed up, and after that—my life was a hell on earth."

Olivia felt a tremor run through her.

"I'm sorry," she remarked, knowing, though, that no sympathy could compensate for such a frustrated existence, and that words were futile.

Lillith dragged her attention from the two women and went toward the door.

"I must be going now," she said, "you two'll be wantin' to talk. You've heard 'nuff from me, an' the flood's clearin'.'"

But not all, she thought heavily, an' why drag up old tales anyway? There'd been too much lying and deceit and wickedness going on. Let the waters of time take the dark things away—and memories too, that were none of her business. Before she went out, she turned and faced Olivia with a long intent look in her shrewd eyes. "Later I'll be movin'—up-country Birmingham way where some of my folks be. You

tek heed o' that Justin, girl. His father was a comely
gorgio gentleman, an' Justin will be, too. But finer
still, and with rich warmth in him. Born of me he may
have been, but not to be of my kind. Yours he is—an'
was destined for et from the day he come here."

She lifted her hand, making a sign in the air, and
was gone.

Olivia waited stiff as a marionette for some seconds, then with a sudden quick movement rushed
after her. But Lillith was already making her way
down the steps to the drive, and when Olivia called,
she did not even look round, simply shook her head
and went on—bent forward, shawl flapping round
her shoulders like the wings of some giant dark bird
already bound for another land.

Olivia sensed with queer regret that she would
never see her again.

When she returned to the lounge, Elaine was
standing by the chest with her hand fumbling in her
pochette. She was smiling; a bright color tinged her
cheeks. There was a flask on the table, and a faint
smell of spirits tinged with eau de cologne in the air.

Olivia sighed.

Elaine held out a hand placatingly. "I just had to,
my dear," she said. "It's too late now to change. I'm
not brave like you, I'm—I'm a silly weak creature."
Tears flooded her eyes. Olivia put her arm around
her and eased her into her chair.

"It's all right, Mama. I understand. Try and rest.
You must need sleep after such a terrible day. Why
don't you go upstairs?"

Elaine smiled gratefully, drew out her handkerchief, and dabbed her lips. "I will, dear—I will. And
I'll have a peep at the baby. He—he's no one but us
now—and Justin—the poor sweet creature." In passing the chest she reached automatically for the flask.
Olivia pretended not to notice and helped her slowly

upstairs. When her mother was ensconced with
Jenny to attend her in her bedroom, she went down
again to the kitchens, where her cloak and boots had
been put to dry. They were still damp, but she pulled
them on, dragged her hair back and tied it with a
ribbon, then went to the stables for Moonbeam.

No one was about, but of course there wouldn't be,
she thought. All the men would be trying to salvage
any wreckage there was from Boscarrion, or at Crannick.

Crannick!

Her whole body lurched. Supposing something
had happened there? It was so near the sea—the
main adit drained straight from the granite into the
waters below. She hadn't been there for many
months now, but she'd heard the mine was working,
with its quota of tut workers and bal maidens, and
that a certain amount of copper had already been
brought up. She'd heard from a groom at Boscarrion
that folk said a large level was none too safe, and that
a drive was starting in another direction. Supposing
—at that point she determinedly checked the dark
thoughts threatening her and proceeded with the
business of saddling Moonbeam.

A few moments later they were off. The mare galloped gleefully despite the soggy ground, its heart
beating a joyful response to the well-loved, well-
remembered young voice. "Come on, Moonbeam,
good Moonbeam—good girl, then—"

They sped down the track from Penraven to the
right, and when she reached the high lane winding
to Crannick, Olivia reined the mare and looked back,
scanning the view where only yesterday Boscarrion
had stood. There was still no sign of it—only a formidable mountainous erection of sand and darkened
earth where granite had been plundered from the
elements. Not even the remains of a chimney or tur-

ret could be seen. The contour of the coast was completely changed. The dots of men had dispersed. No indication of life was there. It was as though a dead land lurched over the sea, and with a shudder Olivia knew that no one possibly could have lived through the holocaust. In the flash of an instant she recalled Mara's slim shape running to Rohan's arms—that one moment of passionate beauty and acceptance, which she knew would remain with her for the rest of her life.

And now—sand.

Sand, and stone, and desolation, leaving no living memento of what had once been there.

Except the child who must now have all the human care it was hers to give.

With sudden fierceness she turned and headed Moonbeam toward Crannick. At certain points she had to slacken speed, making detours around piles of stones and rubble. The moors on her right were dark and lonely under the fading late-afternoon sky. Trees and bushes had been crushed everywhere. Streams still trickled from the hills over what roadway had been left.

And there was no chimney stack standing near Crannick. Only a mass of damaged workings and a group of men standing by the cliff edge.

Justin?

Olivia kicked Moonbeam to a gallop.

When she reached the mine site, she swung herself from the saddle and rushed over the oozing ground to the dejected area.

Faces turned slowly—pale discs of ravaged faces—and looked at her. She was aware of a terrible constraint and dumbness around her, an inability to express emotion of any kind. Just defeat was there, and a long-drawn-out bitterness.

Then she saw Justin.

For a second neither of them moved.

She felt cold and frightened, because he made no gesture toward her.

"Oh, Justin," she whispered. She forced herself to his side, and lifted her arms. "Justin, I'm so sorry—"

He did not speak, just stared at her. The men, discomforted, walked away.

Then he spoke, in queer stilted language.

"It's all gone, you know. There was flooding. The ground between the workings gave—between the old and the new. The adit's just a gully now. There's no structure left. Nothing. And one man died; one precious life—" One hand went up to his eyes. He shook a little.

"You couldn't help it," she said.

"I tried to warn them, I tried. But it wasn't enough."

"But just one—Justin—it could have been so many, couldn't it?"

He lifted his head again. His eyes were blazing.

"One life—there shouldn't have been any. One life can be rare—precious, with a wife and children depending on it. Don't stand there talking in that aloof way as though it can be wiped off casually as just a minor loss. It can't, by God. It's something—" He broke off, shaking his head. "Oh, Olivia—you don't understand," he said more gently. "Why should you?" He turned away as though to leave her.

She pulled him back by a sleeve.

"Justin—"

He shook himself free.

"Leave me, Olivia. Just leave me—"

"I can't, I won't. I love you. I've always loved you, and I don't care however tasteless it is to say it now, I shall—"

A cynical unbelieving smile touched his lips.

"Don't be childish. You married Rohan."

"And you married Mara." Her voice broke. "Poor Mara."

She shrugged, although the sudden aching in her was almost unbearable. "All right, if you—If I'm no use, I'll go. There's no point in anything, is there?"

She turned desolately toward the side of the road where Moonbeam grazed and slapped her on the flanks. The mare lifted her head and whinnied softly.

Olivia swung herself into the saddle and, not looking back, started the journey back to Penraven.

Hours passed. Night came, throwing a leaden pall over moors and sea.

News had been brought to Penraven that rescue attempts in the vicinity of Boscarrion had been abandoned. No living soul remained there. Not even an animal, cat or dog. The hungry dunes were satisfied and reigned supreme.

Gradually the wind had died into intense silence.

Penraven itself had withdrawn into lonely quiet. The servants and all in the house had fallen into exhausted sleep, except for Olivia, who paced the hall and rooms downstairs, waiting for Justin.

It was past one o'clock when he came. He looked haggard and defeated, and had a scar running in a jagged line across his forehead. Olivia met him in the kitchen. She had the fire still going and food in the oven, but he would not eat.

"Then you must drink," she said firmly.

He took a glass of brandy from her mechanically, and presently a faint color tinged his face.

She waited, not wishing or daring to intrude, forcing herself to leave all the initiative to him.

He spoke after a while.

"I suppose you know everything—how I'm—"

"Lillith's son? Yes, I know."

"A bastard, and a bloody failure on top of it," he said grimly.

"You're Justin," she told him, "that's the important thing."

He looked at her then—not with amusement exactly, but with a slow glowing warmth softening his strong chin and dark eyes.

"You always were a damned stubborn pain in the neck, Livvy," he said. "If I'd known what I know now, I'd have taken you properly in hand long ago, with either a halter or—"

"Yes?"

"Put you firmly over my knee first, and then—"

"And then, Justin?" she prompted.

"Oh, Livvy, Livvy." His arms were suddenly round her, his lips hard, softening gradually into deep hungry caresses on her mouth, cheeks, and at the gentle hollow between her firm young breasts. Then just as quickly he drew away.

"We mustn't. Not yet. There are terrible things out there. Boscarrion gone—and Mara—"

"I know."

"She was so beautiful. Perhaps too beautiful for her own good and that of ordinary mortals. Then Rohan —" He paused, staring hard into her eyes. "I'm not going to ask if you cared for him. He's gone now, and maybe we should try to—to grieve—even if we don't. But I can't pretend, Livvy. I never liked him, and never could. Perhaps everything's happened for the best; except Crannick!" He sighed heavily.

"Try and forget that—just for tonight, Justin," Olivia urged. "You must get rest. Tomorrow we can talk."

His voice was wry when he said, "There's very little to talk about anymore. Crannick's gone, Penraven's no longer mine, all I have is a morsel of pride

and a load of debts to face. But I'll do it—somehow.
Damned if I won't. I'll join the army—or take off
somewhere adventuring. You'll be safe here with
Elaine, at Penraven. It's yours, Livvy, you realize
that, don't you?"

"It will be ours," she said. "Somehow together
we'll make it a happy place. There's land to be
worked, had you forgotten that? Everything's ahead
of us, Justin. Oh, my love—my love—I need you so,
comfort me—please hold me close—"

He did just that.

When they went upstairs later, a rim of light already pierced the far horizon where a pale sun was
rising.

Their eyes were bemused, ringed and dark from
the experiences of the previous day. But in their
minds and hearts, despite sadness and the inevitable
reaction, confidence and assurance of the future was
already spreading its roots toward the new life ahead.

They were together at last.

Nemesis and the sand had brought the pattern to
its preordained conclusion.

Epilogue

Many years later I returned to that remote coastline
where Boscarrion had once stood. Time and the elements had made it forever their own. No trace remained of the cave or ruined doorway. Only the

rushes moved over the high line of dunes reaching toward the moors.

The autumn sunlight streaked mellow gold over the scene, and it seemed to me then that all haunting of evil had gone for good. Perhaps its darkness had never really been. For ultimately knowledge must erase despair, and the pattern of a broken life find understanding.

There is one curious addition to my macabre experience.

As I was searching among cracks and hollows of some protruding rocks, I found a small tin box wedged between a ledge of the cliffside. It must have been there for a very long time—centuries, perhaps. It was rusted and tightly shut.

I prised it open.

Inside was a small book with its leaves half rotted away. But some of the writing was decipherable.

At the top of the first page was a name which I made out to be "Ann Trellis"; and below—

> Today is [I could not make out the date, but the words continued in illiterate English] I hav to see my sun at her murcy. But i can do nuthen. She is bad an' Ellis shud not hev marid her. O dear Lord, help me to bare et. I shud nevur hev let er tek my babe. Ellis shud av sed to everywun e wus ours. Now e is a big fine boy, an I do hate er with all my hart. She is so crool to im an do beat im awful. But wot can I do dear God wen evrywun do think im ers. They wud send me off an I wud not see im agane. Ellis sez wun day I will be a reel housekipper. But I don bleeve et. Praps sheel tek the flux or sumthen praps wen my sun es growed up Ile tell im hoo I am an God wull fergive me—

After that the words died away, the corner of the paper disintegrated in my hand; but the impact of the pitiful confession moved me to replace the book carefully in the box again where no other curious eyes could see it. The sand grated in the hinges as I closed it. It was as though I had sealed some small sacred tomb.

I turned, and for a moment or two stared out across the quiet sea. Then on impulse I threw the relic as far out as I could into the water. Soon there would be nothing left of Ann Trellis's diary but a wad of quickly decaying ancient paper.

A gull cried as I walked away. Then all was silent but the gentle lap of waves on the sand. I knew then that Rohan Tregallis, if he'd ever existed, was at peace.

And Mara? She was surely everywhere—in the light and shadows of that sunlit shore, her face the epitome of all that was fair and fey and symbolic of that haunted place.

Cornwall.

But I knew that I would never return.

Some things are best left as dreams and a retreat from the real world in which they can endure forever.

Illusion and reality after all are but two sides of the same coin—and who can say which is the truth? Certainly not myself.

THE DARK HORSEMAN

Marianne Harvey

author of *The Proud Hunter*

Beautiful Donna Penroze had sworn to her dying father that she would save her sole legacy, the crumbling tin mines and the ancient, desolate estate *Trencobban*. But the mines were failing, and Donna had no one to turn to. No one except the mysterious Nicholas Trevarvas—rich, arrogant, commanding. Donna would do anything but surrender her pride, anything but admit her irresistible longing for *The Dark Horseman*.

A Dell Book $3.50

THE WILD ONE

by
MARIANNE HARVEY
bestselling author of *The Dark Horseman*
and *The Proud Hunter*

Proud, beautiful Judith—raised by her stern
grandmother on the savage Cornish coast—
boldly abandoned herself to one man and sought
solace in the arms of another. But only one man
could tame her, could match her fiery spirit,
could fulfill the passionate promise of rapturous,
timeless love.

A Dell Book $2.95   (19207-2)